Countryman KARL BLACK

Neville Farki

COUNTRYMAN KARL BLACK

Countryman Karl Black

by

NEVILLE FARKI

Published by
Bogle-L'Ouverture Publications Ltd
London

First published by Bogle-L'Ouverture Publications (1981)
Written in 1973
141 Coldershaw Road, Ealing, London W13 9DU.

© 1981 Neville Farki.

Distributed by Bogle-L'Ouverture Publications
141 Coldershaw Road, Ealing, London W13 9DU.

ISBN (cloth) 0 904521 21 4
ISBN (paper) 0 904521 22 2

Printed at the Press of Villiers Publications Ltd., Ingestre Road, London N.W.5.

CHAPTER 1

'Yes, time to dig up from this place'

'Karl, . . . Karl,' Kojo called. The spring on the bed in the other room started to squeak as Karl awoke and turned on his back.

'K . . a . . r . . l,' Miss Birdie called.

'Yes, mam,' he replied.

'Get up, man,' she said, 'and wake up the other ones.'

It was about six o'clock Monday morning in late September. Day had just begun to break and, every now and again, a cock would crow. For most people in Guys Hill, this meant that it was time for them to get up and start the day's activities. It was the same thing for Karl's family. Kojo was his father. He was black, medium built, and had a few strands of grey hair to the side of his head. Kojo was married to Miss Birdie. She was a little shorter, slightly darker in complexion, but much fatter than her husband. Both people were in their forties and had been living together for over twenty years. Kojo was a farmer and Miss Birdie a higgler. Although they were poor, they tried their best with the children.

Karl was the first child. He was twenty-one years old, about the same complexion as his mother, five feet ten inches tall, well built and wore a little beard. He looked much older than his age. Tom was next and, although two years younger, he was nearly as big as Karl. Pat and Geney were the two girls, with Pat being the elder and bigger of the two. Junior was the last child. He was nine years old, and his small face bore a close resemblance to his mother's. Although Miss Birdie loved all her children, she had a tender spot in her heart for the 'wash-belly'.

The little house in which they lived had three rooms. One was used as a hall and dining-room, and the other two as bedrooms. It had a long narrow veranda, with strips of board about three feet high around it. The house was painted outside in bright pink, with dark green on the veranda strips. The few banana trees to the front, almost hid the house in the early morning.

After about five minutes, Miss Birdie called again from the room, 'Karl, . . . Karl.'

'Yes, Aunt Birdie.'

'You don't get up yet?' she asked in a stern voice.

Karl got up and then sat back on the edge of the bed. He

slapped Tom and Junior, then stretched over to the other bed and pulled the sheet off Pat and Geney.

'K . . a . . r . . l, they get up yet?'

'Yes, Aunt Birdie.'

Karl had got into the habit of calling his mother 'Aunt Birdie'. He had left Guys Hill when he was about six years old and lived in town until he was thirteen. He lived in Kingston with Kojo's older sister. Her name was Hilda. Because Karl could not pronounce the name when he was small, he used to call her 'Aunt Da'. The woman worked as a 'ward-maid' at the Public Hospital. She did not have any children and had asked Kojo and Miss Birdie to send Karl to stay with her. A child living with her might change her luck, change it so she could bear one for herself. Aunt Hilda lived in August Town and used to send him to the primary school there. Every holiday, Karl would go back to Guys Hill to spend the time with his parents. As a boy, he believed that Aunt Da was his true mother and Miss Birdie was a good aunt. Nothing more. Although when he grew up, he realized the truth, he still called his mother 'Aunt Birdie'.

Karl came out of the house. The night dew was heavy on the low grass around the building. Water was still dripping from the zinc roof of the house onto the little kitchen behind it. He moved to the water drum beside the house. 'I don't feel like going work today,' Karl said to himself. He took the big mug and poured some water in the face basin. The tank was nearby. For years Kojo had applied for a pipe, but till now, no pipe.

'I don't feel good at all. Me mind mix up bad.' He started to wash his face. 'Cho—I feel like a bag of shit.'

Karl put the soap in the dish and the toothbrush into his back pocket. As he started to dry his face, he looked up and noticed that the sun had just peeped up behind the nearby hills. It had a beautiful colour looking like a bright mixture of red and yellow. There was more yellow than red. Between the sun and his mood, there was so much difference.

By this time, Junior had gone with Tom to get some milk from the cow and to move the old donkey that Miss Birdie used to help collect her load on week-ends when she was going to market. Kojo was getting ready to go to his field. He had to be early as Mass Joe, an old friend, was coming to help him for the day. Tomorrow he would also have to be up early, but this time to work on Joe's farm. Pat was sweeping out the house and Geney was washing the plates. Soon she would have to help Miss Birdie prepare the breakfast.

6

'Karl, what happen to you?' Miss Birdie called from the kitchen window. 'Why you not getting ready to go to work? Come, man, carpenter trade is not too bad. Time for . . . ' Miss Birdie turned away from the window as the dumplings she was frying started to burn.

'Yes, time to dig up from this place,' Karl completed what he thought his mother should be saying to him. He thought for a while, 'After I come back from town, spend two more years in school, I reached class six. And although I don't have any big brain, after two years with Maas Charlie, I could put up any three room building.' He walked towards the big ackee tree at the side of the house. 'And now after four years with this man, him still want to treat me like bwoy learning the trade.' Karl started talking to himself. 'Yes, the person who did give him the name Charlie never do a better thing. All that man know to do is to f . . . . ' He shut up quickly as his father was just passing by.

'What you saying, Karl?' Kojo asked.

'I was just saying a not going to work today, sah, as all Maas Charlie know to do is f . . . . ool 'round people. I don't feel like a going back to work with him.'

His father looked at him and shook his head.

Karl leaned on the ackee tree and watched his father pass him and went into the house. A few minutes later, Miss Birdie was carrying Kojo's breakfast to him. And about ten minutes later, he left for his field down the road. As Karl sat down at the foot of the tree a cling-cling bird enjoying his early ackee dish, started to sing a merry tune. Karl looked up just in time to see the little bird lifting its tail feathers. A soft, wet bit of mess landed on his bottom lip. In one action Karl jumped to his feet and picked up a stone. He threw the missile at the bird. It hit a limb, bounced back, crashed through a pane of window and landed on Miss Birdie's bed. Karl felt like cursing some bad words.

Miss Birdie bellowed from the kitchen, 'Bwoy, you drink mad puss piss . . . Een?!'

But Karl did not answer. He did not know what to say. He just moved to the basin to wash the mess from his lip. When he reached, the soap was not there. Someone had carried it into the house. Karl shook his head, 'Yes, yes, two trouble better than one.'

It was now about half-past seven. Tom and Junior had come back with the milk but Karl left the yard without getting his breakfast. He just was not in the mood to eat. His mind was on the way Maas Charlie was treating him.

7

As a young man, he had to plan for the future. Maas Charlie did not get jobs often and when he got a building to put up, Karl and four other men did most of the work. Sometimes after they laid the foundation, Maas Charlie would come to see how they were getting along, one or two times each day. Despite this, they were only getting eight dollars a week. When they complained, Charley used to say that it is because they were lazy and did not want to work.

'What use eight dollars have to a working man these days? I don't want to live with the old people all the days of my life. I would like to have a house and a family too. With the way cost of living going, eight dollars can hardly buy food for me.'

He walked down the road until he came to Maas James' shop. As he went inside he noticed that although it was so early some men were in the bar drinking rum.

'Give me another whites,' one of the men said.

'Yes,' said another.

'The white rum really good to wake up the spirit.'

Karl thought for a minute, 'Yes, white rum really good. Good to wake up you duppy when the blood in you alcohol stream burst you heart string.' He looked across at them, 'Rum must kill some of you, must!'

The first man spoke again, 'Yes, Maas James, give me another shot of the whites.' He paused to finish what was in the glass. 'But, man,' he continued, 'you have to trust me this one.'

Karl looked again at the men. Were they sane, when on Monday morning they wanted to trust rum? These same men had women and children at home suffering! Then why did they want to drink so early? And why did government allow rum bars to open all day to sell this drug? Why?

Maas James saw Karl and the other people waiting on the grocery side.

'Young Kojo, how the morning? What you want?' the shop-keeper asked.

'Sell me a pound of flour, quarter pound of salt fish, big gill coconut oil,' Karl paused, 'and sell me a box of matches and half pack cigarette.'

Maas James had started weighing the flour but stopped when he heard him mention cigarette. Karl used to smoke before but used to ask someone to buy it for him.

Maas James spoke, 'So you start with this one, you soon move on to the other one.'

Karl knew that the man was talking about ganja. 'But, Maas

8

James, you shouldn't surprise that I smoking cigarettes. Is the example you older ones set for me. If is something bad, why nearly the whole of you do it? And 'bout the other thing, I wonder if is because you and the estate owner don't get nothing from it, why you so much against it. Is you same people sell rum twenty-four hours a day during the week, forty-eight hours on Saturday and on Sundays after church.' He stared at the shop-keeper, 'No true, sah?'

Everyone was looking at Karl. The three men who were over the bar came to look also. Each one was clinging to a glass with a little 'devil soup' dangling in the bottom. Karl got the things, paid Maas James and left the shop. He was going down to the river to spend the day. He wanted to be alone, to decide what to do, how to get away from Maas Charlie and to make his life better.

It was now after eight o'clock. The morning was still young. The sun had come from behind the hills and was spreading its rays over the whole district. The sunlight, passing between the leaves, formed a beautiful patchwork on the road. As Karl passed under a cedar tree, a cling-cling bird flew off the tree. It made a frightening sound as it disappeared into the distance. Karl wondered if it was not the same bird that had messed on him earlier and now seeing him feared for its life.

'Two twos are four.'

'Mary had a little lamb, little lamb.'

'Jesus was born in Bethlehem of Judea.'

Karl looked up. He was passing the primary school. The buildings were so full that some classes had to be held under trees. There was so much confusion. Stopping for a while, Karl saw Levi Annan teaching a class under a tree. He was Junior's teacher and sometimes came up to their home. He had just been teaching at the school for about three months, but was very friendly. He mixed quite easily with the poor people of the district. The youths loved him for that.

As Karl looked over at the school, he wondered how on earth children learnt under those conditions. The government was emphasizing education to build the nation. Literacy, high school and all was great, but primary education was the basis. It was the foundation of the educational system. Without good conditions in the primary schools, we could have . . . nay, we will need a million adult literacy classes. Karl gave a lazy wave to Levi Annan and moved on.

Further down the road was the biggest church in the district. It was empty and had a deadly silence around it except for the sound of a rat-bat squeaking from the roof every now and again. An overcrowded noisy school, an empty quiet church, what a difference . . . ! But yesterday the parents were all shouting for the Lord to help them to have a better life. Wouldn't the Lord agree to help the parents by first giving the children a fair chance to learn in school? Wouldn't he have allowed the church to be used even as a basic school for five days a week for nine months a year?

'Yea, the Lord would agree,' Karl thought, 'although parson may not.' He looked towards the house below the church. The front door was closed and the car was still in the garage. 'Wonder if him wake up yet?' Karl asked as he continued down the road on his way to the river.

He soon passed Maas Charlie's house. The door in the front room was open but he did not stop. Why? An argument may start and in the mood that he was in, a few bad words might just hit the ageing Negro.

As Karl passed Kojo's farm, he could see his father and Maas Joe hard at work, still fighting with the cutlass and the hoe. What else could they use when the most of the land was hillside? Certainly not a tractor. Every now and again they had to peel the corn from their hands. With the prices they were getting for their produce, the cost of things they need on the farm and not to mention the cost of living, the two farmers might have to start saving the very corn.

'From I know my father and, Maas Joe, I see them working. Man, I really hope my trade treat me better than that field treat my daddy. First them don't have any good land to work on. I really hope the carpenter trade turn out better, because if it don't . . .' he took a deep breath, 'ah, bwoy!'

Karl turned off the road, down the little track. Soon he was face to face with Guys river. The stream was very important to the community. Some farmers who were nearby could get water both for their animals and for irrigation. When there was little water in the tank that supplied the district, most of the women went to the river to wash. After they had finished washing, some of the braver ones would take a bath. It was on one such occasion that Karl got his first glimpse of naked mature female body. He would never forget that incident. It had set his mind on fire.

There was no one in sight when Karl reached the river. Just the big body of greenish-blue water slowly passing by. All was quiet except for the ripple of the stream as it flowed over one bolder after another. The silence was broken occasionally by the cry of a gull as it cruised over the water in search of careless fish. Every now and again, a coconut, a few fingers of stray banana, a bit of bamboo would float past and disappear around the corner. Karl and his friends used to come to bathe and catch shrimps almost every weekend. However, when he wanted a little peace and quiet, he came here by himself.

Karl sat down on a stone, took out a cigarette and lit it. Maas James would probably tell Kojo that he bought the cigarettes. Karl still did not feel comfortable smoking. He took up the paper bag with the food he would cook for the day. A little pan which was usually used for cooking was hidden further down the stream. As he started to walk along the bank his mind went back to his trade. If he left Maas Charlie, what would he do? There was no other carpenter in Guys Hill that could give him a work. What would he do then?

'Blood!' shouted a voice from behind the root of a nearby guango tree.

A frog landed flat on its belly on the bank in front of Karl. The cigarette dropped from his hand. The frog jumped back into the stream. Karl came back to his senses.

'Ha, ha, ha, ha, ha, a, a, . . . ,' the voice laughed as a head appeared from behind the tree. The person had been in the water and as he raised his head, Karl could see the water trickling from his locks.

'Ras Bongo!' Karl caught his breath, 'Man, you really frightened me.'

'Yes,' said the Rasta man, 'I man could see the brethren was in deep thoughts.' Bongo had stopped laughing. The man spoke slowly as he came out of the water, naked as the day he was born.

'Trying to catch two fish in this little net when that serpent came across I path. Anyhow, I don't mean the brethren no harm. Seen?'

The Ras did not have to say that as Karl knew very well that the man would not hurt him. Besides, knowing Ras Bongo very well, he knew that the locksmen who worshipped Rastafari were mostly peaceful people—so peaceful that many times, they suffered persecution from police, church and even some of their own district people. These were people who had been brought up to believe that low cut hair, well brushed or burnt to hide the kinks, looked good; that any form of worship, apart from Christianity was ungodly; that Afrika is a country of cannibals; that talk of loving oneself meant hating others; that talk of freedom from oppression meant useless bloodshed. These people saw Ras Bongo as a member of a group that was a disgrace to their race. No! Most hardly thought about their race as it would mean that they hated

11

other races. But surely these people saw Rastafari as a disgrace to the community and to the whole country.

Ras Bongo had come out of the river and was standing beside Karl. He was used to the man as the Ras came to his home quite often to talk with Kojo. Bongo must have been about ten years younger than Karl's father, yet he could behave as companion to both father and son. He also used to carry shoes he had repaired for the family. The Ras was the finest shoemaker in all of Guys Hill. Besides being good at making chairs, baskets, mats and hats, he could make decorations from wood, coconut shells and all kinds of local materials. Often Karl wondered if schools could not be made where men like Bongo could pass on these valuable skills to some of the youths. A big industry could develop around this, which could provide employment and at the same time supply people with these things at reasonable prices.

Karl used to spend a lot of time talking with Ras Bongo. The Rastaman always had much to say as he used to read and meditate a lot. Miss Birdie did not like seeing him with the Nyah as she feared that her son, like many youths in the district, might become a Rastaman.

Ras Bongo, slightly taller and slimmer than Karl, still had water dripping from his body. He put down the fishing net on the river bank, then began to use his hands to wipe the water from the black skin of which he was so proud. Karl had taken up the cigarette that had dropped when the Ras frightened him.

'The brethren have any more of the ital,' the man asked.

Karl took a cigarette from his breast pocket and put the butt between the man's lips. He then raised his cigarette and lit the Rastaman's. Bongo pulled on the cigarette, then he relaxed. Smoke streamed through his nose like a chimney. The two men sat down on a stone under the big guango tree, their faces turned to Guys River.

'Ras Bongo, man, I having a hard time on the job. Is nearly four years now since I working with Charlie. And guess what?'

'What happen?' Bongo asked.

'Although I have to work so hard, I get only eight dollars to carry home Friday eve—.'

But before he could finish the word the Ras started to chant.

'Death to all down-pressers. De . . . a . . th to those who trod upon the children of Afrika. The day will come when I and I shall rise up and smite them down.'

The Rastaman was dead serious as he chanted. Karl always felt nervous whenever he heard the man speak in that way. There was silence for a while.

'Yes I,' Bongo said in a calmer tone, 'the day will soon come.'

Karl took another pull on his cigarette, then he said, 'Brethren, I am thinking of leaving here.'

The Ras looked excited. 'Where to? Afrika?' he asked. 'The big General in Uganda and many other states want I, specially the skilled Afrikan, to come and help to build the mother country, I and I should want to go and build our own.' He looked at Karl, 'No true Jah man?' he asked.

Karl nodded his head to show that he agreed.

The Ras smiled and stroked his beard. 'True, true.'

'Yes, brethren,' Karl continued, 'I thinking 'bout going to town, thinking to go and stay in Kingston with Aunt Da.'

'Who that?' Bongo asked.

'Aunt Da is my old man sister who I kind a grow up with. She come up Guys Hill here a few times and always want me to come back and stay with her.'

The Ras threw a pebble into the stream. 'Yes, I man think I know the woman. One Sunday Kojo man, did carry her up to the shop, so that I man could sight her.' He smiled, 'Nice woman. If I was clean-face man and hold a few more years, I man prob'ly could capture a daughter.'

Bongoman had always lived by himself, leaving the district every week to take something for his mother in Benbow.

One of the fish that was in the net jumped out and landed beside Karl. He was frightened as for one minute he thought it was another frog. Taking it up and putting it back in the net, Karl then put a stone on the mouth of the mesh.

'So what you think 'bout it, Ras?' the younger man asked, taking back his seat on the rock.

'Well,' Bongo began, 'the city dread. It wicked and vile. The country parts bad but not half as bad as the city of Killsome. It just like when this river come over. True I . . . Muddy from top and the mud wash right down to the bottom.' Bongo moved his head from side to side. He continued, 'But if a man can hold a good slaving, that man can make a little dunny. A little something to survive in this wicked land. It dre . . . a . . d . . . !'

Karl butted in, 'Survival of the fittest and the weak get grine.'

'Yes I!' The Ras started to get up. 'But as the father say him hear the cries of him children in captivity . . . in Babylon.' With this Ras Bongo got up, threw his cigarette butt into the water and moved towards the bank where he hid his clothes. He had work to do at the shoemaker shop. When he was leaving he took two of the fish he had caught and gave them to Karl.

'So when the man plan to leave?' Bongo asked.

'I don't decide yet, but it wouldn't be before weekend.' Karl replied.

'Well, when the brethren decide to ride, give I man a sound,' Bongo said.

As he moved off Karl said to the Rasta, 'One love, Brother Bongo.'

The Nyahman turned and replied in his usual cool way, 'True, True.'

Karl spent the rest of the day by the river. He caught some shrimps and cooked it with the food he had bought at Maas James' shop. He thought over his plan to go to Kingston. That very evening, he was going to write his Aunt Hilda. It would be best to go from Saturday and he could start looking work the following Monday morning. He had heard so much over the radio about so many new housing schemes and factories to be built. Karl thought that as a tradesman he should be able to get a work on one of these construction sites in no time. When he got the job, he would save up as much money as he could. In the meantime he could meet a nice girl. They could come back to Guys Hill, build a little house and live. Kojo and Miss Birdie would soon have grandchildren to play around their feet. He got up off the stone, and gazed across the river.

'Yes, I am going to dig. Things mus' better there.'

It was now getting dark. The crickets had started to whistle and a few frogs were coming from the water on to the land. It was now time to go home. As Karl was to turn on the track up to the road, he looked up stream. He couldn't believe his eyes. 'Is a woman bathing?' he mumbled to himself. Karl walked quietly toward the moving object where he could see it more clearly. He stopped dead in his track and hissed his teeth, 'Pswoou, is Maas Joe old brown donkey drinking water. Pswoou!'

The donkey held up its head and spotted him. 'He-haw, he-haw,' the ass brayed as it jumped out of the water and galloped upstream, along the river bank.

After Karl left the river Monday evening he went straight home. He wrote the letter to Aunt Hilda telling her to expect him on Saturday. Karl didn't say anything to Kojo and Miss Birdie about his plans until the next evening. His father did not like the idea,

14

but he felt that Karl as a young man would have to try for himself. It was not so with Miss Birdie.

'No, not a fart! You not going leave here! You believe that after I carry you in me belly for nine long months and then have to stretch out my p . . . stretch out my parts to bring you here, you want to go to town for rude boys and police to shoot you?'

Soon after, the woman's anger had turned into grief. Karl could see tears setting in his mother's eyes. But although he loved her so much he could not let tears stop him.

'Aunt Birdie, I don't want to leave me family. I would like to be here all the time. But, I can't stay here and make life better. Have to leave and try out life, so that I can help myself and help you and the old man when you can't help you'self any more.' Karl paused for a moment and looked his mother in the face.

'Aunt Birdie, I have to go. I have to try and make myself a better man.'

Miss Birdie looked at her son for a while, then turned into her room humming a hymn as she went along :

'Rock of ages, cleft for me,
Let me hide myself in thee.
Let the water and thy blood,
From thy riven side which flow,
Rock of ages, cleft for me . . .'

Karl did very little for the rest of the week. He saw most of his friends and told them of his plans. He also saw Maas Charlie one evening. Karl wanted to leave unexpectedly, so he told Maas Charlie that he stayed away from work because he was not feeling well. Deep down, he felt that Maas Charlie was wicked and just wanted to keep down other people. Charlie's favourite phrase was, 'each man for himself'. He used these words so often that it stuck in Karl's brain like a bad sore mark on a fat leg.

During the week Karl also saw Maas Joe and his wife, Kate. He told them that he was leaving. When he went to see them that evening, the two people were sitting at the back of their house. Miss Kate was helping her husband to learn to read and write. Like many peasants in the district, Maas Joe could not read since, as a boy, he had to spend most of his time working in the field with his parents to help provide for the family. Maas Joe and Miss Kate were so sorry when Karl told them his plans. When he was leaving they gave him some good advice and two dollars.

How these people who were poor could still be so kind? Maas Charlie who was better off, would want to take money from him rather than give.

15

Karl also went to see Levi Annan and Ras Bongo before he left. The Rasta man gave him a pair of sandals and a black knitted tam. The teacher gave him two little history books. Everything was now set for Saturday.

CHAPTER 2

'Laud, I place me son in Your hands'

Karl went to bed from about nine o'clock that Friday night. No one else was at home. Kojo and Miss Birdie were gone to a community meeting. Geney, Pat and Junior had also gone with their parents. Kojo used to take them to the meeting ever since they were small as he felt that young people should take part in every thing that was happening in the country. Karl knew that soon his parents and the children would come home. But as usual Tom would be the last to come in. Miss Birdie used to quarrel because she heard that Tom used to spend Friday evenings playing domino at Maas James' shop. She even heard that sometimes he would drink beer with some bigger men. Karl turned over in the bed. 'What Aunt Birdie don't hear yet is that Tom fooling 'round Maas James' daughter. Hell fall apart when she hear that, 'Karl thought. 'But as a young man, Aunt B must expect Tom to stretch him leg.'

His mind started to drift, 'Going to town tomorrow. Umm . . m . . mph. I hear that when a man short a girls in Kingston that man really short, and I not short. I . . . am . . . not short!' The young man smiled to himself. He turned over on his belly and put his two hands around the pillow. 'I . . . am . . . not . . . short!' Before long he was fast asleep.

Karl did not sleep well that night. He was half awake for most of the night. When he got up, he could not be certain of what he dreamt or had thought about during the night. But his half-dreams had all been about Kingston. Everyone was up early that Saturday. Miss Birdie prayed for about half hour that morning. Like even the most uneducated, when she went to the Lord, Miss Birdie tried her best with the Queen's English as if he could not understand 'patwa'.

As she was now about to end, she raised her voice, 'Almighty, you know how troubled these times are. I beg you to protect Karl. Protect him from the evils and tribulations of these days. Oh, the heart of man is so desperately wicked. Father, you know our every need. Laud I place me son in your hands, Amen.'

Karl was fastening his grip as his mother finished her prayer. He thought, 'You know our every need? Umm. Then why we

17

suffer so? And why we need to pray?' Karl smiled as he tied the grip with a piece of string.

It was nearly six o'clock. Soon the 'Star Bus' would be coming from Highgate. Tom carried out a box with some yam, bananas, ackee and a few other things that Kojo was sending for his sister Hilda. Karl finished putting on his clothes. Pat and Geney put some breakfast on the table for him, but he was not in the mood for food.

'Poo . . o . o . omp, poo . . mp, poo . . o . . o . . o . . omp' came the sound of the bus horn. Karl was waiting at the gate with his grip and the box of food. Kojo, Tom, Pat, Geney and Junior were all there. Miss Birdie watched from the veranda. Since the evening he had told her about his plans, she was like a sick woman. Karl hugged his brothers and sisters and said goodbye to his father. The bus turned the corner and was now approaching the gate, Karl stretched out his hand. The bus slowed down and then stopped right at the gate. The two side men put the box on the top of the bus. As he entered the bus with his grip, he turned to wave goodbye to his family. He could see tears trickling down his mothers cheek. For one minute, Karl felt like getting off the bus. But no it was too late. The Star Bus was moving off.

As usual on a Saturday morning the bus was packed—people going to work, people going to market, people going to look for their families, people going to look for their friends and some to look for their enemies. There was one group that Karl noticed first as he entered through the back door of the bus. Oh, they loved to sit in the kitchen. It was as if the back of vehicle was theirs. These were the market women.

'Laud, who this? Miss Merl, see Birdie son here,' one of the women said as Karl put his grip on the rack over the seats. 'You don't know me?' she asked.

Karl looked at her. She seemed to be about the same age as his mother. Like most women, and unlike most men in the area the woman had on more than her fair share of fat. She was very black. Her polka-dot dress was clean and well pressed, one could almost see the starch in it. The woman had on a bandana head tie which showed up her pure African features. She was just beautiful.

'E . e . eeh, Birdie son, you don't remember me?' the market woman asked again.

'No, mam, I don't remember you.'

'Me name is Elfreda O'Riley. Me and Birdie was school mates

and when she used to go Coronation market, we sell on the same stall.'

Karl used to hear his mother talk about Miss Freda and sometimes the woman sent things for him and the other children. Elfreda O'Riley, Elfreda O'Riley, he thought. Where the hell black people get them names from? If it not English, French, Spanish, Indian or Chinese, it is Scottish. We have every one except Afrikan names. Tell them you name Wantum Enkaka and them laugh you to scorn.

Karl finished fixing his grip and stood over the seat where the woman was sitting. 'Yes, Miss Freda, a going to town, mam. Going to stay with me auntie at August Town.'

'Then when you is going to come back?' the woman asked.

'I don't know, mam,' Karl replied. 'I am going to see if I can get a job to make life better. Can do carpenter trade, but I don't see no progress here. Every day only working to build up another man. I want to build up meself so I can care for the youths when a have them.'

Freda looked at Karl from head to toe. She smiled. 'Then, young Kojo, you is thinking about children already?' Freda asked.

Karl was about to answer when he noticed that the woman sitting beside Miss Freda was going to say something. Like Freda and nearly all the other market women in the bus, she was well dressed and wearing a head-tie.

The bus was about to descend that steep hill known as The Devils Race Course. The woman looked up at Karl and then across to Miss Elfreda. 'Freda, don't ask the young man no fool-fool question. How you mean to ask him if him thinking 'bout pickney? You don't know that from the boy is sixteen him can plant him seed. And I hear 'bout a fourteen-year-old father up at Benbow. Don't know if is waiscoat or jacket, but that is what I hear.' She stopped talking and looked through the window.

Miss Freda slapped her on her hand.

'Merl, you too out a order,' she said with a short giggle.

Karl did not know what to do. He kept looking serious.

As the 'Star' moved slowly down the steep hill, it passed the dwellings of many poor people perched precariously on the hillsides. They stood like posts a furlong apart on The Devil's Race Course. As the bus stopped to take up a passenger, the woman stopped talking. When the bus moved off again, the woman started talking again.

'Freda,' Miss Merl continued, 'I have a son, you see, and him going to Junior Secondary School down Bog Walk. And miss'is, as

19

soon as the boy little bit bigger, I going to tell him 'bout life. Me know that young people is young people and like to have them fun. But I going tell him, beg him, preach to him, that after him reach sixteen, him must be careful, put on him guard. Because if that boy should trouble a woman daughter, a . . . '

Miss Merl could not finish the sentence. A goat had run across the road and the driver of the bus had to slam on the brakes. Cries came from all around.

'Maasa God, save me!' 'Laud have mercy!' 'Jesus save me!' The side-man at the back door hit his head on the door. 'Raas-claute!' he cursed. He followed through with two more in quick succession.

The bus stopped briefly, but seeing that no one was hurt, it soon moved off again. Miss Merl started to talk again. 'Yes, Freda, I would like me son to get a good education, because we who don't have the education, have life too hard. It is only them who have the big brains, only them and the backra pickney that don't have it hard.'

'True you talking, Merl,' Miss Freda said.

Miss Merl continued, 'Look at we . . . we carry food to market—the staff of life, important to the whole country. If you don't think is true, make all we market woman stay 'way from market for one week. See if teacher, doctor, backra wife and pickney dem don't eat them shit! Yes, eat them dung. Yet we the producers—the farmers, higglers, dressmakers, masons, carpenters—get the dregs.' Then, looking up at Karl, 'See Birdie son here, him have to run way to town. You see.'

The bus was coming down the last hill before it reached Linstead. It was moving slowly, but the engine was revving under great pressure. Karl knew that it must have been in first gear. The brakes alone could not hold such a heavy loaded vehicle, so heavily loaded for a bus that was far from new. The more people, the more load, the less safe, but the more money.

As the bus came off the hill, Karl could see the level land before him. It was covered for acres with oranges on one side and sugar cane on the other. Karl's mind went back to Kojo, Maas Joe and many small farmers he knew at Guys Hill.

'Look that,' Miss Merl said, pointing through the window. 'All on this side, is one man own it. All on the other side, him son own that. Legacy from slavery time, pass down from one generation to the other. Poor black people like me and you work over there for pittance, buy the orange them at high price to make Mr Goyle and him son fat.'

The woman mentioned the name with scorn. Karl remembered Maas Charlie's favourite words 'each man for himself'.

Miss Merl twisted herself on the bus seat, 'White on top, brown in the middle and black at bottom, is so here stay!'

'Merl, you chat too much!' Freda butted in. 'You don't see that you soon reach Linstead. You not praying that the market not too bad there?'

'Yes,' Miss Merl replied, 'but as I did say, I want me son to get a good education. Him won't have to fret 'bout market. When that boy breed a daughter, I want him to be able to take good care of himself and him family.' She looked up again at Karl, 'I really glad to see that Birdie son thinking ahead and planning for tomorrow. I love the young man them with good studyration.'

The bus soon reached a railway crossing—no gate, no lights, no nothing. The driver stopped a good distance from the line, as a train was passing. Good thing it was a careful driver. He was not the one who used to stop on the line to see if the train was coming. The train had now passed—eighteen carriages of aluminia on their way from the Bauxite Works. 'Whose bauxite works? Where was the aluminia going?' Karl thought as the bus crossed the line.

Soon the 'Star' reached Linstead market. Many people were taking up their things to get off the bus. Miss Merl got up. As she stepped out of the vehicle she looked at Karl.

'Good luck, son. All the best and don't fe'get Kojo and Birdie! God bless you.' Then she turned to her friend, 'Freda, a hope market good so you go home to you man early tonight.' She said teasingly, "Member is Sat'day nite tonite, hey, . . . hey, bam . . . bam!'

Karl sat beside Miss Freda for the rest of the journey to Kingston. He did not say much to the woman along the way. Karl used to go to Linstead fairly often, but it was quite a few years since he had been to Spanish Town and Kingston. A portion of the road near to Flat Bridge was still being worked on.

Just outside Spanish Town the bus stopped near to where a big housing settlement was being put up.

'Low Income Houses,' Karl's eyes glimpsed the sign. '$10,000 for two bedroom units, down payments as low as $3,000 and up to 6 years to pay the balance.' The bottom of the signboard, 'E.D.Y. Lyn & Co. Ltd.' A few of the houses were already erected. They were well placed as the settlement was placed on good farming land.

'Food must can grow inside house too, for if not . . .' Karl shook

21

his head, then worked up a smile.

The bus soon reached Spanish Town. The old capital was well located near to three sugar estates, Cayman to the east, Inswood to the west, and Bernard Estate to the south. The town looked like a place that had gone to sleep for some time, only to wake up later and find that it had too much of one thing, and too little of another. Too much of what?

Spanish Town had gone asleep and woke up to find that it had too many old, broken down buildings to shelter the mass of its people. And yet, Karl thought it strange as the old capital was lucky to have three of the country's largest estates, rather three of the largest estates in the country, near to that old town.

As the bus was about to move off from the market gate, Karl glanced at a clock. It was nearly eight o'clock. Like Linstead on a Saturday morning, many of the narrow streets were very crowded with people going about their business, most of them going to buy or sell something at some kind of market place.

Miss Freda sat still beside Karl in the bus. She looked as though she was wrapped up in her thoughts.

The market woman would go back home that night as she did not have much load. She, like most of the women from Guys Hill area, carried oranges, coconuts, mangoes and ackee when the season was in. Some also carried vegetables and food crops like yams and bananas to the market. In those bags and baskets on top of buses, trucks and cars, the higglers carried life blood to the towns. Most times these women, with the help of their men folk, would pick the load and buy the rest on Thursdays. Sometimes the bigger children would stay home from school to help. When Miss Birdie used to carry things from Kojo's farm, Karl suffered because of this. Sometimes on Thursdays and Fridays he had to stop from school to help his parents. If it hadn't been for this, he might have passed some J.S.C. subjects. He might have been a teacher and not a carpenter, although a district with a teacher and no carpenter was like the people in town without higglers from the country. Life might have been better.

Karl's mind went back to the women. There were not so many as when he took the 'Star' at Guys Hill, but they sat still sat in the 'kitchen'. After a higgler got her load, if it was plenty, she would have to go to market from Thursday night. She would usually have to spend Thursday and Friday nights either in the market or under a shop piazza. There they would half sleep, covering up themselves in crocus bags. They had to half-sleep or else they might wake up the following morning and find that every-

22

thing down to the bag had been stolen in the night. When market was bad, higglers like Miss Freda would have to stay in town Saturday night as well. If they did not sell all their produce by Sunday they would have to sell the remainder very cheaply or give it away. The money that they got after living like this for three days might be able to buy some things to take home, pay their grocery bills and throw their 'partner'. This was the 'poor people's co-operative bank'. Usually ten to thirty 'partners' from the same community would throw a 'hand' each week. This money would go to one member this week and another next week and so on, till all members would get their 'draw'. A partner had helped many a poor family to eat bread, wear clothes and sleep under a roof.

'But how farmers and higglers can have life so hard?' Karl thought as the bus raced passed Cayman estate. 'How higglers can have bad market when we import so much food? On one hand, the small farmers don't have no good level land to work on.

On the other hand, this estate, owned by persons unknown to us from slavery time, has miles of level land. Higgler and farmer can't find market for food while many people go hungry—and we still importing more and more food from places that also have them hungry people. Funny,' Karl thought. He gazed out of the window at the land on either side of the Kingston road.

The bus was now moving very fast. As it passed two cars most of the people looked back. Karl looked back too. Another bus was trying to overtake the Star bus. The other bus was now beside the 'Star,' neck and neck, but could not pass. Miss Freda was sitting very stiff in her seat. Karl could see the tension on the people's faces in the two vehicles. They were now approaching the roundabout. A car, coming from Kingston, moved around that intersection. The people in the Star bus braced themselves as the other bus swerved to avoid hitting the car. The driver of the 'Star' jammed on the brakes and swung over to the soft shoulder. The people in both vehicles were cursing. The two drivers laughed and waved to each other.

The bus was now approaching Six Miles. They were driving on the new four-lane highway. Although Karl was about to drive on the overhead bridge for the first time, from the moment the bus approached the bridge he recognized it. He had seen such a roadway in many foreign magazines. It was even built by a foreign company and paid for with foreign loans. The bridge looked magnificent, but wouldn't factories be a better investment? Superhighways or factories, which do we need more? One—more employment, the other—more taxes. Where are our leaders? Where are they leading the flock to? Along the super-highways of eternal debts! True a few factories had been built since the last time Karl had come to town. But these, like most of them were owned by people from America, Britain and Canada. 'How these people so kind!' Karl thought, 'so kind to leave their country to come and develop ours. Apart from the reward on earth, them cup of milk and honey must flow over when they reach beyond the skies—must flow over!'

Miss Freda turned in her seat and woke Karl from his day-dreaming.

'O God, this part I can't stand.' Miss Freda said.

She had kept so silent when the bus was speeding, but as it started to slow down, the woman's mouth got life again. 'On the broad road, things no too bad, but from you reach this round about, is pure chuck up business. Everything start moving like them going to funeral.'

Karl looked in front of him. The bus that had nearly caused the accident was just in front, crawling like the 'Star' it had been racing. They were three miles, from the centre of the city.

'And beside,' she continued, 'up here so stink.'

Karl looked out of the window. People were busy going about their business. Every now and again they would pass a pool of mucky water and a heap of garbage nearby. Some must have been there for weeks. One or two hogs and dogs with their ribs looking like guitar strings would be busy digging up the garbage, digging for life. But were these animals alone? Every now and again a squeal would be heard, as one animal would hit another to take away something precious from his fellow hustler. What a sight! But what Karl was seeing was not the best. If the bus had travelled along the highway along the sea front, he would have seen a better sight. There the fellow hustlers were not dogs and pigs, they were the beautiful bald headed big black birds, nicely called 'john crows'.

As the bus crawled along Spanish Town Road, he could not help looking outside. Behind the sidewalk were the shanty houses. Some looked like dirty old pieces of board and zinc nailed together. The people on the side walks and in the homes were all Afrikans.

'How people live like this?' Karl thought. 'And why them all have to crowd up here when so much idle land in the country? Besides Cayman estate have so much land just three miles from here, Why?'

The bus slowed down, then came to a stop. A man was sitting in the doorway of one of the shacks. He was a shade darker than the door he was leaning against. 'Wonder if him did come to town to make life better? I wonder?'

Karl was brought out of his deep thinking by Miss Freda. The market woman was getting off. The bus did not stop at the gate, as this would just cause everything to come to a standstill.

'Birdie son, God go with you,' the woman said as she got off the bus.

Soon the bus was unloaded. As Karl looked back to wave goodbye to Miss Freda, he could see a young boy standing beside the woman. The boy had his hand on a hand-cart. Karl remembered what Miss Merl had been saying on the bus. He remembered his brother, Tom who was about the same age and size as the youth with the handcart. 'Wonder, if him or him parents did come to town to make life better?' Karl thought.

Soon the bus reached Parade. Karl was now in the heart of the city, box in one hand, grip in the other. The big clock on the church tower struck ten o'clock.

CHAPTER 3

' . . . could see that you is a country man'

'Thief! thee . . eef!' screamed a woman from across the road.

The woman's cry made Karl jump. It was as if someone had hit him on the head with a hammer two times. He held on tighter to the box in his left hand and the grip in the right.

'Me purse, me purse, laud God a bwoy pick me purse! See him going up the street there!' The woman was pointing toward the corner of South Parade and King Street. 'Yes, see the man in the blue shirt. See him there. Help me somebody. Hold the damn the . . ee . . eef!' the woman shouted.

Two vendors selling on the piezza joined the woman in crying for thief. A man who was standing near to one of the vendors started to move in the direction to which she was pointing. Another man joined the first, then a woman, then another woman, then a little boy with a bag under his arm. In a short while, it was as if the whole street was chasing and shouting 'thief'. Karl looked further up the street. He could see a youth in blue shirt and black pants running across King Street. Two beefy policemen who were standing at the traffic light moved after the youth. The boy nearly ran into a bus that was moving off from the lights. He tried to turn up King Street to avoid the bus, but stepped in the slippery gutter and lost his balance.

The pick-pocket started to stumble. The crowd was closing in on him. One of the policemen in front kicked him as he struggled to regain his balance. The youth hit his head against the base of a statue and fell flat on his face. Karl moved in the direction of the crowd. One of the policemen was stepping on the boy's hand. Another man was taking off a heavy leather belt. He had a grim look on his face, the look that nearly every one wore. That wretched look, fixed by hard life, birth to death, was now hardened a hundred times. They had caught one of the real enemies, one that had so often taken away their pittance. Those who gave the pittance were respected, were feared. They had committed no crimes, 'Damn thief them, if is even a sweetie.'

'Kill them rass!' the man with the belt shouted.

He was striking the boy with the buckle of the thick belt. The crying boy was trying to explain that he came from Spanish Town

26

Road. He did not have a job and did not get anything to eat from the night before. He had been begging from morning and got only four cents. The youth wanted to buy a patty and soft drink. No one seemed to be listening to him.

'You born . . . a teef. So take licks in you rass cla . . . ' The belt finished the word.

The woman whose money the boy had stolen took off her shoes. The heel flattened the boy's nose. Blood spewed from it.

One of the vendors said, 'Is just a youth. Don't kill him.' Then she turned to the policeman who held the boy, 'Corpie, go on with him, sah.'

But the woman who the boy had picked was still furious. 'Them too dam thief. We must kill them out. You think is little hell I go through to get this little penny. Me don't have no man, no work, and to make him thief me two penny.' She was now holding the purse she had got back. 'Is Beverly Hills them must go with that.'

The policemen were putting the youth in handcuffs.

The man with the belt shouted, 'Don't send them to any damn prison, when them go prison, we taxes have to feed them. And when them come out tomorrow, them start holding up bank and shoot people.'

Another man who had just arrived on the scene was holding up his fist in the air like Mohammed Ali ready to deliver a knock-out. 'I want me own. I want to land this in him jaw bone. We must kill them out. Catch them and keep them in jail in the week. Then every Monday morning, tie them, one by one, on a police jeep, and drag them on the road from Constant Spring to Parade.' He was now holding up his two fists. 'Bet we would get rid a them!'

The two policemen by this time had draped up the youth. A big new police car arrived on the scene. The officers pushed the boy into the car and moved off with barking sirens. Karl looked behind him. He was standing under the statue of Sir Chief.

Sir Chief and his cousin Mister Menlie were the two men who led the country from the mid-forties to the late sixties. These leaders had laid the foundation for the country. After they resigned from active politics, two younger members of the family took over. Mr Reaper and Mr Joshua, both great men, continued to build on the foundation that the older ones laid. They continued in the good tradition of the family and were doing very well for themselves.

The statue of Sir Chief had been put in place of Queen

27

Victoria. It was at South Parade facing the sea. Mister Menlie's statue had replaced that of King George. It was at North Parade, facing the hills. As Karl looked at the bronze image, he thought that it was a pity the statues were positioned in that way. It would have been better for the two to be placed side by side facing the same direction. This would be a symbol to show that the two men had fought together to help to make the country what it was. When the younger cousins died their statues could also be placed beside the elders. This would be a great national gesture.

By this time, the crowd had dispersed. It was nearly eleven o'clock and everything was back to normal. The Saturday morning sun was pelting hot. Karl moved across the street to the bus stop. He was waiting for the number six bus to August Town. The heat of the sun, the bustle of the people, the wailing and screaming coming from the many small record shops together with the smoke from passing traffic gave Karl the feeling that he was on his way to hell. But the devil had taken such a long time to send the cart. It was nearly one hour since the incident with the pick-pocket. Karl had been thinking that an hour later he would be in Aunt Hilda's house drinking a little cool water. 'A soft drink cost fifteen cents and a patty about twenty. It is just a matter of time before each of them cost fifty cents. The drink is full of little sugar, a little gas and a lot of water. The bottle must cost more than the drink.' Karl thought, 'Not even a few long benches to sit on and wait for the bus, although people have to wait so long, no public place to get a little cool water to drink. Why should a youth have to pick pocket to get a drinks and a patty? Why life so hard for most of the people in this country? No wonder Ras Bongo call it BABYLON.'

The sidewalks were now lined with people going to different places and waiting on different buses. People waiting with their shopping bags coming from market, while others had empty bags going to some other market. The vendors, some merely children, were very busy selling little more than nothing. Karl had put the box on the sidewalk and rested the grip on top of it. He still held the handle of the grip in his hand. Now feeling exhausted, Karl was dying for a bus to come. He was waiting for over three-quarter of an hour before the bus finally came. Everyone at that stop, started to take up their belongings and rushed towards where it was stopping. The bus stopped and the passengers came out through the front door. The driver closed the back door and got up from his seat. He came down to where the conductress was sitting and the two of them started to talk and laugh.

A woman with a shopping bag in one hand and a little girl in the other started to curse. A man who was standing right in the door way started to beat on the bus door.

'Conductress! Conductress!' the man called. 'Open up the bus door and make we come in. Is over a hour we waiting and now you and the driver sit down and a chat.'

Neither the driver nor the conductress paid any attention to the people. The company must get its money. The workers must get their pay, although it's small. Why worry about the people?

The man was now angry. 'The driver must be you man? Or you planning to give you man bun. Him mus' going fuck you tonite!'

No sooner were the words out of his mouth than the conductress looked around angrily, her moon face through the bus window.

'You must know,' she began, 'you should know! You look so frigging weak that you woman mus' give you bun!'

The man was about to answer the conductress when he looked behind and noticed that two other buses had just come in. After waiting for nearly one hour to get a bus, three had come within five minutes. When the driver and the conductress saw the other two buses, they got up. The driver went to the front and the conductress went to the back of the bus. Karl thought that they were only changing the sign to show that the bus was now going to August Town instead of Parade. He did not notice that after the sign was changed, more people had moved to the two buses that were parked behind.

The conductress was still quarrelling. 'Damn fasty shit-house! You think a going kill out meself to suit anybody?'

The driver had opened the door and people were now entering the bus.

She continued, 'Think I going kill out meself to suit any of you? I have me five pickney and the father don't business with them.'

An old man was going up into the bus.

'Come up, come up quick, sah,' she handed him the ticket. 'On this blasted bus from five thirty this morning and have to stand up every trip from Parade to August Town four times since morning. You think it easy? E-e-een, think me have elephant foot?'

She was now moving her hand very fast. Money, ticket, change, was the order. More and more people were pushing to reach into the bus. What a great difference a line would make! Line up, line up when the bus might drive off anytime? Line up, line up when one might have to wait for hours to get another? Line up when the whole life of the people had known only 'each man for himself'?

29

How can one tell crabs in a barrel to line up? How the people lived under it daily? Yet government after government had given the company ultimatums: 'Run the bus service good, or else . . .' But it turned out each time, that the complete statement was: '. . . or else we give you a fare increase.' So the bus company just made the service worse and worse and gets rewarded by fare increase, after fare increase.

Karl reached the doorway at last.

'You don't know that this is not a country bus?' the conductress said as she saw Karl struggling to enter the bus, box in one hand grip in the other.

He did not answer the woman. The important thing was to get into the vehicle and out of the boiling midday sun.

'How much the fare to August Town?' Karl asked.

The conductress put her hand on the bunch of tickets and stared at him. 'I don't believe you parents did send you to school,' she said.

Karl was puzzled. He could not understand why the woman had said such a thing. He wondered if he had been rough and she thought he did not have any manners. Other people were boring to enter the bus.

'Sell me a right through ticket,' Karl said as he handed the conductress a fifty cents note.

The woman sold him a twelve cents ticket and gave him back his change. Karl moved to the back of the bus. The conductress started to quarrel again. She was dying to send off the bus, although more people wanted to come in.

'You think it easy to stand up to work the bus for six or eight hours. And when me varicose vein burst, what the bus company going give me? When I work out me soul-case to death, what will the white man who own the bus give me?' she asked.

A male voice answered, 'Flowers. One red bunch from England, one white from Rhodesia and a blue one from South Africa. Three nice bunch.' It was the man who had caused her to start quarrelling at Parade.

The bus moved off and was now moving up Orange Street. 'Flowers,' the conductress looked at the man. He was sitting near to her on one of those seats with the back turned to the window.

'You think flowers can feed me five children, send them to school and pay rent?' The conductress asked. 'Flowers? eh, ehay . . .' she laughed mockingly.

The bus was about to pick up some people at the next stop. As the driver touched the brakes, the conductress was losing her balance. A man who was nearby, held her up.

'Thank you, sir. Them can't even make the bus with a little seat at the door so we can sit down and collect them money,' the conductress complained. 'We is human being too. And not even the big union that take we money every week don't see that.'

'But how come you want the company to make the bus with seats for you to sit down, and you won't run the bus good?' the same man asked.

'Run bus good? You expect me to run bus good when me have to stand up six days a week collecting the white man money, and me can't see what me working for. You must be mad!' she exclaimed.

A youth was sitting next to Karl, short locks under his cap, started to talk. 'See here, dread. The man who own them, don't drive in them, and the man who drive them and drive in them don't own them. Sight?' He continued rounding up his mouth and biting his lip as he spoke. 'Cho. From them and the politricksters driving in them big car, cho . . . the poor black man on the bus could dead. Until we own and control you know . . . cho.' The youth kept silent for a while.

When it was not the conductress, it was him. Although he spoke in the style that most rebellious youths had adapted and developed from the older Rastafarian, his message was clear. Own and control. Pay workers better. Profits would no longer leave the country to go abroad to kill black people in Britain and Afrika.

'It stay here to improve this land. Sight? People of this land must unite. Unite and drive out the invaders, drive the imperialis into the sea and let those who use it own and run it—not the capitalists from here nor from there.' The youth looked at Karl, 'Seen?' he asked.

Karl nodded in approval.

The youth rounded up his mouth once more, 'Cho, cho . . .'

By this the bus had reached Cross Roads. Karl could tell this from seeing the Careb theatre and the big clock opposite the cinema. While in town as a youth he had been to this cinema a few times. When going to visit Aunt Hilda, he would always look to see what film was showing. As the bus stopped, Karl looked at the posters advertising the films. Most of them had Africans playing the leading role.

Compared to his boyhood days, some things had certainly changed. There was still the great white Tarzan, brought up by an Ape, and still king of the jungles. From South Sahara to the Cape of Good Hope, the white man was king of every striking jungle in

31

the Afrikan continent. But Tarzan was not all, the great white Phantom the one who could never die, also ruled Afrika, even when he went to New York to look for his white woman Diana. Tarzan who was more fortunate, had his white woman Jane saved from the wreckage of a plane. No black woman good enough to be even their concubines! Oh, those poor black skins when they came across the path of any of these white heroes. Licked, kicked, a thousand defeated in a single battle by one of the white heroes. White heroes! But black heroes too!

As a youth Karl was sure to see a Tarzan or a Phantom every week. If not, he had to see even one film of his favourite cow-hand, Big John, killing off the American-Indians for their land. Black people used to cheer as much for Big John as they did for Tarzan and the Phantom. There were still other films in these days which had a few black people in them. They were usually sixty-year-old Toms calling five-year-old white kids 'master' and big fat black nannies taking care of white babies. But now after the awakening of the sixties in response to the shouts of black power, Afrikan faces, many though twisted from super-tom to super-niggers, were filling up the cinema scenes.

When the bus moved off from Cross Roads it turned on Half-Way Tree Road instead of August Town Road.

'Conductress, the bus is going the wrong way,' Karl said getting up from his seat.

The conductress turned around and looked at him. 'Going the wrong way? The bus not going the wrong way, you going the wrong way. From you come on at Parade with that big box and that tie up grip . . . could see that you is a country man.'

People were hearing the argument. They were staring at Karl. Most of them had a miserable look on their faces, as they simmered in the bus, packed like sardines under the mid-Saturday sun.

'This not a number six bus going to August Town?' Karl asked.

The conductress waited for a while before she answered. 'Man, this is not a six bus, is a thirty-six bus. You can't read? You didn't see when I did change the bus number and some of the people move to take the bus behind. It seem like most country people illiterate and fool-fool.' The conductress turned her face towards the front of the vehicle.

As the bus sped up Half-Way Tree Road, Karl felt like cursing. What was he going to do? Would he have to get off and have the trouble to go back to Cross Roads with the big box and grip. He started to get up from the seat. 'You see people like you? You know why you so fat?' Karl asked the conductress. 'Well, you fat

32

because you full a shit, full a shit like may-bug'.

He was about to stop the bus when the youth told him that he did not need to get off there. He could go to Half-Way Tree and then take a bus from there to August Town.

'Yes dread,' he said to Karl. 'Is so them wicked when them dealing with them same brethren.'

But Karl was still angry with the conductress. 'From I come on the bus at Parade, I hear the woman quarrelling 'bout how company treating her bad. True. But you can't fight the Bus Company by treating the poor people who take the bus like dog. If anything, try to treat passengers good, and them will back you when you fighting the company.' He pushed back the box under a seat. 'Imagine you change the bus number and when I ask the fare to August Town, you couldn't tell me the bus not going there.' Karl shook his head and uttered a big sigh.

The conductress looked at him without saying a word. The bus was well on the way to Half-Way Tree.

Karl got off at Half-Way Tree. The same conductress directed him to where he could get the bus to August Town. She warned him to make sure he took the right bus this time. Karl did not have to wait too long to get the bus. He waited for just around half an hour.

It was now almost one o'clock. He had left Guys Hill from six o'clock that morning and still had not reached his destination. He was hungry and bought something from one of the vendors at the bus stop. There were so many of them selling the same thing. The hardships of their lives were printed on their faces. So many people selling sweets and biscuits, while the sugar estates and big land owners had the best land and the country imported millions of dollars worth of food.

As the bus moved off, leaving the vendors behind, Karl mumbled to himself, 'People must have work and houses to live in, then we can start think 'bout big high-ways and over head bridge. Work, house and schools first.'

But the country was not all slums, bustling crowds and pick-pockets. Karl noticed a great difference between what he had seen coming to Parade and what he saw coming to Half-Way Tree. The sidewalks were not as crowded. The buildings were a thousand times better. The banks, the stores, the shopping centres, the same owners as down town, but here every thing was much better. And most of the people, a shade paler than those who flocked down-town looking for 'Sale'.

As the bus drove towards Papine, the difference between where

33

the poor and the rich lived became clearer. It was the same thing in the country parts. Look at Mr Goyle who owned the plantation on the way from Guys Hill. The people who worked in the citrus and cane fields were often crowded together in rent houses. The Goyles lived in a big house of several apartments with acres of idle land lying around the building. They called the acres of wasted land a 'lawn'.

The bus continued its journey up Hope Road. 'But why the government allow this? Why one family have such a big house and so much waste land, while other people crowd up in slums. Why?' Karl was looking at a house on the left hand side of the road as he thought: 'All that idle land can cultivate instead of waste labour and water to grow flowers and grass. Sorry something like a donkey couldn't get way over there.' He looked around and noticed that the man sitting beside him was looking at him, the box was under the seat and the grip was in front of them.

Karl turned to the man, 'If me old man did have a piece of land like that I wouldn't have to leave country to come here. Sure I could work it and make meself into a man. Why the government allow such people to have so much idle land all over the place? Why sah?'

The man stared at Karl for a while before answering. He looked like an old school teacher with his neck tie. For a minute Karl thought the man was dumb. Then his lips started to part.

'Young man, *don't* you know who lives there?' the man asked as if he were surprised. 'Well, if you don't know, just keep quiet and stop asking darn stupid questions. Do you expect our leaders to live in cardboard boxes pitched on a square of land?'

The man paused and Karl spoke, 'No, but the people them lead sh—'

But the man would not allow him to finish. 'Well, our leaders need fine houses and space to entertain foreign diplomats, and even once in a while to entertain the people, entertain the people so that they get the feeling that the place really belong to them. Then, of course, when the nation's business becomes pressing, leaders need a fine lawn to run around and keep body and mind in good shape.' He was dead serious.

'Then them need . . .' Karl tried to get in a word, but the old man would have none of it. He seemed to be hurt by the question that Karl had asked. The bus had passed one residence and was now passing another big iron gate. There were guards also at this gate.

He pointed a shaking finger towards the window 'And that is

the residence of a great son of the soil. A man of humble parentage, black like any one of us. We should be proud that the colonial days have passed when we had a white governor to rule over us. Don't get me wrong, I have nothing, absolutely nothing, against white people. Forget slavery. Now we are independent, we have our own flag, anthem, even our own national bird and we have a black Governor General. We should all be proud of him.' The man was looking quite pleased with himself.

Karl took a good look at him—his brown shirt turning white, . . . no his white shirt turning brown, but his tie looking brand new. Karl finally got his chance to talk.

'Them live in palace, get fifteen to twenty thousand dollars a year, allowances, cars, drivers, maids. But we the poor people who put them there . . . You hear why I on this bus now, sah?'

He looked at Karl as if slightly angry, then a smile. His mood had changed to a teacher looking in compassion on an unruly student.

He spoke. 'Think not what you country can do for you, but what you can do for your country.'

But before Karl could say anything else the bus was stopping at the Matilda's Corner stop. The man was getting off. As he got up, Karl noticed two big patches on his pants bottom, his shoes were well polished, but his little toe was peeping out of the right shoe. As he walked towards the bus door, he repeated his little memory gem. 'Think not what your country can do for you but what you can do for your country.'

Before long, the bus had passed Mona and reached Papine. There many people got off. Some, coming from the market, came in with their bags and baskets. The bus now looked so much like the 'Star' bus coming from Guys Hill that morning. The bus passed through the University and would soon be in August Town. As it entered the town, Karl could see the same thing he saw all along his journey—tall and short, fat and slim, brown and black, mansions and shacks. He got off two stops before it reached the terminus. Luckily for him, with the grip and the heavy box, it was a short walk from the stop to his aunt's home. Karl looked at the number on the gate post.

'10 July Road? Yes, right here.'

CHAPTER 4

'Evening Aunt Da'

Kingston is a town of many towns—Allman Town, Whitefield Town, Trench Town, Jones Town, Rae Town are just a few. August Town in many ways resembles most if not all of those towns. It has its stores, shops, rum bars, supermarkets, big houses and its fair share of slums. Its people, like those of the other towns, are largely working people. They provide their share of labour for the factories from Spanish Town Road to Rockfort, the business places from Papine to Parade, the public places from Mona to Three Miles and the residential homes from Beverly Hills to Constant Spring. But although in so many ways August Town resembled any other town in Kingston, it had one outstanding difference. As the people living there often say, 'August Town is far from town'.

It took Karl nearly three hours to travel the five miles from Parade to August Town. This was nearly the same time it had taken him from Guys Hill to reach Parade, a distance of over thirty miles. But at last, he reached his destination. Karl walked into the yard and up to the door of the little house. He knocked on the door and stood back as he heard footsteps inside.

'Karl,' the woman said as she opened the door and saw him. 'Karl,' she paused with opened mouth, 'Karl, I can't believe that is you grow so big!'

'Evening, Aunt Da,' Karl said as he put down the grip and the box in the doorway.

By this Aunt Hilda was hugging her nephew. She tried to kiss him on the cheek as she had always done, but this time he had to bow his head for her to kiss him. Although Kojo and most of the other brothers and sisters were fairly tall, Aunt Hilda was a short woman now approaching her late forties, being few years older than Karl's father, and although Hilda was fat and looked well, her face showed that she was not a kitten. But she was still strong in body and in spirit. The two people still stood at the doorway. Aunt Hilda stepped back from her nephew.

'Karl, you mean you grow so much over the few years I don't see you? How is Kojo? How Birdie, how Tom, Pat, the other girl and little Junior?'

36

'Everybody alright, mam, and them all say to tell you how-de.'
Karl paused, 'Aunt Birdie, the old man send this box with some
things for you.'
She looked at the box with the food. 'Ah, Birdie and Kojo always
sending things for me. Come, come inside. You must be tired after
that long journey. Come, come man.'
The two people entered the house, Karl carrying only the grip as
his aunt had the box.
'Karl, I so glad to see you. Just day before yesterday I get the
letter that you write me. I was telling Rachael . . . remember Miss
Rachael, from over the next yard?'
Karl nodded, 'Umm . . . yes.'
'Well, I was telling her that you coming back to stay with me'.
They were now in the little kitchen. Two pots were boiling on
the two burner kerosene stove in one corner. Karl remembered
that since leaving Guys Hill he had eaten only one five cents bun
and drank a pint of pale yellow coloured watery liquid from a box
labelled, 'orange juice'.
He put down the grip to rest near to the table with some plates
on it. 'Yes,' Karl said, 'I remember Miss Rachael. Sometimes
when you did have to go to work on night shift, I used to stay over
her yard with the children and her husband Mr—' But he could
not remember the name.
'Stone, Mr Stone,' his aunt reminded him, opening one of the pots
as she spoke. Steam gushed out of it.
Karl was surprised that he had forgotten the name. When he was
a little boy growing up in Aunt Hilda's home, he and his playmates
used to nickname the man 'Mr Tone'. He used to have a terrible
bulge in his pants. Many people thought he had a 'bowson' but that
was not true. The man was merely gifted. Vernal Stone had been so
kind to Karl. To him as well as Miss Rachael, Karl was like one of
their children.
Aunt Hilda pushed the box under the table and then turned off
the stove. Karl still had the grip beside him. The woman turned
to him.
'Put the grip in the next room for the time being and come and
eat a little something.'
Karl left the kitchen to put the grip in his aunt's room. The house
had two small rooms with the kitchen, bathroom and toilet in the
back. Aunt Hilda used the bigger room as her bedroom and the
smaller one as a kind of living and dining-room. But she had a
small folding bed in one corner. As a youth Karl used to sleep on
this bed and when he came to look for her that bed was his.

37

Not much of a house but it was the best the woman could afford. And she tried to make herself comfortable.

As Karl put down the grip, he looked around his aunt's room. It was as usual clean and tidy. On the bed were two well pressed green uniforms. These were the clothes that all the ward maids at the Public Hospital wore on the job. Yes, when he has his family, his house has to be a bit bigger, but his woman would have to keep it just as tidy as his aunt kept hers.

He went back into the kitchen. Aunt Hilda had taken off the pot and started to share out some food in two plates. Rice and two pieces of yellow yam in one plate and stew peas and pigs tail was about to go in the other. She held the plate over the pot, spoon resting in the stew.

Aunt Hilda turned to Karl, 'You eat pig's tail?'

'Yes, Aunt Da,' he replied.

'I have to ask as I know all the young people now a days don't eat pork. All a them seem to want to turn Rasta.' Then taking up one plate in each hand, 'Let me put it on the table here for you. Sit right here and eat from the old woman again.'

Old woman? If Aunt Da had a man, then she would just be in her prime, Karl thought. He smiled. His belly smiled too.

Karl sat down and started to eat. He was so hungry, he did not even remember to rest for a while and fool Aunt Da that he was saying grace.

'Eh, eh, you forget how to say grace, Karl?' the woman asked.

Karl looked around. 'No, Aunt Da, but I feel re . . eely hungry. The Lord will understand.'

The woman blinked her eyes twice. She moved her short fat black healthy self nearer to the table.

He dipped the spoon into the stew-peas. 'The food like Satan before me, tempting me. Just that a not strong enough to resist Satan on a hungry belly.'

Aunt Hilda opened her mouth, but no word could come forth.

Karl put another spoonful of rice and stew peas in his mouth. The food tasted wonderful. It was so much like Miss Birdie's cooking, except that Aunt Da seemed to know more ways of cooking a dish well. And she had no man or kids to cook for? There was a man when Karl was a boy living with her. He had even promised to marry her. But how could he marry her when he already had a wife? Wasn't that what they called bigamy? Aunt Hilda never tried seriously again. Also Karl could remember that once his aunt and a woman had a quarrel. The woman had called her a 'mule'. Aunt Hilda had cried all day.

38

'Karl, you don't know how a glad you come back to stay with me again,' she sat down with her plate of food. 'Tell me 'bout the country. What happen down there?'

As the two people sat around the table, Karl started to tell his Aunt about Maas Charlie, how he was working for the man for a miserable eight dollars each week. He told her that he wanted to be able to take care of himself and his family when he had one. If he did not get a work that would pay him more, he would not be able to make himself into a man. Karl told Aunt Hilda that Maas Charlie was interested only in robbing them to make himself and his family better. Maas Charlie did not care about the men who worked with him. When they complained he used to tell them that they were lazy. He told them that black people were too lazy and did not want to work. He could not afford to pay more. Most times Maas Charlie would tell them that next month he would give them an increase. But next month never seemed to come. 'Each man for himself,' he lived by this, it was close to his heart.

Karl also told Aunt Da that Miss Birdie did not want him to come to town as she was afraid that either criminals or police might kill him.

'Yes, the crime really serious in town here.' Aunt Hilda cut in. 'Everyday you take up the newspapers, every single day you see robbery and killing and raping and all manner of evil. When is not thief kill policeman, is policeman kill thief. Sometimes is either thief or policeman kill innocent people. It serious.'

Karl was almost finished eating. Aunt Da put another spoon full of the stew peas and rice in her mouth. She swallowed the food. 'But . . . what . . . to do . . ummm? If you want to make life better, you have to take the chance in town here. But, Karl,' she paused and looked at him across the table, 'is nearly twenty years me in town here and working every day. And see me here, sometimes is hell to buy a dinner. And you see this little fowl coop,' she looked toward the ceiling, 'a can hardly turn in it, have to pay forty dollars a month for it.'

Karl suddenly moved the glass from his mouth. 'Forty dollars a month for what. For this? Forty dollars!'

'Well, I live here for nearly ten years now. Up to five years back, I used to pay twelve pounds a month.' Aunt Da paused and looked down to the floor as if she was thinking over something.

'Yes, twelve pounds. It was not dollars time yet, so work out five years and at twelve pounds or twenty four dollars a month and another five years at forty dollars a month. See how much rent I pay since a live here.'

The woman got up from the table and searched a bottom drawer in the cabinet in a corner of the room. She gave Karl a bit of pencil and paper.

'Work it out and tell me, you read to higher book in school than me.' Aunt Hilda gave off a hearty belch. 'Pardon,' she said, then started removing the empty plates from the table.

Karl took the paper and pencil and began to work out the amount of rent his aunt paid in the ten years.

Aunt Da had taken all the dirty plates and other things from the table. After a few minutes, she called from the kitchen. 'You finish yet, Karl?'

'No not yet, mam,' Karl replied.

But it did not take him very long, 'Aunt Da, for the ten years . . . ,' Karl paused as his aunt came into the room. 'You pay three thousand, eight hundred and what?'

The woman looked at the paper, her mouth wide open, 'Eeen, three thousand, eight hundred and what? Laud God. Poor we poor people. No wonder we life can't better.' She shook her head. 'And this landlord, him own this house and four more in the settlement. Karl, I hear is seven hundred pounds him pay for this house. And me son, him only pay down two hundred pounds. Four hundred dollars in today's money. But as soon as him pay down on them, him rent them. So with the rent money, him pay for the four house in the settlement and the hell ever one that black backside and him red woman have in Mona.'

The man had borrowed money from the bank. He had security. The bank demanded that. What security did the poor have? If they do not get loans to start life, how can they ever have security? A poor woman paying nearly four thousand dollars in ten years. She still did not own a pane of window in the house.

Karl spoke, 'And the government know about all them things and allow them. Then they talk 'bout helping poor people'.

Miss Hilda shook her head, 'Umph, poor me, Hilda pay two thousand pound worth a rent to keep a man and him malatta woman in a big house.' She started to walk to the kitchen as if she was mad. 'Me . . . me . . . ' she said slapping her chest with each word, 'me, red up this finger, . . . me vote, when nobody don't business with how me live till election time?' She stopped in the kitchen doorway and looked back at Karl. 'Me Hilda vote again! Must be a new set. Not the same one family from '44. Not me.' Miss Hilda stepped into the kitchen. 'Maasa God, come take you world soon, come quick, cause I know what going happen here.'

Just coming from the country, hoping to make life in town, Aunt

Hilda's revelation was no encouragement. Karl got up from the table and followed his aunt to the kitchen.

'But, Aunt Da, from the time you working till now, how much they pay you as a ward maid down there? You couldn't save enough money to buy a piece of land and make up a house for yourself?' Karl asked.

'Buoy,' Aunt Da said in a stern voice. 'Land selling here from two to five thousand dollars a square. In country it little cheaper. But is when you can get it'. Then turning from the sink and staring at Karl, 'You hear that? Is when you . . . can . . . get it. Then one block cost twenty cents to buy and lay it. Ten pound a hundred. How you expect twenty dollars a week to pay rent, buy food, clothes and at the same time save up money to buy house and land. Eh! Tell me how!'

Karl did not, rather could not, answer. Only a fool or a crook, someone like Maas Charlie, could answer.

Aunt Hilda did not say anything else. She just turned to the sink and continued to wash the dirty things. Karl offered to help her. He used to help Miss Birdie sometimes in the kitchen. But his aunt said that she would wash the things and he should unpack his grip in the mean time.

Karl would have to keep his clothes in her room, but he would sleep on the little bed in the next room. He could keep the grip with the other things under the bed. Karl was glad as in the nights he would be able to sit at the table and read. This was a habit he had got from sitting up with Pat, Geney and Junior when they were doing their home work. With his own room, he could come in late without waking up Aunt Da. True, he would have to come in through the kitchen as the front door had only one key. But it did not matter. Soon he hoped to meet a nice girl. When they meet he would have to go and spend some time with her in the evenings. It was not right for any man to ask a woman to open a door for him when he came home late. A man should open his own door, even if it is a back door.

Aunt Hilda came into the room. 'Karl, you finish put up the clothes yet?'

'Yes, yes, Aunt Da,' Karl replied, jumping out of his little day dreaming.

'Ah right, make us go down the Supermarket and when we coming back, we can stop over Rachey. A going to wipe off me skin and put on piece a clothes. I won't take long,' she said and moved towards the bathroom.

Shortly after, Aunt Hilda and Karl were stepping out of the

gate. It was now around five o'clock and being 'short-day' the sun was going down. They crossed the street and started walking down July Road.

Saturday evening on July Road seemed in many ways like Saturday evening on the main road in Guys Hill. For one, there were many people moving up and down with their little bags of food often held tightly to some part of the body. It was hard indeed, very hard to get. A few had small pans dangling from one hand with a little kerosene oil dripping from the sides. True, there were no donkeys with half-empty hampers coming from market, nor were there many women with baskets balancing daintily on the top of their heads, but to Karl, it seemed as if the hand carts pushed mostly by barefooted teenaged boys, did the work of both hampers and baskets.

On Spanish Town Road, there were bare-footed youths in grimy clothes pushing hand carts, on July Road in August Town, barefooted youths in grimy clothes pushing handcarts. How come, Karl thought as he walked up the street with Aunt Hilda. But he was soon to be frightened by three little boys jostling and pushing against each other.

'Glee-News, Glee-News,' they said one after the other as they stood on the sidewalk blocking Karl and his aunt.

Aunt Da started to open her purse. Karl looked at the boys. The oldest one seemed to be about twelve to thirteen years. He was about the same size as the youth that had picked the woman's purse at Parade. The youngest was about eight years old and about the same size as Junior. But, Junior had on more flesh and his face did not look half so grim. The little youth's ribs were showing on one side where his gansie had a tear. Between the road, the boy's skin and his gansie, there was little difference in colour.

'What on the headline?' Karl asked the boys.

They stopped jostling and started to look at each other, putting their dirty hands with the money over their faces, on their heads as if it were the first time they realized that they had hands.

'We don't know, sah,' the biggest one said.

'Then, you don't go to school?' Aunt Hilda asked in a stern, motherly voice.

'No mam,' the second size boy answered.

'Then you parents don't send you to school?' she asked again.

The smallest youth started to move away as if he was expecting Aunt Hilda to grab him for a beating.

'Well, we don't go to school, mam, because we muma don't send we, mam. She say she don't have any money to buy food and pay rent much less buy clothes to send we to school.'

'Then you mother no—' but Karl stopped talking suddenly as he noticed the two smaller boys dashing out into the street. Into the middle of the street they ran as two cars came up the road. The bundle under their arms, each boy held out a single *News* as if the paper had the power of stopping each vehicle from bouncing out their little senses, and reducing them to mince meat. Neither their shouts nor their papers stopped the cars. A hard way to make a living, but what else could they do in a democratic country. They had the freedom to live like dogs or die like dogs. The two youths came back on the side-walk.

'Then you mother don't work?' Karl asked.

'No, sah,' the biggest boy said.

But the littlest one did not agree.

'A lie him telling, sah.' He came nearer to the group. 'She work election time and Christmas gone she did work down Mr Wong Supermarket. And is him we selling the *News* for.'

Malnutrition, probably from in the womb, was showing on him.

'Him give we twenty cents every evening and sometime two patty. But sometime the patty dem too stale and we can't eat them.'

The other two youths laughed. What else could they do?

As Aunt Hilda paid for the paper, Karl looked at the boys. He remembered the youth that picked the woman's purse, the bus conductress, the youths pushing the hand-carts, and now these selling the newspaper.

As Karl and his aunt left the boys, the woman began to talk. 'The little boy them sell the paper for Wong. The Chineman don't give stale patty to him dog. Him give them tin food. But him give the stale patty and only twenty cents to them for selling so much paper every evening. And him never even think 'bout giving some money to help to build a community centre where the same little boy them can go and learn to read and write and have a little fun!' The woman paused. 'But him don't even live in August Town!'

'Where him live?' Karl asked.

'Wong live at Beverly Hills. Right up in them heaven. Him children, bright and dunce, go to high school and all kind of big school. And when them want to have fun, them go to YMCA centre and to New York and Miami every holiday with them mother. One or two black people children, and only the big shots pickney go to the YMCA centre. And when Wong don't want them to mix, him send them to Chiney Club down Mona Road.' She glanced across at her nephew as they approached the shop. 'You don't see the Chiney them even have them own cemetry?' Not even them duppy to mix with our dead. You don't see that?'

Miss Hilda stopped, they had reached the supermarket. She looked at the sign. 'Umph, I don't know what going to happen to we black people down here. We fart if the Chiney-man, the Jew-man, the white and malata man them decide to lock up them place, we eat one another like how crab eat dead donkey— Umph.'

As his auntie went into the Supermarket, Karl stood at the door and waited. The supermarket was packed with people buying what little their money could for the next week and almost every single person was black, down to the palm. Mr Wong and his wife, looking down from the little room at the back of the building, were the ones that rescued the super-market from total blackness. The three cashiers were collecting money all week, yet they had none—so much like the men who built the hotels, but could not buy a drink in them, or like the ones that built houses, but had none of their own.

It was now sunset and, although a hour before the place was so hot, Karl could now feel the cool evening breeze as he waited for his aunt. A man came out of the supermarket, with his bill in his hands. He stopped near to Karl, looked at it, then just shook his head moved on. Others went in and out as if all was well.

It was more than ten minutes since Aunt Hilda had gone into the super-market. Karl waited patiently. What to do? Oh, he had the 'Glee-News', he could glance at the head-lines: 'Two murderers hanged this morning'; 'Two detained in killing of shop keeper'; 'Rail strike, no trains leave city'; 'Ministers off to U.S. and Canadian talks'; 'Cops to be upgraded'; 'Robbers take $400 from housewife'; 'Black man appointed to senior White House position'; 'President refuses to hand over tapes—Watergate'; 'Government boasts of growing economy'; 'Foreign bank makes $1 million profit last year'; 'Gonorrhoea can affect babies', 'Boy saved from stream'; 'Twelve granted decree nisi'; 'Question of the week—Should rapists be castrated when caught?' The headlines were bold and easily read. Many people had criticized the 'News' for carrying such items. But if that was the news of what was happening in the country, and that of other 'free countries', why not report it? Wasn't that what a free press in a free country was all about? If not, the Anglo-American lords who owned the paper would not have set it up a century ago.

Karl could now see his aunt in the supermarket. The cashier was checking her groceries. His mind came back to himself. He had

44

to leave Guys Hill because he was building houses for Maas Charlie. The conductress could hardly pay her rent, the youths selling *Glee-News* could not wear clothes. If he had stayed with Maas Charlie, then later in life he might be worst off than the conductress. His youths might not have even newspaper to sell. But what could happen to him here in town? Would things be better? 'Yes, it must be better!' Karl muttered to himself. After all the government and opposition were working to make things better. They travel abroad every week to get loans. Loans were helping the country so much. Look at the super-highway that ran into the slums. Forget the slums for the moment. Another loan will take care of them in the next five year plan, as well as with all those experts that came with those loans!

Karl looked at the people making up their faces as they paid for the groceries, no luxuries, just bare necessities. He thought, things must be better, if not for anyone, for me, or else, somebody going get fuck! He folded up the newspaper. 'Must better here than down country, must!'

Aunt Hilda came out of the supermarket, her bag of groceries held tightly to her waist. It was precious, precious like gold.

When Karl and his aunt left the supermarket, it was getting dark. The few street lights on July Road were turned on, and light could be seen coming through windows and doorways of many houses. It was not a long walk to where Miss Rachael lived, but Karl was feeling tired from his day's journey. His aunt, although still strong, was not able to walk with the speed that Karl knew when he was living with her before. Many things had changed since then. Some ten years ago, at that time of evening, August Town, wasn't half as busy. Then, most people took home their groceries in handle baskets. There were no supermarkets, but Wong still had the biggest shop on July Road. Now most of the women wore pants, shorts, mini and micro mini skirts. These exposed parts of the body that ten years ago were seen only in bedrooms. Ten years ago men wore roomy double-cuffed pleated pants. Now pants were nearly as tight as the women's underwear. Probably the cost of living had something to do with these changes. But despite the absence of a few bulbs that had got in the way of flying stones, the lighting on July Road, and most of August Town, was much better. The Electric Service made sure of that. The government paid the bill well.

It was a fairly short walk from the supermarket to the gate of Aunt Hilda's next door neighbour's house. As Karl and his aunt started to go through the gate, two miserable looking mongrels rushed towards them from behind the house, probably hungry, but surely angry. The dogs were barking mostly at Karl as they seemed to know Aunt Hilda.

'Hilda,' a woman's voice called from the side of the house, 'come nuh!' Then it continued, 'Stop, you have company.'

The dogs were still barking behind Karl. 'Don't worry 'bout them, man. Is only the pure head that have life. Scrape after them and see if them head don't reach under the house leave them body.'

Then turning to the dogs, 'Go way! Move! Damn dawg! Move!' The meager animals disappeared as quickly as they had appeared.

'Rachey, what happen?' Aunt Hilda said.

'Good evening, Miss Rachael,' Karl said standing beside his aunt and taking a good look at the other woman.

She took a step back and looked Karl over from head to foot.

'Hilda, is Karl grow so big? I can't believe me eye. Stop, him all have little beard. The same little Karl that used to eat out of me pot and sleep with them boys when you on night shift. It can't be him?'

The three people began to walk towards the verandah.

'Is me same one, Miss Rachael,' Karl said.

The veranda light gave him a better view of the woman. Miss Rachael looked very much the same way, a few strands of grey hair here and there, but much the same as when Karl used to eat from her pot. Although Aunt Hilda was a few years older, she had no grey hair. Miss Rachael was a bit more light skinned, taller, but not as fat. Indeed, she was slender compared to Aunt Hilda. Life seemed to have been more unkind to Miss Rachael than to her friend, although life was also tough with Aunt Da. As the woman moved to sit down on one of the two wooden veranda chairs, she looked so much like Miss Kate. But Miss Kate didn't have six children; she used to drink a lot of milk from Maas Joe's cow, yet she was slim. After all, maybe it wasn't hard life that made Miss Rachael slim.

The three people sat down on the little veranda, a woman in each chair and Karl on a ledge near to the step. He put down the groceries.

'So, Karl, me dear, what time today you come?' Miss Rachael asked.

'About two, mam. Leave Guys Hill from about six this morning.'

'Then how is the other one them?'

'All of them well, Miss Rachey.'

She looked at Karl for a while, then smiled, 'Buoy, you grow nice, sah . . . Umph.'

No one talked for a brief moment, and then Miss Rachael stirred. 'Just finish put on the pot to cook the dinner. Nobody not here but me. I send three of the boys them gone round May Road to take up the grocery as I just get the little pittance six o'clock this evening when a leaving work.'

'What kind of work you doing now, Miss Rachael?' Karl asked.

'Still on the maid work. Working for some white people name Mayer, man, woman and little boy. Rich people them, own the cement factory out Fort-Rock. And me have to work like slave every striking day.'

'I know the factory you talking 'bout. I hear 'bout it plenty times.'

Miss Rachael sat up in her seat, 'Karl, that life not easy,' she began. 'Have to work Sat'day day time when him and him wife gone to gamble at race track. Then Sunday them in front seat a church putting some of the race horse money in collection plate. One Sunday in the month, one single Sunday I get off. And for how much? How much you think I get?' She sat back in the wooden veranda chair.

'Hilda you tell him for me.'

Karl's aunt hesitated for a while, then she turned to her nephew. 'Is twelve dollars a week.'

'Twelve striking dollars! One de-gey . . . twelve dollars!' Miss Rachael said, beating her fist on the seat after every word. 'Five dollars can't even buy grocery. And besides,' she continued, 'the earliest I reach me yard . . . ' she belched. 'The gas you see,' she eased her body. 'Excuse me, manners,' she said and got up.

Miss Rachael came back soon after.

'Yes, the earliest I reach home, Karl, is four o'clock Sunday day time. Sometime is six, seven before I can leave to come home.' The woman stopped talking. She looked towards the gate.

Two boys were coming towards the house each carrying a small shopping bag of groceries.

'Is round the road you go?' Miss Rachey asked as the boys pass the side of the house.

'Yes, mam,' the bigger one replied.

'Evening, Miss Hilda. Evening, Miss Hilda,' the two boys said as they passed the veranda.

Miss Rachael spoke, 'Is way round May Road them coming from, I don't buy either at Wong or at the damn black nayga down the road. Them treat poor people like dawg and them never do one single, not one shit to help August Town! And when . . . '

But Aunt Hilda interrupted the woman. 'You know that the

47

only time I buy down Wong, is only when him have something that I can't get round the road. The little half-naked boys them that sell *News* for him only get twenty cents and two stale patty from him.' She paused. 'Then at the same time, them sell things so dear. Want to get rich quick.'

Miss Rachael sat up in her chair and started to pull off her tie-head. Karl looked at her well plaited kinky hair. She, like Aunt Hilda, Miss Birdie, and many other older African women, had never put fire on their heads.

'Hilda,' the slim woman began, 'them is wicked people. Murderers. Them is robbers, worst than the pick-pocket them. Because at least the pick-pocket is a sufferer. Him have to scuffle to eat sometime,' she continued, perched on the edge of the chair as she spoke. 'Some of them people, you work with them and them don't pay you nothing. Yet them sell them things so dear. Them is legal robber. Nobody trouble them, but make one of the little boy who sell paper for him put a pack of biscuit in him pocket. Umph . . . Police murder the poor thing. Murder him to death.'

Miss Rachael's stomach was still giving her trouble. Over the years she had not been eating right. Sometimes the gas would come up, at other times it would go down . . . down with a loud sound. Rachey continued, leaning back in the chair with her head-tie folded on her lap.

'People like that nyam dawg and the fowl-friggin, bald head nayga down the road too thief.'

Karl wanted to laugh, but the woman looked too serious. She must have had reason to talk in such vicious manner.

'Them so thief that them must thief milk out a coffee. I wouldn't too frighten if I hear that some of them thief them daddy off them muma already.' The woman looked at Karl as if she had forgotten that he was there. 'Pardon me, you hear, son.'

The two boys who had just come in with the groceries had to put them down in the kitchen and come back to the verandah. Miss Rachael told Karl that they were the two youngest children. She had six with her husband and all of them were boys. The fourth boy was giving her a lot of trouble. He didn't want to go to school nor to help with anything in the house. He spent most of his time gambling with some other boys down the river. Almost every Saturday, from morning till night, he would be over the whole August Town moving from one betting shop to the other. The boy was only fifteen, but knew the name, trainer, owner, groom, of every horse that run at Cayman Park. Furthermore, the boy used to say that he did not have to go to school to have money. Several

48

of the richest men in the country could barely sign their names. Many of them had got their riches from gambling.

Miss Rachael could not say much about her eldest son. He had left home when he was just over twenty years old. She heard that he had been to America as farm worker, but had broken the contract and did not return. That boy did not send anything to them as he said that his father did not give him anything. They tried their best with the boy, but what did they have to give him?

'And you remember John?' Miss Hilda asked.

'Yes,' Karl replied. 'I remember we use to play together and go to school, although him was a little older than me.'

'Yes, him is about twenty-six now and still here. Him help me with the children a lot.'

One of the boys who had been hiding in the front room to get a look at Karl said, 'Is not John him name again, him name Kwame.'

'Kwam . . . what?' Karl asked as it was the first he had heard the name. But he was only surprised that he actually knew someone with that name of one whom Ras Bongo often spoke.

'Kwame,' the boy said.

Miss Rachael pushed the door, 'Go turn on the stove in the kitchen.' She turned to Karl.

'Yes, me son, him say him don't want to bear the slave master name no longer. Him want to have Afrikan name. One that him can feel proud 'bout, proud just like how the damn thief down the supermarket proud of him Chiney name.' The woman smiled. 'Yes, Karl, and if you want him get vex, call him John. Him say, the first John him come cross is in a history book and him is the first slave-trader, John Hawkins. According to him, this white man not only a pirate and a criminal but a rapist too. Him rape Afrika.'

Karl did not know what to say. He had learnt about the man in school, but not even Ras Bongo, called him a rapist.

Miss Rachael continued, 'Then, my big son say that the surname 'Stone' is not even a name. It is just a word, a common noun at that.' She paused. 'So the name John Stone don't make sense, any sense to him.'

As Miss Rachael spoke about her son, her smile seemed to express a mixture of amusement and pride for him.

'But, Karl,' Aunt Hilda said, 'don't ask if Kwame is not one nice young man, you know.'

The other woman butted in, 'Don't ask Hilda, him is like a son, father, brother, husband all in one, but although I don't agree with some of him idea, him . . .'

Karl's mind went back to Guys Hill. He missed the rest of the sentence. Kwame was such help to his family. His mother was proud of him. How long would Aunt Birdie have to wait before she could say things like that about him?

The sound of something frying came from the kitchen. Miss Rachael got up. She moved towards the front door.

'Then what about Mr Stone?' Karl asked. The woman stopped dead in her tracks, one foot in the room, one foot on the verandah.

'Him, him. That s-h-i-t,' she said dragging the last word as if it was new to her. She turned towards the kitchen without saying anything else.

Rachael did not stay long as it seemed that her two sons were taking good care of business. They had to know how, or most nights they wouldn't be eating until after eight o'clock when she came home from work.

Miss Rachael came back and asked Aunt Hilda to help her sons to share out the dinner as she was still feeling sick in her stomach. She said that Hilda should also share out food for herself, Karl and Kwame.

He would be coming in later although some nights he used to stay with his girlfriend. If he did not come in that night, the food could be fried up for breakfast the next morning.

'Yes, Karl,' the woman said as she threw down her slim frame in the veranda chair. 'Yes, you ask 'bout Vernal.'

Karl could see the tiredness in the woman's face. He wondered how she could be getting so little pay for washing, cooking, cleaning, ironing, in short, being the houseslave of Mr and Mrs Mayer and their son.

'Yea, that man Vernal,' the woman began. 'Karl, I can tell you 'bout him, because while you was here as a little boy, you was just the same as Kwame or any of the boys to me.' Miss Rachael took a deep breath and sat forward in her chair.

'Karl, although you was small, you remember that Vernal used to do a little painting. Him is the man who paint some of the house them in this settlement, plenty more round August Town and as far as Papine. You 'member that. Eh?'

'Yes, Miss Rachael.'

'Well, Karl, you 'member too that Vernal was a nice trying husband. I used to proud of him.'

Karl nodded his head and glanced at Aunt Da who had just come out of the kitchen.

50

'Well, me son, about a year after you leave town, Vernal go down
him country and borrow the title for him father dead-left land.
Then him use the paper and borrow some money from the bank to
pay down on this little house here. You understand me, Karl?' she
paused.

'But you know when a poor man borrow money from bank, if
one month pass and him don't pay, him in ants nest. Them ready
to crucify him.'

Aunt Hilda butted in, 'That is why I prefer to fight me own
battle. I don't have any land paper, but if I even have, I don't
want nobody to put prison on top of me. No sah!'

'So, Karl,' Rachael continued, 'Stone borrow this money suppose
to pay ten pounds a month. Was still pound that time.' She uttered
a short belch, then leaned back in the verandah chair. 'Um. Then
there was a man from round May Road. Him was the MP chief
henchman.'

'That bitch still live there, Rachey?' Aunt Hilda asked.

Miss Rachael turned to the older woman. 'Yes, a believe so,' she
replied, then faced Karl again.

'Yes, Vernal and this man have some woman quarrel. I never
hear fully how it go. But him carry news to the MP. Almighty! For
over a year, not a work on no settlement building! Not a job to
even brush up a skerting! Not even a window. Not a penny from
the settlement house!'

She stopped and looked at Karl as if she wanted to make sure
he was hearing everything. For apart from the people and the
vehicle passing on the road, a sound-system was warming up for
a dance down the road.

'So guess what? The bank move in and sell off the land in
country. And him nearly go mad. Bellevue nearly call him. Me
husband start to stay out late and when him come in, him don't
know him muma from a broom stick. Drunk . . . like . . . bat.'

Rachael looked towards the kitchen then back at Karl and Miss
Hilda. 'You want we eat the little food right here?' she asked.

They all agreed to eat on the verandah. It did not take long for
Miss Hilda to come back with the food. They had eaten at
around four o'clock and it was now approaching nine. Even a
cricket whistling somewhere outside, sounded faint as if it were
hungry.

Miss Rachael began to talk again. 'Yes, Karl, me husband turn
rum bum. And all I talk to him from him lose the land is just rum.
Him is a disgrace to me.'

She started to eat from a basin, 'Tired eating this damn rice every day. Cho, man can hardly get food to eat. When is not rice short is flour. If is neither rice nor flour, is sugar. Imagine sugar short when we have so much sugar factory. Bet it not short over England. I don't know what poor people going to eat.' The older woman lowered her spoon, 'Then to come up to bump now, apart from food shortage we have water shortage too. Every day them lock off the pipe, say water in the dam "critically low". Critically low?' Miss Rachael asked. 'Is the marrow in them head critically low. How can water low and every day Mayer and all them shit up on the hill, watering lawn and a swim in a pool. Not critically low for them to put in them pool? But critically low for we to put in we bath pan.'

Karl sat down and listened to the two women. He had a hard day from Guys Hill. Sleep was seeping over his eyes lids. The food kept him awake. Many people say that most women love to chat. Might or might not be true, but certainly for these two in their late forties, it seemed true as hell.

'But, Rachey, is something I always wonder 'bout.'

'What, Hilda?'

'Down Spanish Town Road, one drinks factory have about two, yes, two well. Then if government collect so much water rate and taxes money, why every year we have to suffer this way? A few wells and couple more dams, that's all. Laud man.'

Miss Rachael added, 'And as soon as rain done fall everybody forget that another drought will come.' She was finished eating first and had the empty basin in her lap. 'Wicked as them say Castro is, at least the people have water to them satisfaction. At least that.' Miss Rachael gave off a loud long belch. 'Excuse me, manners,' she said and moved towards the kitchen.

It was not long before one of the boys came for the empty plates. They seemed to be of great help to their mother. The two women looked as if they could sit and talk for the whole night. But it was now after nine o'clock. There were now less people moving on the street. Some were gaily dressed as if going to a dance. Karl could feel the sleep more and more in his eyes. It had been a full day. He was hoping that he would see Mr Stone and Kwame before he left. Miss Rachael told him that he could rest assured that he would see Kwame the next day. Being Sunday, he would not be going to work and if Kwame spent the night with his girlfriend, then he would come home early the next morning.

The two people said goodbye to Miss Rachael and left for their next door home. As they entered the gateway, they saw a man stumbling with a bicycle and coming towards them. Aunt Hilda and

Karl stood at the gate and as the man passed, they could hear him in deep conversation with the cycle. It was difficult to say whether he was leading the bicycle, or the bicycle leading him. The half-drunk man passed without even seeing them. He stopped at the next gate for a short while spat out a few bad words, then continued talking to his companion as he went through the gateway. The dogs did not even bark.   Aunt Hilda looked at Karl. He looked at her expecting that she would say something.

The woman uttered a low groan and said, 'Poor Rachey.'

Soon they were inside the little house. Karl pulled off his clothes and lay down on the single bed in the little room. Aunt Da was in hers but was not ready to sleep yet. But Karl was too tired to stay up anymore.

'Good night, Aunt Da,' he called to her.

'Night, me son, sleep good, you mus' tired.'

The woman's words were so true. From Guys Hill to August Town, 4 a.m. to 10 p.m. was more than a full day for him.

CHAPTER 5

'Kwame, man is you that'

'Karl, Karl,' a woman's voice called.

Karl turned in the little bed.

'Yes, Aunt Birdie,' he said and turned over on his back. He opened his eyes slowly and was a bit frightened when he realized that the face was not that of his mother. The sunlight beamed through the top of the two windows in the room. Aunt Hilda was dressed in a tall white frock with a small black straw-looking hat perched dandily on her head. A bible and a 'hanky' were in one hand, and a fat looking little purse was in the other hand.

'Karl, a going to church. I should come back by 'bout eleven or near that.' Then looking towards the kitchen. 'A little something on the stove for you. When you ready you can light up the stove, careful with the kerosene, and warm it up. You hear me?'

He was now fully awake. 'About what time now, Aunt Da?' he asked.

'Is after eight o'clock now.'

'Eight?' Karl said and started to sit up in bed. He was used to getting up early even on Sunday mornings. Miss Birdie used to make sure that all of her children, despite the trouble that Junior sometimes gave, always got up early.

'Yes, is after eight now, so a leaving. If you going anywhere before I come back, lock the door and leave the key over Miss Rachey. You hear, man?' she asked, and then went through the door.

As his aunt left, Karl thought a little over the days as a youth when she would never, never leave him behind. He just had to go! But now, not even Miss Birdie could get him to go, even for a wedding. After all, they didn't usually have the eating part in church. But many people would go to church, so that it did not appear that they went to the wedding only for the food.

But Karl was not a man particularly fond of church. First, he did not quite believe everything he heard in church, like Samson killing those forty thousand Philistines with the jaw bone of a donkey, or Jonah in the belly of a whale for three days. More than that, most leaders, and most followers he knew, turned him off from going to church. 'Let your lights so shine before men, so

that they might see your good works.'
Where were their lights? And as for their good works! Loving,
kind, holy on Sundays . . . back-biters, malice keepers, hate-
mongers, hypocrites for the rest of the week. 'Love thy neighbours,'
they preached. 'Hate thy neighbours,' they practised. Where was
the church leading the fight against injustice and oppression? Indeed
many were not only sliding, but like Maas Charlie were first-class
blood-suckers. If Christ were alive today he would have to be
careful how he went into some of those ivory towers. And if he were
not careful, if he did not deliver the right kind of sermon—that is
one suitable when dignitaries sat in the front seats reserved
for them, he might have to face a second crucifixion. These
'Churchians' would crucify him, Karl thought. 'Let your lights so
shine before men, so that they might see your good works.' He
smiled to himself as he played with his little beard, 'Aunt Da beat
me to learn that.'
    Karl got up and spread the bed. He then went into the bathroom
and had a bath. After that he went straight to the kitchen, only in
his brief. Then he lit the kerosene stove, and heated the breakfast.
As he ate the food, he felt a bit depressed. He was so used to
having his Sunday morning meal with Geney or Junior pestering
him for some. When they were not around, one of the other two
would do the job. After breakfast, Miss Birdie, and if the spirit
moved him, Kojo would leave for church. Tom went only now
and then, and somehow Miss Birdie could not keep Junior in the
building until the end of the sermon. Sometimes the boy would
slip out and before she would realise it, Junior would be down at
Guys River with Karl and Ras Bongo catching fish.
    Karl took another sip of the tea that his aunt had prepared. He
smiled as he remembered Ras Bongo. How the man had always
been kind to him and many other youths in Guys Hill. Between
the Rasta and the young teacher Levi Annan, the youths in the
community were learning a lot. Annan was trying to organise a
youth club where the young men and women would not only play
games, but would also study national and international affairs, both
past and present. But Annan wanted to encourage the young people
to study things that would help to make them and their country
better. Although people like Maas Charlie were opposed to it,
Annan wanted the youths to know more about places like Cuba and
Afrika. They were not taught much about Afrika or Cuba in
schools or in church except that in Afrika the Afrikans were back-
ward, some still eating people, and that in Cuba, Castro pulls out
toenails and fingernails daily. According to Maas Charlie, Castro

55

cuts off men's balls so that they would not have many children to feed. 'One flour bag drawers for every woman for a whole year!' Karl smiled as he remembered Charlie saying this.

Soon Karl finished eating the breakfast. He washed the plate, cup and little teapot that were used. Karl then went to his bed-side and pulled out his grip. As he opened it, the first thing that caught his eyes was the black tam that Ras Bongo had given him. The sandals were packed at the bottom.

Boy, it would really be good if the Ras could help Mr Annan with the club, he thought. That man could not only teach the youths some history and so on, but could help many of them with a skill. Karl took up the tam—knitting, shoemaking, basket-making, if only that. Even a few might be better off. He put the tam on the bed. 'But the Rastaman so funny, he don't seem to want to take part in anything here. Him head so full up with Afrika. Him say him hate down-pression, him hate slavery, him hate Jam-down. Bongo hardly want to have anything to do with what happening here. Nice if him could help with . . . '

A sound as if someone or something was at the gate broke Karl's thoughts. He listened for a while but he heard nothing more. Besides if it was someone the person would knock. His thoughts went off again, back to Guys Hill.

'But him want Guys Hill and the whole country, anywhere black man live to be better. Can't really understand him, still hope him help with the club. The Ras funny.'

Someone knocked at the door. 'Bongo funny bad . . . wonder who that?' He reached for his pants. 'Coming.' As Karl buttoned his pants he muttered to himself, 'But who say if Bongo even help, and some youth learn a trade, that would make them better? After all, I have a trade, but still have to run leave country come here.' He moved towards the door. 'It tough, tough like rock.'

When Karl first opened the door, no one was in sight. He stood at the doorway for a while. Oh, what a lovely morning it was. No late rising cocks crowing and apart from a lonely grass-quit flying across July Road, there were no birds. Yet for 9 o'clock it seemed wonderful to him. No frogs croaking down the slopes, no rain clouds hanging overhead. The place was sunny and looked so lively, so full of life.

A girl walking up the sidewalk kicked an empty tin. The sound rose above the hum of engines passing round May Road. The empty milk tin stopped spinning and rested almost in the middle of the gateway. The girl reaching it, kicked it aside. Karl's mind was caught between the empty tin and the plump legs that kicked it. The tin had come from the overnight garbage, but where had the legs come from? His mind raced back to Guys Hill. 'On a Sunday morning like this, I sure to be at Guys River. And if I unlucky, I would see plump legs. But if I was lucky, I would see a whole bird.' The young woman had passed the next gate, but down to her waist was still visible.

'Wonder how long before I get a job? Hope is soon. Cause I want to be a better man in every way,' he thought. 'What a nice, nice, swe . . e . . t sister.'

Karl got up and walked towards the gate to take up the empty tin. It came from the garbage that Aunt Hilda had put out about two or three days earlier. Every morning the woman had to scrape up the rubbish as dogs would scatter it during the night. They would make a mess of the place. But like most of the people in the settlement and most other parts of the town, his aunt could not take in her garbage at nights. What would she do with it, and besides the truck might come any day or better yet, any night. Unemployment in the country, yet the garbage pile up. 'What a situation,' Bongo would say, 'I and I die, for salvation.'

His aunt must have been hurrying to reach church early. How else would she have missed this tin. Karl opened the big paper bag. The smell from the garbage hit him. But it was nothing like Spanish Town Road, and no one, not even white roaches lived in this paper bag. But people, or so they are supposed to be, lived on Spanish Town Road. Karl managed a twisted smile. For those on Spanish Town Road were only degrees poorer than the mass of the people in Guys Hill.

'Karl . . . ' someone called.

He looked up.

'You never hear me knock at the door about five minutes ago?' the young man said as he came closer to Karl.

'Jo . . . ,' Karl cut the word short, 'Kwame, . . . is you that?'

'Umm . . mm, same one,' he replied.

The difference of the few years in Kwame's favour, did not show very much in the two faces. He had always been a bit thinner from the days when both of them were attending primary school. Kwame must have got some of the leaness from his mother, Miss Rachael. Karl could have got his shape from either Miss Birdie or Kojo. Not much difference.

'Then, Karl, how is life, brethren?' Kwame asked patting his hair as he spoke.

'Life not treating me too good, Kwame,' Karl replied. Kwame had what looked like a note book in his hand.

He was still combing his hair. Unlike Karl with a little beard, Kwame had a clean shave. His shirt, well tucked into his pants and as Miss Birdie would say 'looking like a decent young man.' Surprising! Changed his name to an African one! Wasn't he a rebel? Then where was his beard? He looked more like a Sunday school teacher than a rebel.

'You going to church?' Karl asked.

'No, man.'

'Then you going to check the sister?' The two men, Kwame slightly taller, were now walking towards the door.

'No, Karl. I want to go up to the garden. Hope Garden I mean. Put on you clothes and we can go together, you know, go together and talk 'bout life.'

Karl agreed to the suggestion. 'I was just wondering what I would do for the day. Kwame, give me fifteen minutes.'

The two went inside the room.

Karl took out the tam and the sandals that Ras Bongo had given him. He told Kwame a little about the Rastaman. He took out a new shirt that Miss Birdie had bought for him in Linstead. He told Kwame how his mother did not want him to come to town. Karl then took a two dollars from the bottom of the grip. Kwame did not know Maas Joe or Miss Kate, but he had heard about them from Aunt Hilda. It did not take fifteen minutes, more like thirty, for Karl to get ready. Soon they were leaving for Hope Gardens.

Karl and Kwame got off the bus. They crossed the street and walked towards the two large grey concrete pillars each bearing part of the name 'Hope Gardens'. An arch made of half-inch steel, linked the two pillars. Lodged somewhere near the middle of this arch, was a well-designed crown, sitting atop the initials ER. The symbol seemed to be there to remind everyone passing below, they were entering the most beautiful garden in an independent country, with the queen that had donated its independence, still as head of state. Such a fine fairy godmother, greeted her children as they came.

The two young men passed through the gate. They walked through an avenue lined on both sides by tall cassia trees, which had grown to form a kind of arch over the roadway. But this was not a man-made arch and bore no symbol of who ruled the country. The yellow flowers that dropped into the road, were being crushed by what seemed an endless flow of people. People in cars, trucks, buses, bikes and bicycles but most, like Karl and Kwame going into the garden by way of 'walkers transport'.

'Kwame,' Karl spoke, 'this place really cool. For eleven o'clock on a sunny morning it really cool. Is only one place that I can think of that so cool at this time of day.'

Kwame looked at his younger friend. 'Where? Dead house?' he asked.

'No, man, down Guys River. On a morning like this or almost anytime of day, no matter how up the road hot, down the river just cool. One day I would like we to go up country and we can go down the river.'

They came off the roadway and started to walk on the lawn. It looked as if it had been cut one or two weeks earlier, and was now springing beautifully. Oh, how well kept, not even a bit of paper . . . , yes, one small bit of reddish looking paper, wrinkled as though someone had folded it up and sat on it. Only about ten yards away, the fifty cents note must have dropped from someone. The two men raced for the money. But Kwame, much slimmer, slightly taller and only a few years older, reached it first. A pack of cigarettes—forty cents and a pack of biscuits—ten cents, was all the money could buy. But didn't it come in handy? Fifty cents in hard times, sure did.

Karl and Kwame came off the lawn, and continued walking in the road. They approached a little bridge, a number of short rounded concrete columns bulging in the middle and tapering at the ends. On it were no arches, neither natural nor built by the subjects of their Royal Majesty. They crossed over the bridge and turned a bend. Before long, they were face to face with the full splendour of Hope Gardens. Hibiscus, Croton, Joseph-coat, Zinna, Sun-flower, Gerbera, Allamanda, Oleander, were a few that were in full bloom. The flowers seem to have all the colours of the rainbow. But just as the shades of the rainbow merge to form a complete and beautiful body, so the different flowers, planted in rows and in circles, formed a patch-work that made a wonderful whole. A sight, that on first meeting the eyes always pulls the tongue.

It was Karl's turn, 'If Maas Joe donkey ever get in here, him eat what him don't see. I never see a animal eat flowers so. Because of that old donkey, Miss Kate can hardly plant anything 'round the house.'

A strange screaming sound was coming from an area of very tall trees, to the right side of the garden. Kwame smiled as he looked at Karl's puzzled face.

'Don't run, man,' he said.

'Wha . . . what that, Kwame?'

'Is peacock, man.'

'Peacock?' Karl asked. 'Then I hear that them so pretty, how come them make such weird sounds?'

'You can't ask me that,' Kwame turned to his friend. 'You would have to ask them.'

Karl pointed his thumb at his chest, 'Me? me? Me go near them? You must be mad!'

The two men walked further into the garden and looked around for a while. They soon found a concrete bench under a big tree. It was a Wild Fig. As they sat down, Karl began to talk.

'The peacock sound like something I used to hear as a little boy in Guys Hill. A dread sound, a terrible screaming, some nights especially in the rainy season.'

'What that was I?' Kwame asked.

'Umm . . . mmh.' Karl began talking. 'Buoy, is a funny story. From I was a youth I hear say that a man and him woman over Benbow, catch a fight one night in the October rains. The two used to quarrel every living day. Day . . . and night. The woman claim that the man won't give her enough money to take care of herself and the children. The man him claim him couldn't do no better and that the woman keeping man . . . '

Kwame interrupted, 'So one night the quarrel lead to fight. Same story everywhere.'

'Yes, them start fight one rainy night. 'Then in the fight, the woman take off her draws to beat the man.' He paused for a second. 'Blood claute! The man reach for him 'lass, and one blow, the woman head fly off her body.'

Kwame looked at Karl his mouth half opened.

'Raas! Chop off her head?' he asked in amazement.

'Yes. Then when the man finish, guess what him do?'

'What,' Kwame asked.

Karl looked up into the fig tree as if wondering whether or not the tree was listening. He continued, 'Because him 'fraid that someone might find the head if him throw it with the body in the river, or find the body if him buried it, him throw the body in Guy River and bury the head. People find the head bury in a yam hill, but nobody find the body.' Karl took off his tam.

'Government hang the man and leave the youths with neither mother or father and nobody to take care of them. Now them beat from one relative to the other. I hear that one of the biggest boy get mad. Him is like leggo beast in the district.'

As Karl paused, his friend spoke, 'Is town here you have them like beast on the street. Can't decide whether Bellvue in Kingston or Kingston in Bellvue.'

'Country and town, Kwame . . . But make me finish tell you the story.' He continued, 'Most people in the area, when them hear this wailing sound, them say is the woman duppy. People say that them see the head looking for the body.'

'So how the head move 'bout without the body?' Kwame asked.

'They say it roll. Hair peel off, eyeball missing, skin paste on to skull, teeth grinning, but still the head screaming as it roll. One man say that it roll under him foot one night him coming from bush in the rain. Cold sweat wash him.'

'Cold sweat wash him in the rain? You not joking?'

Kwame looked at his friend for a while. A wild fig fell from the tree.

'Karl, you ever see duppy?' Kwame asked as he picked up the little yellow fruit.

'No, I never see it. Sometimes especially walking late, I see some funny things. But to see duppy, if you don't born with the power, you have to wipe dog matter in your two eyes. I never do it.'

Kwame leaned back in the bench, looked at Karl and shook his head.

'Karl, you serious, man?'

'I don't really know.' Karl replied, 'But if a man can believe that Oral Graham and Billy Roberts can heal people and Jesus raise from the dead, I don't see why him can't believe in obeah and duppy.' He sat forward on the concrete bench. 'A man believe in the power of God, him must believe in the power of Satan too.'

People were moving all over the garden, moving from one area to the other. Guides could be seen showing white and brown folks around, pointing out things of interest to them. But black people? Only when their accents showed that they were visitors to the country, if they were in a group of goodly white or mulatto folks, then they would not be pushed out. A people turned against itself, born and grew up with this, accepted it as natural . . . , of course, the guides were all black.

Neither of the friends said anything for a few minutes. Karl started to look at how well the sandals he had on fitted him. They were the ones Ras Bongo had given him. Like the tam, it fitted well. From looking at his slippers, he started to notice the root of the tree under which they sat. A good portion of the root was spread out above the surface of the soil. Secondary roots, criss-crossed in some parts, side by side for a while, then fused in other parts. It was as if the trunk of the tree was placed on a large round mat. What an intricate mat it was! Made over more than fifty years of bending, knitting, twisting, fusing, but ever growing. The limbs grew in a fashion that made the canopy low but with a wide spread.

Kwame broke the silence. 'Talking 'bout man chopping off woman head. I don't know if is the man or the woman going do the chopping, but I almost certain that some chopping going to happen, if things go on the same way.'

Karl looked at him. 'Who you talking 'bout?', he asked.

'Talking 'bout my old people, Miss Rachey and the old man. Buoy, for the last couple years at least two nights every week, the man come in drunk. And when him come in drunk, you can rest dead sure that war inside the house.'

Karl broke in, 'Yes, Miss Rachael was telling me a little 'bout that. It dread.'

'Karl, man, you can be sure that war in the house every Saturday night when him come in. That is why I usually stay out Saturday night time.'

Kwame threw the fig on the grass in the direction of a group of girls. He took the pack of cigarettes from his pocket, handed one to Karl and put one in his mouth. Karl took a lighter from his pocket. He had bought it at Maas James's shop. They lit up the cigarettes. Kwame took a draw, and inhaled it.

'Then the old lady never tell you . . . ' he let out the smoke slowly through his nostrils, 'she never tell you about what happen week before last Saturday night?'

'No. No, she never tell me,' Karl replied taking a pull on his cigarette.

'Well, man, last Saturday night, the man drunk.' Kwame paused, 'My old man so drunk, so drunk that him have to put down the bicycle and lay down in a bus stop on May Road.' He took another draw then turned to Karl. 'So what you think happen?'

'I don't know. Somebody thief the bicycle?'

Kwame smiled, 'That would be bad and not too bad.' He stared at the bed of roses nearby and then back at Karl.

'You notice a lot of youths running all over the town like stray goats? Some of them sell *News* for Wong, the man who own the supermarket.'

'Yes, I notice them, more and dreader than in country.'

Kwame continued, 'Well, about three of them see Daddy in the bus stop, fast asleep with him mouth wide open.' Kwame took another puff. 'A man who was coming up the road, say that him see the three little boys beside the bicycle in the bus stop. One of them was standing over the old man face with him buddy in him hand.' Kwame looked up in the tree and sent out a cloud of smoke. 'The man say that by the time he reach up to the bus stop, the boys disappear and Daddy swallowed all the piss.'

'What!' Karl remarked, then said nothing else.

For the next few minutes, the two men just sat in the garden smoking their cigarettes. Karl remembered the morning when he first bought cigarettes from Maas James. On a Monday morning, men had to credit rum. They had the freedom to do so, yet Maas James had asked him about ganja as if it were the worst evil. But the herb was illegal while rum was legal. Ras Bongo never had to trust ganja on Monday morning, neither did anyone piss in his mouth after he had smoked it.

One was legal and the other illegal. Does that mean that one is good and the other bad? OR, were they both evil? If they are both evil, then how is one legal and the other illegal? OR is it that one benefit one class of people more and is therefore legal? But even with the herb, it is mostly the man smoking or selling one or two sticks that goes to jail for it? What about those in the trade? What about Mr Big?

Rich and poor, mansions and slums, profiteers and pick-pockets, white and black, rum and herb, legal and illegal—does our society have double standards?

Kwame threw away his cigarette butt. 'When the man help daddy to come home and tell the old lady what happen, she get mad. She take up a piece of board and slap him in him face. Then them start to fight. Break up everything in them bed room. Is you auntie Hilda and some other people have to run over and part them. The next day when the old man sober up, him cry like a little baby.' Kwame paused.

'That is why I say, government should make rum illegal too just like how ganja . . . '.

But Kwame interrupted before he could finish. 'Yes, yes. That might well be true, but make it illegal would be like fighting crime by increasing the police force. Beat them today, prison them tomorrow, casterate them the next day, give them life sentence the next, hang them the next and you know what next you will have to do? Ee . . e . . en!' Kwame asked with his eyes wide open, 'You know what next you have to do?'

Karl did not know what to say.

'Well, you would then have to kill them children too,' he emphasized. 'Yes, to get rid of crime, you would have to kill them children and, funnily, when you increase the police, you have to take in more criminals in the force. Why? Because is the children of the poor, the poor, not the rich that make up the police and the army.'

But where was the argument straying to. They had been talking about making rum illegal. How did crime and police and army get into that?

Kwame eased off the bench, and looked at some people walking in the roadway, then back at Karl. 'Making rum illegal is like making ganja illegal, is like making crime illegal. It don't solve anything. Yes, it might keep it down for a while, but it don't solve one fucking thing!'

He sat down on the concrete bench again. His mood seemed to be getting back to normal. Kwame stared at Karl taking the last few puffs of his cigarette.

'You ever see a man trying to kill a tree by picking off the leaves?'

'No,' Karl replied, 'but I can remember, one time Kojo did try to kill a big guango tree by cutting off the limbs. But it never work. After a few months the tree start spring back. Even after him chop it down, it start send up new shoots.'

'So how him finally kill it?'

Karl threw away his cigarette butt. 'Kojo, get Maas Joe and some other men help him to dig out the root.'

'So, Karl, you see what I was dealing with now?' Kwame asked. 'No need to make rum illegal, that not going to help. We must find out what in the country forcing so many youths to turn to crime. What forcing so many people to turn to herb and rum.' Kwame put up his foot on the bench, 'You see what I dealing with now?'

For about ten minutes the two sat without saying much to each other. They just sat watching the people as they moved about in the gardens. Then they talked about work. Tomorrow Karl would have to start looking for a job. Kwame was working with Electric Service. After he had left primary school, Kwame went to evening classes at a technical school and was now an electrician. He promised to help him find a job. Pity he wasn't an electrician or it might be easier to get one. Really? That was only what Karl thought.

'It not so easy, you know, Karl.'

'Why?'

'Because for over a year, there had been so much trouble at the plant. The company was not employing any new people. The workers had formed their own union. There had been complaints that the big unions had sold them out. Workers had paid thousands

64

of dollars in dues. They did not know what had become of it. Then after a strike last year, some of them lost their jobs and their demands were not met. Yet, the union delegate, who was riding a bike before, was driving a car two weeks after the strike.' Kwame explained to Karl, 'But by law, while workers have the right to have a union of their choice to represent them, the management not forced to recognise that union.'

'Funny law. Funny indeed!' the younger man said.

'So we win the poll and the damn management don't want to recognise the union.'

'Why?' Karl asked.

'Well, the management say that the leader of the union and me, the secretary, defend black power. And not only that, them say we is communist.'

'Black power? Communist!' Karl exclaimed.

'The only sin was that we say a thing as important as electricity in the country shouldn't be owned by no capitalis company. And a foreign one at that! We say that is the people and the government should own them things.'

'So that is why them don't want to recognise the union?' Karl asked.

'Yes, just that and them don't want take on any new man. But we won't give up the struggle. Not until we win our rights.' Kwame took up his note book. 'And we mus' win.'

Karl started to open the pack of biscuits, 'But mus'.'

Hope Gardens was splendid. So natural, so cool, so pleasant. But why wasn't the splendor spread more over the whole country? The garden occupied about 400 acres of land. There were many places in other parts of the island where even ten acres could be used to make a garden. If government would provide the land, the community organizations could make even a dozen more mini gardens in different parts of the country. The few 'flower-beds' that were located in some townships were chained down until tourists visited. Profit-making reserves for the white 'backra'. What of the 'natives'? Are the tourists more important than them? Why can't people get the land?

'Karl, man, the same kind of question, I ask myself when I see the youths on the street in August Town. I don't see why we can't even get a piece of land to have a good playfield. So for most youthman July to May Road is them play field. Talk about crime?' But not until the people in general and the young in particular have things constructive to do, not until then would the country start to solve its real problems.

'Roots, man, roots,' Kwame said in a pleading tone. 'We must get down to the roots. The roots!'

It was now early evening. Shadows were becoming taller than the people and the things that cast them. There were many more people in the garden than when Karl and Kwame came in. Some not able to find seats, sat on the grass. Others sat there merely because they were in a picnic-mood, and in such a mood, they seemed to prefer things nearer to nature. They wore clothes of different colours and shades, sometimes matching, sometimes different from the flowers nearest to them.

People in small groups were chatting gaily with one another, single persons were sitting alone pondering over their troubles, or just enjoying the fresh air and the beautiful scenery. But in all this, the lovers stood out heels high above the rest. One such pair was walking between a row of variegated hibiscus. Holding hands then, hugging then, kissing now. Between the kisses, the two were chatting and laughing as if they owned the garden.

The pair was passing where Karl and Kwame sat. The man was tall and had a slender frame. He wore a checkered purple and white tall sleeved see-through shirt. As he put his hand around the girl's neck a gold plated 'chapereta' glistened. On the other hand was a watch. Did it belong there or on the clock tower at Parade?

Between the kisses came the laughs which showed a gold tooth taking its share of the sunlight. The man had on red bell-bottomed pants with four large white pockets. Resting gingerly on the side of his head was a white broad-rimmed cowboy hat. How it stayed in place as he walked was a mystery. But how he walked was a greater mystery, as the man seemed to have only enough strength to lift the first two inches of his platform shoes. But the shoes had a double platform, each of about two inches. He was little more than able to drag the pair of shoes. He looked like a real lanky 'cow-poke' from the Mid-west, with a walk that would make Sidney Poiter look like a creeper. Perched partly on his nose and partly on his top lip was a pair of wire-framed dark glasses. He looked good, real good! The two lovers had passed Karl and Kwame. They were now moving towards the group of three girls sitting on the grass nearby.

The girl was more soberly dressed. Her blouse was not much more than a little piece of purple cloth with a few stitches here and there. It was one of the fashionable rib-ticklers, which covered little more than her two rounded tits and a few square inches of her back. Her white shorts stuck tightly to her body. It stuck so tightly, that a part of it, stuck right between the fat jaws of her

66

buttocks. She did not wear any two-colour shoes. Hers was a bright red bootie laced all the way up to the thighs. The woman did not wear a hat. She wore instead a wig with a straight blonde main flowing to her shoulders and had light pink powder, black eyebrow pencil, light purple eyeshadow, fire red lipstick and nail-polish completed the mascarade. She too looked good, real good! The pair of lovers were now only a few yards from the group of girls. Kwame and Karl watched anxiously. Between the hugging and kissing, they didn't see the three big women.

'Hey!' one of the girls shouted, 'you no see you going step on we.'

One by one they got up.

'You look like you blind? Is love you in love so, Mr and Mrs Dress-puss?' one girl asked.

The man looked over his glasses. It must have been made in Japan.

'Say, baby . . . was you adre . . . eesing me? Cause nah nigger could be talk to me like tha . . aat.' His speech was a cross between St Elizabeth patwa and Texan slang.

The first girl, now in an awful mood spoke again.

'Go way, boy. Who you calling niggar? You think because you go to America for two days, get the white man crumbs and him wear-and-left, you can come to call we niggar?'

The female lover was still holding on to her man. She stepped forward stroking her blonde piece. The dye must have run short in the British factory that made the wig.

'Listen, gal. Don't fuck with me, man!' She minced the words as she pointed in one of the girls face.

'Don't fuck or I will kill you raas. You hear me!' she held on tighter to her lover.

'Hey, he . . ey,' another girl laughed, 'look on her talking 'bout man. Her face look like alligator love bump. Look her! Lord, if you not busy take a step over here. Hey, he . . ey,' she laughed.

'Aligator love bump, aligator love bump. You want stand up there and talk 'bout aligator love bump.' She let go of him ready to fight. But he held on to her.

'Forget 'bout these fools girls, baby,' he pleaded.

People were looking in their direction. One or two had started to move towards them. Kwame and Karl watched from where they sat.

The first girl spoke again. 'What, what you think, gal? You think we 'fraid a you?' she asked. 'You think we 'fraid of you because you look like you come from Hanover St.' She screwed up her face as she spoke.

'What's they talk 'bout Hanover?' the man asked. 'What's the . . ey talk 'bout Hanover as if them better than Hanover,' he continued in his St-Elizabeth-Texas accent. 'Them, them so dam blaa . . ck.' He was a shade darker than the blackest girl.

'Go 'way with that,' one of the girl jeered.

'Go 'way with that batty buoy!' another said.

They turned and laughed with each other.

'Go 'way, boy. Black is beautiful. The children of Afrika are beautiful people. She pointed to her afro hairstyle, 'Look on this,' she said.

The natural kinks stood out in the Sunday evening sun. The people watching mixed beaming smiles with outright laughter.

But the woman was not finished with them. The man could no longer hold her. She went up to the biggest girl taking out what looked like a long nail-file from her bosom. She pointed it into the girl's face.

'Is you talking 'bout Hanover St.?' she asked. 'Yes, I might look like a whore. But learn this, you have to look good to whore.'

Sweat was now pouring from her forehead washing the false eye brow, in streaks over her oily pink-powder face. The woman continued hawking, 'Yes, you have to look good to whore or the white sailor man don't want you. Look at you!' she said still pointing the nail file in the girl's face, 'You head dry like dry-up cocky.' The woman raised the weapon to cut the girl but the man held on to her as the girl jumped back. One pulled off her thick heeled slippers, another reached for a piece of stick and the oldest one with her bare hands, they moved in for the kill. Karl and Kwame were beginning to get up but . . .

'Come on, baby. Let's split this scene. It kinda gets up-tights,' the St Elizabeth-Texas negro said, his cool was wearing thin. 'Gal, why the blood-hole you no come on?' he shouted pulling the woman by the hand.

She lost her balance and slipped. Her blonde mane fell off, leaving her inch of burnt hair exposed to the sunlight. The girls started to laugh. The people joined in.

'Hear that one woman use her wig to fan when she hot. Your own would be better. Take it up!' someone shouted to the fat Kingstonian negress.

One of the girls called to the wig-less beauty, 'You must wear wig on you pubic parts. Eh, he . . . ey!' 'Go 'way. You don't have any culture, you don't have anything.'

The woman was now moving away under the pull of her lover,

but still fighting. 'I have more than the three a you put together,' she shouted. "'Cause I have me two big milking stations and a aerial base between leggy mountain. Go way. Man soon mash the three a you fucking gear box. Bus' it up.'

The negro still pulling the negress disappeared behind a row of crotons. Two policemen on horses arrived on the scene to find out what was happening. A patrol car stopped near by. Policemen seemed to be everywhere these days. Soon one will have to be in every house. They quickly left but not before they had menaced two youths walking barefooted and wearing locks. They suspected that they were pick-pockets.

'Even in the garden on a Sunday evening?' Karl wondered. The roots. The roots Kwame had said. Not until we get down to the roots.

People and police had gone back to their business. The girls moved to a shadier place chatting and laughing over what had happened. Kwame took out two cigarettes, as they sat back under the tree. He lit both and he gave one to Karl. Then he took a bit of pencil from his pocket and opened the note-book he had with him. Kwame began to write. His friend watched.

'Wee — Maay'
Bumpy Ma . . ry bought a long wig,
Bumpy Ma . . ry had a fat pig,
Bumpy Ma . . ry once lost the wig,
And where did she find it,
but on the fat pig.

Grumpy Tom . . my bought a white coat,
Grumpy Tom . . my had a black goat,
Grumpy Tom . . my tried the white coat,
And where did it fit,
but on the black goat.

CHAPTER 6

'If only I could get a job'

Karl spent the first two months in Kingston without a job. During October and November, sometimes walking in the boiling sun or in the pelting rain, he went to almost every construction site in Kingston. In some cases a sign board at the gate would do the trick. At other times, a bulky security guard would spare a few more words. The times he got through the gate and spoke to the foreman, Karl would be asked who sent him and if he had a letter. He was to find out that this meant a letter either from a big man connected with the site or, better yet, from a politician. The thought of a man with skills having to batter to get a job made him mad at times. Wonder if it was things like this that helped to put so many people in town and in country, out of their minds?

But in a country where nearly a quarter of its people have no job at all, or worked for two or three months each year, where some got work only at Christmas and election time, then even the skilled must help to make up this number. There was talk that some girls looking for jobs, had to lie down for it. But so far these men who gave out jobs were not brave enough to ask men to lie down for theirs. And well, how many women give out jobs in a society that boast equality for its people? If the women were to ask Karl to lie down for his job, he gladly would. But money for either man or woman, Karl did not have. That was why he was looking for a job!

Many times the condition made Karl ask himself certain questions over and over again. His mind had become so active of late. One day he sat outside a site at Half-Way Tree. 'Why I leave Maas Charlie?' he thought. 'Why I leave?' He leaned on the fence, looked at the concrete columns of what was to be a shopping centre. 'Why I leave Maas Charlie? Charlie is a fucking robber. No matter how long I work with him, I would never be able to make myself into a man. Never able to care for myself and a family, much less give Aunt Birdie them something.' He looked at the faces as they passed on the sidewalk. They seemed to know nothing of a smile, but were much more pleasant than those at the nearby bus stop. 'I wonder if it really going to better than with Maas Charlie?'

He felt so tired, walking so much that morning. He couldn't help noticing that it was the same names repeating themselves on most of the business places he passed in his daily hunt. But it was the work, the work that was heavy on his mind.

'A . . a . . ah,' he let out a deep breath. 'I don't know. God know I really don't know. So many hungry, mad and naked people I see in town come from country too. But you still have plenty fat, sane, well-dressed people . . . living well. Is true that you have more bucking hell, but somehow I must get a job.' Karl leaned up off the fence and started walking to the bus stop.

'Only if I get a job, I must make life, I must . . . make . . . it. If only I get a job.'

The little money that Karl had carried with him went like butter against hot bammy stone. Although he paid no rent, the forty dollars he had carried from country disappeared in the first six weeks. First, on the road he had to buy food. A plate of food would cost a dollar. A few pieces of meat, sometimes more bone than meat, a cup of rice, a leaf of lettuce or a slice of tomato was all. Kojo and Maas Joe were not getting anything for their produce, nor did the cooks, nor the people who served the food get good pay. So where does the money go? To help build a better country for the mass of poor people? Then how could one help the poor, by sucking out their guts with high cost of living, low pay, no work! Or . . . or . . . or this country only help to fatten the fat few.

Karl thought about his position. 'Two months, no work, twenty cents out of the dollar. Aunt Hilda give me this morning.' He shook his head.

'But I must get a job and get it soon at that. Mus!'

Kwame, Miss Rachael, Mr Stone were trying to hear if there was any work that Karl could get. His own Aunt Hilda was also helping. During the first six weeks, Karl had been looking mainly on construction sites. He wanted to get a chance to use his trade and to learn more, so he could become a better carpenter. Now, survival was more important, Karl was prepared to do anything, anything to get a bread.

He had written home several times to his parents. He had also written to Maas Joe and Miss Kate. The man could not read or write well, but the woman had replied and said that they were longing to see him.

Karl also wrote to Ras Bongo and Levi Annan. The reply from the Rastaman was encouraging.

On Saturdays, he had to go down to Coronation Market. Miss

Freda would always bring either money, food or some other thing from his parents. That made him more and more eager to get a job and be able to help himself and his parents when they got older and would no longer be able to work. Oh how Kojo and Miss Birdie, despite being poor, had cared for their children. Kwame was more than a brother. Most evenings he could not come home until late. Sometimes he was working overtime, other times, attending union meetings. Man was he serious about that! But no matter how late Kwame reached home, he was sure to come over to see Karl. They had to talk about what had happened that day. When Karl was in difficulties sometimes, it was because he was ashamed to go to his friend. Kwame even tried to get a girl-friend for him.

Several times, it came across Karl's mind to try and leave the country. He discussed the matter with Kwame who did not oppose the idea, but was not very encouraging. He kept telling Karl about 'staying here and fight.' Put Kwame aside, where would he go, and how would he reach? When he was a boy, hundreds of people used to go to England and America each week. And although their lives were miserable, and although white people piss on them and put them in ghettos to live, most could send back a little something for their families even if only at Christmas time. But here life was miserable, white people still treat black people like dog, kept them out of their heavens, hotels and beaches, and here there was nothing to send home, not even at Christmas!

'What trouble I would have to go through to make a living,' Karl had said to Kwame.

'Make a living?' Kwame asked. 'Make a living or make a dying?'

Karl looked at his friend as they sat in Kwame's room that evening. 'Ras Bongo always talk 'bout it, and if I could get the chance, I would go to Afrika. But how?' Karl asked.

Kwame shook his head, 'Karl, I don't know, I really don't know. We have British and American and German and Canadian and French and Spanish and all kind of embassy, but I don't even know 'bout any African place where I could check out 'bout immigration. I don't know.'

'Kwame buoy, it dread. Wicked when a man have to think 'bout running way from the country him born and grow. Why? Just to make a living.'

'But everyday, you know, Karl, everyday I have to laugh when I hear 'bout life hard in Cuba, so hard that America send plane to carry out people to—'

Karl cut in on his friend, 'Well, man, if America, England,

Canada, South Africa, any one of them send plane here to take out people . . . anyone, anywhere, and by tomorrow morning, half this country would gone. I can bet any man . . .' Karl said, pushing his hand in his pocket. It was empty not even a red cent.

The next day was the first of December and Karl feared that Christmas would find him without a job and no money to spend. So starting from early that morning, Karl walked through most of August Town. The sandals that Ras Bongo had given him were going. He took a bus up to Papine and spent the other part of the day still looking for work. At times he felt like giving up and going into one of the many rum-bars to drown his troubles, even for a time. But he still managed to resist.

The evening when he came home Aunt Hilda told him that Miss Rachael wanted to see him. He did not even stop to eat his dinner although he was so hungry. He stepped out of the house and moved towards the one next door.

'Karl, you just coming in,' Miss Rachael asked. The light from the front room shone dimly on the verandah. 'Is after eight now and you just coming.'

Karl stepped up on the little verandah. 'Yes, Miss Rachael. The whole day, walking from one place to the other and still don't raise anything yet. Sometimes I feel like giving up and just . . . '

But Karl was interrupted by a voice from inside the house. 'Kwame did have more trouble than this.' It was Mr Stone. He turned on the verandah light as he came out. 'Until a man help him to get the job at the Electric Service, him did have to batter more than this.'

Mr Stone was drinking less since the incident with the little boys. He had also been getting a few jobs of late.

He continued, 'We old body almost done already. But what 'bout the youths, where is the tomorrow for them.' Stone came out on the verandah. 'Talk and promise. Promise and talk. Any man who think that them going to fool the young people today signing them own death warrant.'

The man, a little taller, a little fatter than his wife, sat in the other verandah chair. Karl sat on the concrete ledge, facing the two people. He was anxious to hear what Miss Rachael had called him for. His anxiety was soon quenched.

'Karl, you remember Mr Mayer, the man I work for at Beverly Hills?'

'Yes,' Karl replied not wanting to take up too much time.

'Well, I was talking to that bitch yesterday. Him have a few new windows him want to put into the house before Christmas. I tell

73

him that I know someone who can do it cheap.' Miss Rachael
paused and shifted her slim structure in the chair.
'You have you tools?'
Karl nodded, smile on his face, but laughing in his heart.
'Well, tomorrow morning, six o'clock on the dot, come with me
and carry you tools, ahright?' she asked.
'Yes, Miss Rachey. Yes, mam.'
Karl said thanks to Miss Rachey and Mr Stone and left. Kwame
had not come home yet. Must have been at union meeting or
stopped at his girlfriend. Karl could not wait to break the news to
Aunt Hilda. When he told her, she just looked at him and said,
'Thank the Lord.'
The following morning, Karl and Miss Rachael got off the bus
at the foot of Beverley Hills. It was somewhere near to seven
o'clock. They had waited at the bus stop for nearly half hour. The
woman was supposed to be at work at seven. They had to hurry
up Beverley Hills.
The 'Hills', as some of its inhabitants and their companions like
to call the place, is famous for its houses. Those nearest to the bus
stop are big and pretty. There is little to compare between them
and the shacks across the road from them. But these houses, big and
pretty they may be, are the shacks of the Hills. They occupy little
more space than one wing in some of the houses further up. Even
in heaven there was the big and the not so big. The Hills was but
the heaven of the rich few, and as good Christians, no sin, no
speck of blackness could easily reach a place of rest on Beverley
Hills. At that time of morning, with the sun merely peeping over
the horizon, it cast its first rays on these pale coloured concrete
giants. It could not shine on its inhabitants, since at seven in the
morning, most of them would be getting ready to go back for their
second nap. But the maids and garden-boys walking up the hill were
sometimes glad that the sun could shine on their black bodies. At
seven in the morning, despite the sunshine, the 'Hills' is usually
chilly. And being December, as one climbed further and further
up, the morning breeze was almost as cold as in Guys Hill. The
road was so winding and difficult to climb. It had to be winding.
How else could it be built? And yet for such a well-built and costly
road it was strange that hardly anyone knew whose money paid
for its construction. Couldn't be poor people's taxes money.
Couldn't be!
Karl stopped to rest for a while. 'Then Miss Rachey, it not
hard every day to walk up and down this hill?' he asked. He
put down the tools he was carrying on a gate post nearby. Two

growling baboons, as big as young cow-calves came rushing from a low-lying upstairs verandah. Karl quickly took up his tools and moved on to catch up with Miss Rachael. She had not stopped. It might well have been seven o'clock by this, and Mr Mayer lived near to the top of the Hills.

'E . . een, Miss Rachey, you not tired?' Karl asked again. She looked back.

'You think them count we as much as them dog,' Miss Rachael asked. She still had not stopped to rest the slim legs that had been walking for over a quarter mile.

'Well, if when the dogs them rush you a while ago, you did throw a stone and lick one of them, you would find out.' She turned her head and glanced back at Karl. 'And I tell you . . . tell you that if it was one of them dog coming off the bus down there this morning, you sure to see a car, chauffer-driven, waiting for the dam beast.' Rachael stopped and uttered a sigh of relief, 'Who . . o . . oy. We reach. Is this house.'

Looking at the pink house from outside, it did not seem any bigger than most of the ones around it. As a matter of fact, it was smaller than many further up. True, it might have as many iron grills. True, it looked more secure than the General Penitentry, but if one did not get pass the grills of either window or patio one would not believe that the two stories had only fourteen rooms, sizes from fifteen by twelve to twenty by fifteen; six bedrooms, a living-room on each floor, a study, a dining-room on the ground floor and three rooms that really had no use, except at party-time. In these circles one could not be bothered to count kitchen, bathrooms or maids' quarters. Those could occupy almost any amount of space. And even the maid's quarters were a thousand times better than the homes of most of the maids. It had the only chain toilet in the house, but what else are maids used to besides pit toilet? That would be too expensive on the rocky terrain.

The velvet-green carpet grass on the lawn, and the exotic plants along the edges and in large white pots, made the Mayer's residence a beautiful home in the 'haven of rest'.

Miss Rachael and Karl entered the gate. Three well fed bloodhounds were barking, charging with fangs showing, as they saw the people coming up the drive way. They knew the woman alright, but wanted Karl's liver for breakfast. So much cows and goats, they must have thought it was time to taste the meat of a human being.

Mr. and Mrs. Mayer would not be up until some time after nine o'clock. But young Master Mayer, their nine-year-old son, would have to be ready for school by eight o'clock. Rachael, as the nine-year-old addressed the forty-nine-year-old woman, had to make sure that breakfast was on the table by seven thirty. Young Master Mayer was going to Kings High School which was one of the schools that served black-eye peas soup all day. The eye alone is black in the white dish.

Karl would have to wait in the car-port until Mr Mayer was up. The people did not like 'strangers' on their verandah. What about the Mercedes and the Triumph parked in the port? The Mayers did not mind that so much. When the cars were parked at the Cement factory, workers touched them. Mayer could not afford to make the workers believe that he loved his car so much. Karl could safely wait in the car-port.

While he waited, he gazed towards the sea. It appeared not much more than a streak of blue, tied from one end of the town to another. The buildings looked like just endless rows of roofs parted by streaks of black. Houses further up the Hills stood like monsters on huge concrete legs. If each monster would carry a class, and there were as many classes as are monsters, then the untrained, uneducated youths roaming the streets below, would be gobbled up in a single week. It was a wonder how the monsters managed to stand in place. Their legs seemed to have been plastered in some cases on solid rock. From his knowledge of building, Karl figured that the cost of putting one leg in place was more than putting up a good-sized room for any poor man. The money spent to build one foundation could make ten houses for poor people, then to complete it, that could make another ten. But why should people want to live up here? And why does the government allow them to live up here?

Karl figured that the answer to the second question was that we live in a free society. We have the freedom to eat or die of hunger, to remain sane or go mad, to overcharge or underpay, to become a legal or illegal criminal, to live in mansions or in shacks and, most of all, to inherit riches or poverty. We also have the freedom to vote.

Karl thought for a while that the first question was more difficult to answer. But soon he was able to figure out something. The people came to live on the hills to help the country with the population problem. Away from the poor, the slums could grow. But why does almost every house have a swimming-pool? Karl could still see the sea in the distance.

Although the island is surrounded by water, it also falls in an area that is plagued by hurricanes. It is just over twenty years that we last had one. And when it was raging, no one could bathe in the sea. Then, almost every house in the country could do with a swimming-pool. Besides, with the water shortage each year, the pools could store a lot of water. After a swim one does not need to use so much water in the bathroom. Also, the people who lived on the hills, by storing water, would help make it more available to their 'maids' and 'garden boys' when they returned to the slums in the evenings.

'Hi, you,' a stern voice came from the staircase, shocking Karl out of his deep daydreaming. The man walked further down the staircase leaving the sound of a Christmas carol coming through the half-opened door behind him.

'Are you the young man who come about the windows?'

It was nearly nine o'clock.

'Yes, sir,' Karl replied.

The man, not as white as Karl had expected, was still in his bath-robe.

'Come up here and let me talk with you.'

He had been waiting for nearly two hours. If Miss Rachael hadn't slipped some of young Master Mayer's food to him, he might not have been able to climb the stairs.

'Rachael!' the man called. He had a commanding voice which seemed to be much bigger than his body.

'Rachael, where are you?', Mr Mayer snapped in his firm tone.

Medium built, nearly six feet tall, about forty and with such a voice, Mr Mayer must have been in the British Army at the time of the Mau Mau uprising in Kenya. A voice such as that could be used to drive fear into the Africans fighting to keep their land.

'Rachael!' he called again.

How did workers react to such a voice when they were asking for a raise of pay at the factory?

'Yes, Mr Mayer. Yes, sir.' Miss Rachael came tipping through the front door. To hear the reply, one would have thought that the woman had nothing but fear, respect and tenderness in her heart for her house-master.

'What you want, sar?' she asked gently.

It must have been the same way the house slaves on the plantations used to answer their masters before they put the poison in their last cup of tea.

'Is this the young man?' Mr Mayer asked wiping his thick moustache.

He was not really a white man; he was a mulatto, like most, playing white. He could not piss in a 'whites' urinal in America, much more go to a white church in South Africa. In Britain Mr Mayer would be called a 'golly-W.O.G.', Western Orientated Gentleman.

Rachael looked at the man, 'Yes, Mr Mayer, him is the one, sir.'

He turned to Karl. 'Well, there are five windows, and its four dollars to put in each. Rachael will show you around.'

Mr Mayer was about to say something else, but a woman's voice called from a room somewhere in the left wing of the building.

'Moses, Moses, who's there?'

'Just a minute, Edna dear,' the man replied and entered the building, closing the door, taking the sound of the carol with him and leaving Karl and Miss Rachael.

Mr Mayer had not given Karl a chance to discuss the price. It was hard work as at least one window, burglar-bar and all would have to be taken out and replaced each day. Karl would not be able to work more than twenty dollars for the week. But it was take or leave it. If he could not do it at that price, someone else would be glad to do it for less. Miss Rachael took Karl down to the cellar and showed him where the window and other materials were stored. Take it or leave it.

'Karl, you better take it. Take it, Karl, it better than thief—four dollars a one,' she paused, 'but no wonder so much people thief now a days.'

Karl followed Miss Rachey's advice. But what else could he do? For bad as it was, he would be able to work and even buy a shirt for the Christmas holidays. The three weeks that Karl worked up the 'Hills' was most rewarding. Rewarding? How come? For the first week when he fitted the windows, he got only twenty dollars. After the Mayers saw how well he worked, they gave him the job to make a number of fixtures inside the house—new curtain rods, picture hangers, stands for fish bowls and flower pots. They wanted the house to have a new look for the Christmas.

While working inside the house, Karl could not help stopping to look at some of the things he came across. The furniture, it was something else. The oval shaped tables and the eight chairs in the dining-room cost over a thousand dollars. Miss Rachael was at home when most of the furniture was delivered. She had asked the delivery man many questions. There was carpeting in every room, and furniture and fittings of all descriptions, some hardly of any use, and two television sets, one in the living-room and one in the bedroom that the Mayers shared. Two television sets!

Mrs Mayer seemed to have a hand both in his getting the work

78

for the other two weeks and the better pay. She was even telling her husband to give Karl a job at the factory. Why was the woman who was so mean to Miss Rachael, so helpful to him? He managed to earn twenty-five dollars each week, for the second and third weeks. In all he earned seventy dollars in the three weeks. But he had been living in town for nearly three months now. Anyhow seventy dollars in three weeks was more than twice the amount he would have earned with Maas Charlie and his eight dollars per week. But what of the cost of living in Kingston as compared to Guys Hill? Not much difference, but higher in town. Besides, there were no mango, naseberry, breadfruit, banana and so on to ease the pressure.

But if the three weeks at Beverley Hills did not reward Karl's pocket, how was it rewarding? It rewarded his head. Did he learn more about his trade? Certainly! But this was only the bonus. Because between the hints from Miss Rachael, the arguments of Mr and Mrs. Mayer, and the chatter of their friends at midday or evening 'winings and dinings', Karl had graduated from second to third class. But Mrs. Mayer's hours of daily gossip on the phone had helped him through third class right into sixth class. Karl was in the school of life, the 'Jamaica School of Life'.

Moses Mayer would be celebrating his forty first birthday soon. His grandfather was an Englishman, who had come to the island to run a big plantation that his dying father had willed to him. The plantation, in Westmoreland, had been passed down from slavery days, one generation to the other. But of Mr. Mayer's grandmother little was said. It was no difficulty for Karl to figure out that side of the story. For Mr Mayer's mother and father were 'Jamaican whites,' they never hesitated to say that. And the man was a mulatto. How come? Where was the missing link?

Miss Birdie and Miss Kate never put their hands over their mouths when they talked about how Mr Goyle, who had the estate near Linstead, used to force some, and beg some of the women who worked on his estate to go to bed with him. Some got jobs because of this. Others lost jobs because of European Goyle taste for African women. In the slavery days, many African heads rolled and many pregnant bellies were busted to find out whether or not the child was mulatto. So it was not strange that Mr Mayer's grandmother was an African woman. But the goodly mulatto never mentioned this. He boasted to his friends of how his father, after inheriting a part of the plantation, sold it and went into the cement business with three of his colleagues. Moses was sent to a University in Canada to study Business Management. When he got the degree, he was to come back to manage the factory. But as the man put it, 'because he had such a heavy tan,' he had problems in his studies. There were photographs in the house of him when he entered University, but none when he had graduated. But nevertheless the man was still manager of the Cement Factory.

Moses Mayer's father sold the plantation he had inherited to an American who cut out the cane and turned the plantation into a first-class farm. He grew vegetables and fruit crops and raised chickens. Soon he started a guest house in Montego Bay. In no time it grew into a big hotel. The American had no taste for black women. His children were of pure stock. Edna Mayer, wife of Moses Mayer, was one such child. And although she lived in this country nearly all her life, she still had American citizenship.

It was not so strange to him that the Mayers did not like Africans. The Chinese were alright, the Indians not too . . . too bad. Well the Mulattoes were Jamaican whites, O.K., but the black ones they were something else. Not bad if they had money or were well educated, they might be helpful in business. But the poor uneducated and black? No way. Yet Karl was an African working in their house. Miss Rachael, black like jet, cooked their food and washed their clothes!

Mr Mayer would not say anything about his grandmother. And while there were many large framed pictures of the Queen, the president of America, the governor-general, the Prime Minister of England, the Prime Minister and Beauty queens of Jamaica since 'independence,' there were two pictures missing from the list of 'national heroes.'

True, the people loved their country. They loved its flag. The green stood for the land, the yellow stood for the beauty of the sunlight, and the black for hardship. What else could the black stand for if it was to have true meaning to the black masses of the country? The Mayers loved the motto, 'Out of many one people': 'And this was a multi-racial society, where all the different races lived in perfect harmony,' opening and closing remark at almost every public ceremony. Then why were the pictures of Paul Bogle and Marcus Garvey not there. Is it because they were black. Hell, no!

One of the four Prime Ministers since independence had black skins. The two Queen's representatives of the independent country, had both worn black skins. Three out of the ten beauty queens also had black skins. So if it was not the colour, what was it? Was it what Paul Bogle and Garvey stood for, why the Mayers did not even want even their pictures in the house? Yet the white woman and the mulatto man loved the land, loved the land of wood and sometimes water. But the mass of its people? . . . to hell with those black lazy stupid bitches.

Karl knew that the Mayers did not love African people. Mrs Mayer could hardly stand the sight of Miss Rachael. But she worked well and was honest. Her dignity prevented her from stealing. Karl was dead sure that Mrs Mayer did not like black folks. In good Anglo-American tradition, she did not hide this. She was not British, but every inch Anglo-American.

Karl picked up the whole family story in three weeks. But that was not all. The factory was running into trouble. Two years ago, it had made a profit of nearly quarter million dollars. Mayer used his share to pay down on the house which cost around seventy thousand dollars. Furniture added another ten thousand. He had to pay this off in five years or he would lose the house and would have to go back to live in Mona. What a shame and disgrace that would be to the family. Besides, he had to be paying for the Mercedes for himself and the Triumph for his wife. The two thousand dollars he got from the factory each month as manager was not enough. Mrs Mayer had called it 'little more than chicken feed' but her salary was 'just chicken feed'. Yes, salary! Mrs. Edna Mayer was registered at the factory and paid eight thousand dollars each year as 'personal secretary to the general manager'. And instead of the factory making more money, it was making less. Why was this so?

The previous government was treating the poor people too bad. For the slightest thing, the police and army used to brutalize the poor. Besides there was much talk about corruption. Mayer and others feared that the poor people might rebel, and with so many 'subversives' at the university and all around the place, they might turn the country into a communist one. Cuba was just ninety miles away. So Moses Mayer and many others in the Managers Association gave a lot of money to help the change of government. But what now?

Too many promises had been made in the election. High cost of living was battering the masses and the government, which had promised to control this, was making it worse. Almost every month there was a strike at the factory. Besides, the Minister of Industry was allowing too much cement to come in from abroad. Although he always spoke about developing local industry, a stumbling-block was in his way. His cousin had a big share in a shipping business! Then there was that foreman at the factory.

'That stupid negro, don't know how to deal with the workers,'

Mr Mayer was complaining to his wife one morning. 'That darn fellow,' he continued in his commanding London English, 'does not understand that he has to use psychology on the workers. Knows not a bloody thing about psychology. Does not know what a pat on the shoulder means to a black man,' he emphasized.

The woman, still in bed at 10 o'clock, spoke. 'But, Moses, you're wrong,' the American accent came from the room. 'You're wrong. You shouldn't have told him a damn about promotion.' She sounded almost angry with her husband.

'That promise flew up in his head, and drove him nuts.'

Mr Mayer had started to fit the broad tie around his bony neck. 'I was hoping that if I promoted him, somehow he would get the workers to work,' he paused as he tightened the noose, 'the workers to work a little harder. I mean a fair days work for a fair days pay.' He fixed his cuff links. 'After all some of them get as much as six, seven dollars a day.' Mr Mayer said nothing of how little some got.

The foam matress gave a rustling sound as the woman turned in the bed. 'Six dollars per day? Oh!' Do they really deserve that? Especially now that the business isn't making much profit?' she asked.

Karl listened from the big dining-hall where they entertained their guests. It was the morning when he was putting up a new stand for the big fish-bowl.

'Well, I would love to, but we can't pay them less. And with the big unions, we could make a deal with a few of the big boys. Then we could give a few more benefits without giving them the higher wages, maybe until next year. But with the new union they have formed, it will not be so easy.'

The moment the man mentioned 'new union', Karl remembered Kwame and their union. Same kind of problem between Mayer and his workers.

The woman spoke again, 'Yes, I could tell from the time I saw their leader. That fellow is a black power man.' She squeezed every word. 'He is a communist. Moses . . . you . . . must get rid of him.'

'Then with Cuba and China affair,' Mr Mayer continued, 'We encouraged the government to establish trade links with these countries. We could get things like beef . . . ah . . . I was even thinking of getting some machinery for the factory from them. They sold the things cheaper, and on more reasonable terms. But this damn thing is getting out of hand.'

'What? How?' Mrs Mayer asked curling up herself under her sheet.

He replied, 'Hear that since they set up the embassies, every day more and more people been going there. Want to know about these countries. Want to go to these countries!'

'What the hell they want to know about a communist country for?' she asked. 'They can go to America. What the hell they want to go to Cuba for?' Mrs Mayer shook her head. 'Man, these people are crazy.' She sprawled out in the bed.

There was the usual silence before the man came out of the bedroom. Karl knew he was kissing the woman. How had he done it when Mrs Mayer had not even got up out of bed to wash her mouth? But that was nothing compared to Miss Rachael's complaint that the woman sometimes had breakfast without washing her face. She even wanted her maid to wash her draws. Miss Rachael refused.

After breakfast 'Mistress', as Rachael called her, would have a swim. When she came back in she would head for the telephone. She was addicted to it. It was through her calls, as near as next door and as far away as London, that Karl learnt some of his greatest lessons: about the two men who live as man and wife further up the Hills; about the ganja, no she called it the 'pot' sessions and the man who organized them—he had people planting for him in the country and had contacts with men high up in the police in the island and in America.

About the Ambassador who had the birthday party for his dog and offered a five-hundred dollar reward when the animal was lost; about who was fooling around whose wife in the Hills; about the Minister who had a black wife, but came to spend weekends 'on government business' with the Causausian women he maintained in the Hills; about the woman further down, who made her 'garden boy' bathe, dry, powder her alsatian, then brush its teeth. When Mrs Mayer told the person at the other end, why the woman treated the dog this way, the two giggled over the phone for nearly five minutes.

Karl also learnt that the Mayers had two accounts abroad, and two locally. With the way things were going in the country, they made sure that their accounts abroad were fatter than the local ones. Sometimes, Mr Mayer would go abroad for a few days 'on company business' to add to his wealth. Not even in her wildest gossip, would Mrs Mayer reveal the amount they had saved out of their hard earned money.

The Mayers quarrelled fairly often. One evening, after Mrs

83

Mayer took a few drinks, she began to curse young Master Mayer. The boy used to be at YMCA until late, either swimming or playing some other games. But he came home early. The woman cursed him for always hanging around her like a little 'mamma's boy', and how he had been a mistake. She did not have time for mistakes'. Then again Mayer was spending too much money to keep the boy at Kings High School. She did not like black-eye peas soup herself, and the school did not stand for much of that. But the boy was taking too much money. She wanted to go to Maimi to do her summer shopping.

Mr Mayer could not say much because, although he loved the boy, he was afraid of the woman. Afraid that she might leave him. Strange indeed to Karl. For although his parents were poor, they cared so much for their children. Strange indeed to Karl!

'But from the way she talk to me, the way she smile when she see me. I must be the exception to the rule.' Karl had just finished his lunch, and Miss Rachael had gone back into the kitchen with the plates. The breeze was blowing very cool that evening. It made Karl feel for a nap. No, he had to fit the new curtain rod in the bedroom that the Mayers shared.

Mrs Mayer had just come back from one of her once-a-while, one-hour visits to the factory. The personal secretary to the general manager was very tired when she came back. She was in the room resting. Karl knocked on the mahogany door. At first there was no answer. He thought, 'Since morning she swim, gossip, go work . . . ' he smiled, 'she mus' want sleep.' He knocked again.

'Karl, is that you?' the American accent sounded muffled behind the mahogany. 'Come in, it's open.'

Karl put down the bit and the drill, opened the door and stepped into the room. Not even at Guys River at that time of day, would he expect such a sight. 'Mi . . . miss . . . mistress Mayer,' Karl felt the pores on his fore-head began to open. The sweatglands were now turned on. 'I come to fit the rod . . . the rod, mam.'

'What's wrong, Karl?' the woman asked as she put the cigarette in the ash-tray on the stand beside the bed.

It was one of those queer looking, old fashioned beds. It must be what they called 'antique' furniture. The stereo set near the bed was playing some country and western music. Skeeter was singing in her nose as usual.

Mrs. Mayer turned down the music. 'What's wrong, Karl?' she asked again as Karl moved towards the window.

'Nothing, mam. Nothing.' Looking through the window he could see right into the National Stadium. Mrs Mayer put down the *Woman's Magazine* she was reading and got up off the bed to help Karl who was fumbling with the curtain. 'Is alright, mam. I will take it down.'

'No, I'll help you,' she said now in a soft voice.

Karl tried, but could not help looking. The woman had on a light blue see through shortie nightie. It was so thin, that the nipples of her white breast peeped through at him. In her thirties, Mrs Mayer had legs that were without a blemish. She had known no work. The jaws of her flat behind were a bit too big for her yellow mini draws. Karl glued his eyes to the curtain rod. But the woman was pulling up her end of the curtain towards him. No, he had never dreamt of seeing, much less touching a white woman. And in the state that Mrs Mayer was! He had come to fit only the rod. But now his penis was pushing up the front of his pants. Why did the woman have to come so close? Why didn't she let go his hand? What, so near to him! Her hands on his shoulders. Her tongue on his lips, in his mouth. Good God! Not the bed? She on top of him, he on top of her now. But she wanted to stay on top! Her breast in his hand. Her hand on his penis. But she was sliding down on the bed. Down towards his foot, pushing down his pants, his briefs in one action. Sweating, panting, she moved further down. He was sweating too. Nervous but not wanting to stop. Only once in at least three months. But Miss Rachael might knock! Mr Mayer ! ! ! !

The penis went dead. But not for long. The tender fondling with moist warm lips soon put it back to life. Full of life. Stiff as the curtain rod still lying under the window. Animal from head to foot. Two animals, one white, one black. But she was taking off the yellow pants. Still on top. Ah! now beneath. Legs wide apart. Long red strands of hair moving aside as the slender black serpent lodged its head in a simmering pot of pink flesh. Oooh! A black stallion, a white mare. Animal from head to foot. Animal as hell.

The last week that Karl spent on the Hills was one in which he had to work regularly in the Mayers bedroom. Work or play, it made little difference as he had got his pay with a lot of 'brawta'. But it was much too dangerous. Suppose Mr Mayer should find out. And almost everyday. It was a wonder that Miss Rachael was only suspicious, or so she seemed. But that woman kept talking about 'playing fool to ketch wise!' Now Mrs Mayer wanted him to work at the factory. No way, Karl would rather starve. Yes he wanted a work. He wanted to make himself into a man. But where was he going with the sex hungry, lazy white woman. Yet, they were the very people who were talking about morals in the country. They preached about adultery and fornication every Sunday in church. They cursed Rasta as ill-mannered, without principle and morals. Ras Bongo used to say so many things that Karl was now beginning to understand. But the thing with Mrs Mayer, no one, not even Kwame would know about it.

CHAPTER 7

'Chris'mus a come'

The three weeks of work helped to free Karl of one of his worst fears. Bad as things were, he would have a few dollars in his pocket to last him over the next two weeks. After collecting his pay from Mr Mayer the Friday evening, he went straight home to put it down. He considered going down to Coronation Market to see if Miss Freda had brought anything for him and to give her ten dollars for his parents; but he changed his mind. The pick-pockets would be very busy that evening. Although his rachet knife was always ready for one of them, he might have to spend a night in jail until investigations were done. He would not mind that too much if he had not heard so much about the terror of beasts and chinks in the jails. Karl decided to go home. Later, he could either check out a cinema at Cross Roads or go around May Road to play some domino and drink with Kwame and some other brethren. Next day he would go down to see Miss Freda.

The Saturday morning, as Karl opened his eyes, he saw his Aunt passing through his room and going into the kitchen.

'Aunt Da,' Karl said as he stretched in the bed. ''Bout what time now?'

'Is well past eight now,' she replied from the kitchen.

'After eight! How come I wake so late?'

'Mus' because yu tired, and . . . '

But Karl interrupted her, 'Don't ask if I don't work hard up . . . ' He did not finish the sentence before he started to yawn. 'Aa . . . a . . , I feel like going back to sleep.' He began to pull the sheet back over himself.

His aunt who was preparing their breakfast, put down the spoon and came into the room. With one quick movement she pulled the sheet away. Luckily Karl had on his briefs and as the sheet was wisked off, he managed to roll over on his stomach to hide the 'bone-ache.

'Cho, Aunt Da—' he began.

'Don't "cho" me,' the elderly woman sternly replied. 'Don't "cho" me, I not a hog. Get up and let me tidy me house before I go out.'

'Where you so busy going this morning?' Karl asked as he sat up in the bed.

Aunt Hilda threw the sheet beside him and started back towards the kitchen. 'Chris'mus a come, is just four days left, and I want to start me shopping early.'

Karl raised up off the bed and stretched across to the radio on the table and switched it on.

. . . 'to hear sleigh-bells in the snow,
I'm dreaming of a white Christmas,
Just like the one I used . . . '

But Karl began turning the radio to the other station. 'Pscho . . o,' he hissed his teeth, 'from I am a baby I hear Perry Como dreaming of a white Chris'mas and snow, when the only snow I see here is snow-cone . . . ' By then the dial was set on the other station. The bells began to tingle and then the voices sang:

'Three days left for Christmas shopping,
Three days left to fill the stocking,
Three days left for Christmas shopping,
Only got three days more,
Only got three days more . . . '

As Aunt Hilda finished preparing the breakfast, Karl went outside to bathe in the little bathroom enclosed by zinc and board. As he bathed, the radio in his house, in Miss Rachey's house and the entire neighbourhood blared carols, Christmas music interrupted regularly by commercials and the call to hurry up with the Christmas shopping. As Karl soaped his rag, he thought, 'Nowadays, Chris'mas look like jus' a time when the capitalis' them inveigle poor people to spend out every cent them save from slaving for the whole year . . . and people like Aunt Da, although them is Christian, get caught in the trap. Seem like them more business with shopping than with saying that Chris'mas is Christ birthday.' Then he turned on the pipe, and started to wash off the soap. Karl smiled as he thought, 'But Ras Bongo not going put all him dunny in any capitalis' pocket next week.'

Soon after nine o'clock, Aunt Hilda was ready to go to Half-Way Tree to do her shopping. Next week Wednesday would be Christmas Day and even on Grand Market day she would have to go to work at the hospital, so Hilda had to buy the few things she could afford that day. She also had to buy some things for Miss Rachael who had given her the money the night before. For Miss Rachey not only had to work at the Mayers on that day, but also on Grand-market day. The Mayers said that they would have to give her

Christmas and Boxing Day, so she had to work Grand-market Day.

Karl stood at the doorway and watched as his short, fat, elderly aunt went through the gate and turned down the road towards the bus stop. Before she left, Aunt Da had given Karl five dollars to send for Kojo, Birdie and the children, that was all she could afford at the moment. But it was better than nothing at all, and Karl knew that his family would be glad for the little extra at Christmas time.

Karl himself left for Coronation Market soon after ten o'clock. As usual, he had to wait a long time before he finally got a bus. And with the heavy traffic in the Christmas rush, the bus did not reach Parade until nearly twelve o'clock. The day was not very hot since a strong wind was blowing from the sea. But there was a great deal of activity as the people jostled each other to get in and out of the stores, while the vendors pulled madly at those who passed by.

As Karl passed a snow-cone vendor under the big guango tree near the Country Bus stop, he stopped to get a little refreshment. He noticed that although a policeman stood nearby, some three-card men were busy mingling with the people waiting for transport to the country. One man with the three cards and the board on which he kept shuffling the cards and moving them around, the gold-capped tooth in the front of his mouth glistening, stopped in front of a teenage girl and said,

'This you win, this you lose, this you lose.' He held up the King, the Jack and the other Jack before the girl with one hand. The other hand held the board and a wad of paper money. At first, the girl did not pay him any attention. Then another man stepped out of the crowd and approached them. He took out a five dollar bill. Karl knew that he was the confederate.

The man said, 'Bet five dollars I show you the winning card.' He turned up the King and the man gave him another five dollars, 'See you money here, sah.'

The trick caught the girl for she began to open her purse and began pulling out a ten dollar bill as the three-card man shuffled away. His hand settled and the girl confidently lifted one of the cards. It was a Jack. Her mouth was wide open as the card fell from her hand and the tears began to trickle down her cheeks. In a jiffy, the man and his confederate disappeared. The two strong, healthy men had only exercised their freedom under a 'democracy', the freedom to work or not to work for a living.

Karl left Parade and walked on Spanish Town Road towards the market. He planned to stop and buy a shirt for Kojo, a hat for Miss Birdie and a few little things for his brothers and sisters. He would give Miss Freda the things to take home to Guys Hill. Although he was planning to tell his parents that he might come home for Christmas, he did not intend to go home until after the holidays had passed. For, although it pained his heart, if he went home in this season, he would have to give something to almost every relative and friend. Many of the people in Guys Hill, as in most country parts, did not really know how hard it was to make a penny in the city. Being so kind to him from his childhood days, Karl felt so ashamed to face them in the Christmas or the New Year to tell them that he could not afford to give them even a bottle of wine. After all it was fully three months he had been in town, and should Maas Charlie hear that he had come back to Guys Hill without being able to buy a drink for his friends, that fowl-frigger would be happy.

Karl crossed the street, forced through the crowd on the side-walk and entered a store to buy the few things for his family. There was a 'sale' going on in almost every store on the street. The one that Karl entered was as full as any other, with people busy buying many items for sometimes as little as half the price they purchased them during the year. It was the season of good cheer. Probably that was why the Jew-man who signed the bills and his wife who sat in the cashier's cage were so generous. For two weeks of the year, they were selling the items at much lower prices than they had been selling for the other fifty weeks of the year. And did they still make a profit? To hell they did make a fat profit! Why were they constantly urging people to hurry up with their shopping? And why did the skinny Jew always smile when he signed the bill? Is it because he loves black people?

Coronation Market was a jam. Columns of people moved between the stalls with their bodies almost pasted to each other. The pick-pockets must be having a hard time in deciding who to pick. The stalls had things ranging from common pins to tubs, a lime to a water-melon, red-herring to smoked ham, polyester to old-iron blue, and mini-panty to oversized draws. There were toys of all sizes, shapes and colours. Some of the guns looked so real. Along every stall, people were busily buying and selling, higgling and haggling about the prices. The humming of the traffic outside, the sound of vendors and purchasers all around, made it difficult for one to even hear one's voice. But despite the bustle and the hustle, most of the people seemed to be in a happy mood. For although the things were expensive, Christmas was the time for which many poor people had saved during the rest of the year. And although the masses met hell under the heel of the rich rulers and their puppets for most of the year, Christmas was the season of good cheer.

Karl did not spend much time in the market, but he did not reach Miss Freda until after two. He spent about half an hour chatting to Miss Freda and Miss Merl, who had decided to come to town so that she could also buy a few things which she could not get in Linstead Market. Kojo and Miss Birdie did not send anything as they were expecting Karl to come home before Wednesday. Karl gave the things he had bought to the woman and told her to tell his parents that he may come home.

'Tell Aunt Birdie to look for me with one eye.'

'How you mean?' Miss Merl asked seriously. 'How you mean with one eye?'

Merl was somewhat puzzled.

She began to smile, 'You must come home and carry you girlfriend . . . you daughta so we can see her.'

'Merl, how you so out-of-order?' Freda asked looking at the other higgler, then at Karl.

'But how? Karl can't have daughta too?' she asked jokingly. She leaned back on the stall, rested her hand on the oranges she was selling then asked Karl, 'You don't plant no seed yet, eeh?'

Karl reached back to August Town around five o'clock that afternoon. He wanted to get a little sleep before his aunt came home, since Kwame and himself had planned to go to a dance at Papine. That was all he expected to do for the holidays. However, if his little savings could manage, either Christmas or New Year's Day, he would go to a beach near Rock-fort. But as he came off the bus and walked up July Road, his mind was set on sleeping even for an hour before his aunt came in. He did not expect her to finish shopping, stop at one of her friends in Papine, and reach home before six o'clock. As Karl passed Miss Rachey's gate, he kept his head straight so that none of Kwame's brothers would see him or come to talk to him and prevent him from sleeping. But when Karl reached his gate, the front door of the two-roomed house was wide open. As sure as hell, Aunt Da had already reached home.

'Evening, Aunt Da,' Karl said as he stepped in the house.

But there was no reply. Karl took off his tam, threw it in one of the chairs and pushed the door to his aunt's room. 'Aunt Da . . . ' he called as he looked at the woman sitting on the bed with her head resting on the top of the panel bed.

'Aunt Da, Aunt Da, . . . you sick, mam?' he asked.

'Karl, me son,' she began in a sad tone, 'if I ever tell you what happen to me.'

'Wha, wha . . . '

'Sit down on the bed beside me.'

'Yes, mam . . . ' Karl sat down pushing away a little parcel wrapped in brown paper.

'Karl, get up back and open the window . . . I feel hot.'

He got up and opened the little jalousie window over on the other side of the bed.

'Now, go for some water, let me drink,' she said as he was about to sit down on the bed.

'No, mam,' Karl replied. 'I anxious to hear what happen.'

And so she began to unravel the story of what made her so unhappy. The woman left the house that morning with one hundred and fifty dollars. Twenty dollars belonged to Miss Rachey. Aunt Da had thirty dollars to buy some things for her Christmas. The one hundred dollars was to pay down on a TV set she wanted to keep her company and to see some of the things that were happening around the world. She had saved throughout the whole year to make the down payment, so she could get the TV for Christmas. Why didn't she tell Karl about it before? She wanted to give him a surprise. Rachey was the only person who knew that she was going to buy the set.

Aunt Hilda had taken the bus to Half-Way Tree that morning. There she planned to buy the things she wanted for Miss Rachey and herself. But she did not want to be walking up and down with the money for the TV in her handbag. So she decided to go down to Cross Roads and pay down on the TV set before someone stole it.

She had to wait for about fifteen minutes for a bus in Half-Way Tree. For the buses usually ran badly and with the traffic and the Christmas crowd, many had passed her. While she stood at the bus stop, she noticed a neatly dressed young man in a tie, standing beside her. Soon a bus came and the crowd moved towards the bus door. Aunt Da said that she did not want anyone to pick her, so she stayed out of the rush. The young man was also trying to get into the bus, but he was kind and kept saying, 'Take you time and go in, Mother.' As she reached the door and was stepping into the bus, two other men, 'looking like Rasta,' came up and started pushing the young man. But he was so humble that he did not say anything. So she stopped on the bus step and moved aside to let the 'nice-looking young man' pass her. That was her mistake, for by the time she turned around to rebuke the two 'Rasta-head boys' the nice looking young man had picked her hand-bag. And by the time she cried out, the three of them ran away in different directions.

'The Rasta-head one them couldn't pick me,' she paused, 'for I would be looking for them. But I would never expect such a nice dress young man in him neck-tie to do a thing like that. But it learn me a lesson, not to judge people by them looks.'

The loss of the money was a hard blow to Aunt Hilda, to Karl, Miss Rachey and everyone who knew how it felt to be robbed after working very hard and saving almost every cent for something special. It was such incidents which had caused the people to be so bitter against someone that stole even a cent. For although Karl did not fully understand the feeling of the people at Parade the first day he came to Kingston to live, after hearing his aunt's story, he felt like he personally would support the idea of killing all criminals, even when they steal a pin. But when he looked over his life, the injustices he suffered under Maas Charley, his struggles for weeks without a job, the way the Mayers overworked him for little more than a pittance, the riches of a few while the majority had to struggle for bread, it forced Karl to wonder if he was weaker, wouldn't he too have turned to crime. As Kwame had said over and over again, 'is the system, the capitalis' slavery which make a few rich and many poor, which is at the root of crime. Is poverty that breed crime.'

After Aunt Hilda told Karl and later Miss Rachey, she felt a little better. Miss Rachey said that she would stand the loss of her money. The next morning bright and early, Aunt Da was getting ready to go to church to ask the Lord to forgive the youths who had stolen her money and prevented her from getting her TV set for Christmas.

Karl spent Christmas Day quietly at home chatting with his aunt and sometimes over Miss Rachey with Kwame and the others. Unlike the days when he was a child, the day was almost like any other holiday. To Kwame, it was much the same. But to most people, the day was much more special. They were busy up and down the street, most of them going to and from a fair which was being held on the open lands by May Road. The children were especially gay in their Christmas hats, their new clothes and pretty toys. The only thing Karl did was to go to a stage show at Cross Roads that night.

The following week, on New Year's Day, Kwame wanted Karl to go with him and his girl-friend to the beach near Rock-fort.

Although Karl had earlier agreed to go, he changed his mind the morning. Firstly, he did not have the money to enjoy himself. He was tired of getting money from Kwame. After all, Kwame was just a friend and not his father. And even if he were his father, at twenty-two years old, it was time for him to be able to entertain himself out of his own pocket.

Secondly, Kwame had a girl. He had none. Two or four is alright, but three is a crowd. Although Kwame begged, Karl stayed home all day and all night. He wanted some rest, so he stayed home for the day and read a little book about Marcus Garvey which his aunt had got from a fellow worker at the hospital. He also made a little cupboard for the kitchen. That would protect the food from mice which lived in the roof. Karl went to bed early the New Year's night. The next day, he was planning to start looking another job. His aunt was still next door. As Karl lay in the house alone, he felt so lonely. He would love to be with his parents and brothers and sisters. If not he should be with a girl. It was full time he had a girl-friend. He hoped that the New Year would bring him one.

CHAPTER 8

'Man Man Umm ... mmm'

Karl got into the habit of going to Hope Gardens almost every Sunday. It was a nice place to relax. Although New Year's Day was on the Wednesday, for the whole weekend people were in the holiday spirit. And so the people streamed in and out of the gardens in their glad rags. Kwame was with his girl-friend for the weekend, so Karl went by himself. He had been sitting under a shed near to the gate for sometime. He watched the people as they passed by. They were gaily dressed. To know where most came from, the troubles they left behind, would dullen the very clothes they wore.

It must have been midday, for through the canopy of the trees where he sat, he could see the sun directly overhead. Karl had been thinking of the three weeks up the Hills. Christmas and the New Year had taken away almost all he had saved. Now, the main problem was where would he get another job? Mrs Mayer, yes his Mistress Mayer, wanted him to take a job in the factory. It would not pay much, but she would help him to get some extras. But no, for one, Karl wanted to do his trade. After a time, he might be able to get a job to build a house. After all, Maas Charlie could not build a better house than he. Fat-head Charlie could not even read a plan. And since the man who was working on the school at Guys Hill had shown Karl once how to read a plan, it had become fairly easy to him.

But apart from that, he knew that the woman would want him to do other things besides his work at the factory. No! Karl decided not to take the job. Tomorrow he would have to start hunting again. But now he was in the place he loved so much. Of the ten dollars left, on Saturday he had given Aunt Da three dollars to help buy food. And down at Coronation market he gave Miss Freda a letter with two dollars for his mother, Karl still had three dollars left in his grip under the bed, and two more in his pocket. He felt good about that.

Whistling as he walked slowly into the gardens, Karl decided that he would sit down for a while, then he hoped to go up to the zoo. But a young woman and a little baby boy were sitting on the seat where he and Kwame sat the first time he had come to the gardens. Karl loved to sit there since the spot was so cool, the trees so beautiful and it offered such a good view of the beds and rows of flowers in the finest part of the garden.

Karl approached the young woman, — between twenty and twenty-two years old, he thought. He felt somewhat shy. But nearly four months now and with a little money, it was high time now he make a try. Besides Kwame was not there, he wanted someone to talk to.

Karl went up to the young woman. 'I can sit down beside you, sister?' he asked looking her from head to foot.

Hair straightened, white tall sleeved blouse hanging loosely out of her old iron-blue jeans, She looked up at Karl and pulled the little boy closer to her. Just like mama, neither slim nor fat, the baby looked healthy.

'I don't have any seat here,' she said and went back to playing with her baby.

Can't be more than eighteen months to two years old. Karl sat down. The woman looked at him, neither hostile nor friendly in her looks. Matter of fact, she was not even looking at him. Her baby boy, the flowers, the people passing by, was all she seemed to see. But Karl? He could go to hell and never come back. The three people sat on the seat for over half hour before exchanging another word. The baby was still eating some biscuits from a lunch pan. The little one broke the ice.

'Man, man. Um. mm,' he grunted holding up one of the biscuit to Karl's mouth.

Suddenly she pulled back the baby's outstretched hand. 'No, Huey, rude, don't do that!'

'Why?' Karl asked, 'The baby not doing anything wrong.'

'That may be true, but people too funny nowadays.'

Karl stretched out his hand and took the biscuit from the baby. 'Funny, yes, because the two of us sit down here and if it wasn't the baby, . . . aaa . ay, I wouldn't taste one of the biscuit.'

The baby was opening one of the pans again. 'Man, man, Umm . . mm,' his hand was coming up with another biscuit.

This time she didn't try to stop him. Karl took the biscuit. The woman looked at him and smiled.

'Wh . o . ooy,' Karl said with a sigh of relief. 'At last.'

Doreen was the name, Twenty-one years old. One year younger than Karl. Lived at Papine, just above August Town. But where in Papine? She would not answer. Huey was the baby's name, two years old and was her only child. One more than Karl had. Passed second year exams. Wanted to become a nurse. Couldn't become one unless she had passed third year. After leaving school, unemployed for two years. No job. Nearly became a whore, easiest way out. Finally got a job in a drug store at Cross Roads. Now living with a older cousin. Parents in St James. Did not have a man. Does not want a man!

'But if we couldn't be man and woman friend at least we could be good friends.' Karl suggested this as they got up to walk to the gates.

No. She didn't want any kind of friends. They were all trouble. Could not be trusted. Never sincere. Just a waste of time.

The sun had just disappeared behind the tall trees in the western end of the garden. Karl, Doreen and Huey walked in the cool of the evening towards the gate. And when they reached, Karl pleaded with the girl as they waited for the bus.

'But, Doreen, I would love to see you again.'

'I don't have anything to do with that,' she replied. 'I don't have you eyes.'

The bus was now coming. She took up the baby.

'Baby Huey, you coming back down here Sunday?' she asked. 'Umm, you coming back, my little hussie?'

The bus stopped and the woman with the baby on her shoulder climbed in. Doreen hadn't even said goodbye to Karl. She got a seat near to a window. The baby looked out at Karl as the bus was about to move off. He pushed one little hand through the window and moved the tiny fingers up and down.

'Man . . Man. Ta . taaa.'

Karl could hardly wait to reach August Town. It was just getting dark when he reached. As he came off the bus, he went over to Miss Rachey's house. He had to tell Kwame about Doreen. And throughout the whole week, in his walking from one construction site to another, the woman was at the back of his mind. His eyes caught the sign of almost every drug store he approached. He looked inside, but no Doreen. Not a sign of that woman.

'But the girl said she don't want a man,' Karl said to Kwame. It had almost been the same argument everytime they came home each evening for the week.

'Yes, that is what she tell you,' Kwame replied. 'But as Malcom X say, a good woman might frown the first time, and the second, and the third time too. But then a smile, and a kiss and then . . . ,' he started to smile. 'Karl, I older than you. I know more 'bout woman than you. I don't think you lift up a dozen skirts yet from when you were born.'

Kwame must be making fun. Anyhow he did not know how much work he had done at Beverley Hills. But there was some truth in this question that he asked over and over again. 'Why the hell you think the woman asking the baby 'bout coming back next week?' It gave Karl some hope.

The next Sunday, sure as fate, Karl was at Hope Gardens. Aunt Da had asked him to make a stand at the back of the house. She needed it to put clothes on when she was washing. Because of this he did not reach the Gardens until nearly one o'clock. Doreen was nowhere in sight!

Karl sat down on the bench under the big Wild Fig tree. He started to pull the strands of his short beard.

'I tell Kwame that I wouldn't see the woman again, know I wouldn't see her again.' He hung down his head and looked on the tree root 'Spe . e . e . e . e,' Karl hissed his teeth. The tree and its root was still beautiful. The sandals that Ras Bongo had given him, although they were going, were still nice, but his mind was on . . .

'Man, man,' the sound broke his thoughts.

Karl raised his head and looked around.

'Hi, Karl,' the voice, her looks, a thousand times more pleasant than last week.

What a change! Karl thought. For seconds, he stood just staring at his dream come true.

'Hi, Sister Doreen,' Karl replied trying to hold back the smile. He failed and miserably too.

Huey wore little blue elastic-waist pants and matching shirt, with a yellow knitted tam made in the same fashion as the black one that Karl wore. Doreen wore no pants this time but just a pink and white, checkered, puff-sleeved dress not too short, but revealing as she sat a pair of legs, black, smooth, neither fat nor slim, but pleasing to Karl's eyes. And his eyes did not fail to glance at them at the least chance. They were really a sight for sore eyes. But neither the legs, nor the rounded body that bore them, nor the gay dress, nor the African face above it was the main reason why Karl was so happy to see Doreen. Why then? He was not even sure himself. He just wanted her company. That is not to say that the attractiveness of the woman did not play its part. To hell it did, and a big part too.

Karl, Doreen and Huey spent the day together. This time the lunch pan did not have only biscuit in it, it had a few sandwiches as well. Doreen did not say it but from the way she gave them to him, he had a funny feeling that she had made them specially for

98

him. With the orange juice that Karl had bought at the soda fountain, the three had a fine lunch.

They walked, looked and saw so much that day: the little lake with fishes from 'ticky-ticky' to black perch; the creepers floating above the water, the lilies growing below the surface spreading their broad leaves like huge frying-pans turned upside down. The flowers pushed three, six, nine inches above the water, closed, barely opened, fully opened, made the lake looked like a big vase all set for the wedding. And there was the palm, the banana and a tree that had stem like the palm and leaves like a banana.

Now in the zoo, there was the mongoose, and the monkey. At times it even looked as if the monkey wanted to talk.

'Go way man,' Doreen said playfully. 'I don't believe in no evolution.'

Karl held one of Huey's hands, Doreen held on to the other.

'Hey,' she said looking down on the baby and pointing towards one of the monkeys, 'Hey, see you father there. Um . . mm, See you daddy there . . . '

But Doreen must have forgotten that Karl was there, for the moment she looked back at him, she became serious. And Karl all along, was dying to ask the question. Now was his chance.

'Where's Huey father?' he asked looking the woman straight in her face.

She hesitated for a while. 'I don't know what happen to that bitch. Mus' be dead.'

And so the most touching part of the girl's life story began. Doreen had met Huey's father over three years before the baby was born. She was sixteen then. He was still going to Technical school and by the time he left school, she got a job. The man wanted to go to Teachers' College, as he had always wanted to be a 'big man' in the country. But who was to help him? His father had died when he was young, and his mother alone could not manage. Doreen worked and saved to send him to college. Her parents and cousin with whom she was living, objected, but she pushed on. She loved the man. She denied herself of many things, including other men.

'I provide him with everything. When him wanted to have sex with me I never want to give him.' She continued, 'But we were friends for over a year. And besides, I did love him.' She looked away from Karl and then back at the monkeys. 'But I am a bad luck girl. Bad luck all the days of my life. Born in June so rule under Cancer, a bad sign.'

Doreen paused for a good while, looking at Huey. 'Him wanted me to take abortion. No. I did want a baby, his baby. Then . . . ' she shook her head, 'No fly-by-night doctor, no butcher not going to cut up, cut up nothing inside me body. Not me.'

'Then this is the reason why him leave you?' Karl asked.

'No, not that! Soon after him graduate from college, that time I was six months pregnant, I notice that him come to see me only now and again. Guess what happen.'

Karl gave no reply.

'Well, while I was straining myself to keep him in school, the worthless boy was having fun with one of him college mate.' She spat on the ground. 'Hear that him say—' she broke off and started to speak in perfect English — 'he wants to be a big man in the country and he needs a wife that is in his social class. A woman that can represent him in public.'

They were now leaving the zoo. Doreen continued, lifting Huey to her side as she spoke, 'Yes, him get the woman him did want. One custos from May Pen daughter. But she really represent him in public. Represent him good you see,' she raised her eye-brow at Karl. 'She represent him under every big man in Clarendon. They know every colour draws she wear. Period or no period she represent him. Ah . . a . ay,' Doreen uttered a bitter laugh. 'When that slut sit down in the big cars or the big house, her panty catch a fire. It have to come off.'

Doreen started to speak slower. The thick emotions left her voice. 'The last thing I hear is that him steal school money, she leave him, and him now either at General Penetentiary or at Bellvue. She still leave out here to represent him.'

'So that is why you say you don't want any man?' Karl asked looking at Huey who was playing with a piece of paper, unconcerned about what was happening. 'Yes,' Doreen replied. 'I don't want any man. No woman can trust them.' She pointed from one nostril to the other, 'Not from here to here.'

'But is the same thing with women them today,' Karl emphasized. 'The moment they see a man with a car, or a man who can give them money, them gone. Is a thing in the whole society. The hard life and poverty for most of we, and the riches of couple people. Everybody dreaming to live Beverley Hills life. And as long as Beverley Hills up there, as long as the majority of us man and woman have to struggle like hell to live, man will always leave woman for big life, and woman will always leave man for big

house.' Karl stressed his last sentence, 'You better believe that!'
Doreen spoke, 'That sound true. But I still don't trust any man.
Not me. Trust black man? Me . . . Me, you mus' be mad!'
They left the zoo and went back to sit down.
'Well, here is one black man who you can trust,' Karl said
slowly stretching his hand to hold Doreen. Huey was playing
nearby.
But the woman pulled away her hand. 'Trust a man! Umm . . .
mee? You would have to prove it.'
In the next few weeks, Karl went a long way to getting Doreen
to trust him. She still had her fears about all men and with this,
some weird views about the society. But that would take some time
to deal with, and needed a lot of patience. Karl had also got her
address in Papine. In the first few weeks he had stopped there one
or two evenings. He had taken her to a dance on May Road.
Kwame had met her there. She was nice he thought. Karl could not
let Doreen know he was not working. He had told her that he was
doing carpenter work at Beverly Hills.
When he had completed his 'hunt', some evenings he would stop
at her home. Kwame also dropped by sometimes. They would talk
for most of the time. She had a small record player and quite a few
records too. Her records were mostly reggae. It was the music of
the people, originated and developed from the experience of the
suffering African masses of the country. The hard-driving beat
with the rich mixtures of the drum, bass, horns, strings and 'things',
was full of life and the lyrics summed up the experience of the
people.
The Mayers and their like called it 'nonsense'. But strange when
they have their parties, behind closed doors, they would shake up
their 'ass' to reggae music. The rhythm would hold them! They
had good reason to call the music nonsense, because unlike the
classics, which they claimed to be the finest music, the Mayers
understood the roots of reggae. Was it the music they hated, or
what it stood for?
Doreen had no jazz, she had no blues. She, like most black
folks in the country, was not well exposed to the musical experience
in America. The radio stations played more country and western
than jazz and blues, but bombarded the people with what the big
record producers dictated, that which would pile up profits. Not
jazz and blues, only funky and soul music of the American-
African was popular with most people. Doreen's favourite, which
she played almost every evening, was one by four handsome black
men in that country. The brothers were superb singers, each having

101

a voice as cool as the morning breeze and singing like the evening breeze, whistling through the trees. They were 'TOPS'. Through them she had learnt that her troubles with Huey's father were 'ALL IN THE GAME'.

Doreen did not have Kwame's favourite among her records. He had to buy it for himself. He loved reggae, classics, jazz and blues, Cliff, Beethoven, Basie, Holt and King, but his favourite singer was Miriam Makeba. Kwame had to write 'PRAISES' to her.

> Miriam, oh Miriam,
> Thy music is sweet.
> It rises and falls,
> Retreats and dashes,
> Like waves to the shore,
> To touch some virgins feet.

> Miriam, oh Miriam,
> Thou art divine.
> The flowers bow to you,
> They do the same as men,
> Cause the beauty of thy body,
> The strength of thy message,
> Force them all, old and bold,
> To pay thee homage.

> Miriam, oh Miriam,
> Mighty daughter of Afrika,
> Thou art the supreme,
> Artist of excellence
> 'Naana' of the arts.
> Play your music,
> Till thy brothers and sisters,
> Sons and daughters of Afrika
>   are no longer slaves.
> Then sweet Miriam,
> Go to sleep,
> Thy work here is complete.

Kwame loved the singer, Kwame loved her songs, but most of all, Kwame loved 'THE PIECE OF GROUND' . . .

CHAPTER 9

'Workers run this country'

It was now four months since Karl had stopped working in the Hills. Every week Miss Rachael would tell him that Mrs Mayer wanted to know where he lived. But she had not told her. The odd jobs in August Town or at the university or at the Public Hospital that Aunt Hilda or Miss Rachael, Mr Stone or Kwame helped him to get, could not do. That was not what Karl had left Maas Charlie to come to town for. But the pittance which helped him to survive between January and April came from these odd jobs.

He came home late one evening after another hard day, and as he ate the food that Aunt Hilda had left for him, the thought of leaving the country came back to him. And it came on very strong at that, even if it meant that he had to stow away. The thought that it was his country and he should stay and fight had long gone. Now it was the question of survival. But the same factor that urged Karl on was the same one that stood in his way. It was Doreen. 'Now' that I have a woman, I not going to leave her. I must get a steady job,' Karl thought. 'Must get a steady job that will pay some money. Need enough to send to country to help out me family, to carry out Doreen and to save something for tomorrow.'

Karl got up and wiped off his oily, slightly bearded face. He went to the kitchen to put down the empty plates. 'Trouble to get work, trouble to reach work, trouble to buy food, to find place to live, to pay rent, to save a doctor fee, to see a doctor . . . trouble to live, Karl thought. 'But what to do? Thief!' Many faced with the situation had started to live by that means. But to Karl, to steal from sufferers like himself was a sin that even Lucifer would not pardon. Then to go up to the Hills or to hold-up a bank was more dangerous. It might well come to that, but for now, there was something else.

Karl still had one alternative. He had to make use of it—Edna Mayer, that white bitch. 'But is only the work at the factory I want. Nothing else under the face of the sun.' Karl took off his clothes, turned off the lights and climbed into the single bed. 'Tomorrow I will go up there with Miss Rachey. Just the work at the factory.

Nothing else,' he thought. 'Not one fucking thing else.' Soon he was fast asleep.

The cement factory was at Fort-Rock. It was a fairly large plant employing over two hundred people working on two shifts. The work was very hard. The marl that was used in the making of the cement made the place very dusty. The caustic soda was also dangerous for the lungs. The pay was very low, but better than what Karl had got with either Maas Charlie or in the Hills. Many workers, their women and children at home and living in rent houses, and with the high cost of living, could afford only patty, bun and cheese, areated water or some other light food for lunch. How could that keep their bodies strong to do such hard work? Karl could afford to eat a little better. A good lunch at work and a good dinner when he went home. Not too bad!

Like most workers in town, he had to do two day's work in one. One day's work at work, one day's work to get to work. The first day from Parade to August Town with a box in one hand and a grip in the other was a day's work all right. But the thought that nearly half million lived with this almost daily, was something beyond Karl's imagination. Black people, nine hundred and ninety-nine out of every thousand, are the ones who travel on the buses. Afrikans, and Indians too, worked the most and suffered the most, that Karl had long realized. It was something else that puzzled him.

It took Karl about two hours each morning to travel from August Town to Fort-Rock. This was a distance of about five miles and he used two different buses. It took him the same time or more to reach home. Four hours daily, twenty hours weekly or nearly one day out of every five, spent on the road to get to work. Two and a half working days out of every five and in a year, he would spend about twenty-five working weeks going to work for fifty weeks. True? But Karl was one out of nearly a quarter of a million people, some spending more time, some less, on the buses.

'Can't they be run better, organized routes, express services, a few more buses, and pay the workers better to run the buses good?' He had been working out the figures at Doreen's house.

'But, Karl, they losing money every year,' Doreen had said to him that evening, 'the company don't have any more money.'

Karl turned to his woman. 'Half million people live here in town, at least quarter million take bus. If everyone spent fifteen cent a day, is one dollar a head . . . is quarter million dollar a week . . . is one million dollar a month,' he paused, 'how much of this twelve million dollar a year the company spend to paint old bus to fool people say is new bus, and to underpay the worker? What them do to help the country? Nothing them do to help we. Not even the ticket print out here. Overchange we, underpay the workers and send million of dollars to Britain to make arms to send to South Africa.'

'But suppose say, government or a local company own it?'

'Don't know if it will better, since even the government might just run it like the capitalis' them,' he replied.

'Then, Karl, why the government allow this one company to go on so?' Doreen asked.

It seemed as if she did not know about the ultimatums that government after government had given the bus company. 'Run the bus service good or else, or else . . . we give you a fare increase.'

'Karl, the government not suppose to do things that will help the majority of us in the country? The majority or just a few? Ee . . e . en, Karl?'

There was also something funny about the first month's pay at the factory. He had given his parents a little money. Not much, just five dollars. He had also bought a few exercise books and pencils for his sisters and Junior. It was the second time he had gone home in the five months. At least he now had something to give them and so he felt better facing the family. He had also told them about Doreen and they had all wanted to meet her although Miss Birdie did not feel good about her having a child. A pair of slippers for Doreen and a shirt for Huey was the only other way Karl remembered spending money. Aunt Da did not take anything, but he had only enough money left to pay his bus fare and buy lunch until the next pay-day. Where had the two fortnight's pay disappeared to? His pants all had sound pockets. Where was the money?

Karl began to spend more time with Doreen. Almost every evening they would be together. But after six months, Doreen had not met Aunt Hilda yet. The woman was either gone to church or to work when Karl wanted to take Doreen. One evening while coming from work, he stopped by Doreen's house to take her and Huey to see his aunt. As he approached his gate, he noticed that the door was closed.

'But Aunt Da should be here,' Karl said to his girl-friend. 'Is just quarter to six and she's not going to work till eight tonight.'

'Maas Karl,' it was Miss Rachael's smallest son. The boy came up to the fence that separated the houses. He had a sulky look on his face. 'Miss Hilda not there. She and mama gone down to Public Hospital to look for Brother Kwame.'

105

'Kwame?' Karl asked.

'Yes, him in hospital from today.'

'Ah right, I going down there now.'

Karl went inside the house and put down his bag. In a short while, Doreen, Huey and himself were on their way to the hospital. It was 'brown dusk', just getting dark when they reached.

Kwame went to work at the Electric Service that morning. The leader of their union, he the secretary and three other delegates, all workers with the company, wanted to see a representative from the management. The issues were: first, to gain recognition of the union as the bargaining power for the workers; secondly, that the workers who were fired in the strike before, be given back their jobs; thirdly, that the demands that had caused the strike be negotiated immediately. Their employers had refused to meet the union delegates. Why? They had won the poll. The management had always bargained with the big unions, so why not a union made up entirely of its workers?

Black power, Communists. And not only that, the union would link up with similar organizations. What! Then if they were allowed to grow, anything! no, one thing was sure to happen. Black power and communists would take over the country. Another Cuba! What would happen to freedom? What would happen to democracy? What would happen to Maas Charlie, Mr Goyle, Bauxite Works, Cayman Estates, Mr Wong, Mr Mayer, the Electric Company, and, oh . . . Mrs Mayer! What would happen to freedom?

When Kwame and the other delegates returned to the workers with the news that the management had not met them, immediately they decided to strike. Strike now, so near to the 'Independence' Festival? That was the first Monday in August, exactly a week away. Then what would happen if the strike stretched on to the festival? So many foreign visitors would be present. They had to see the shows: flower show, cooking show, food show, and the 'female puppy' show.

The Electric Service workers started to make up the picket signs. They were ready. 'We have the island's electricity in our hands. We give lights. We can also take it away. Then why should we cringe and beg and fight so that our women, our children can have light in our houses.'

Although there were suitable people in the country, the supervisors were mainly white men from abroad. One supported the strike. Few foremen gave their support. They had light in their houses anyway. But they could not afford to support the strike.

They were foremen. Most of the men were ordinary electricians before. But not only that. What if the company decided to close down for one or two months? They would get no pay. They would have no light in their houses.

A few workers wanted to continue working. They would be willing to accept any good that came out of it, but were not prepared to strike. These workers could not hold back the struggle. Two men with their picket signs: 'Workers run this country,' 'Justice now or else . . . ' stood in the gate way to the main buildings. The rest, most holding their pickets, stood nearby. That was what was allowed by law. Which laws? Who made them? Workers? or employers? The laws said that workers had the rights to be represented by the union of their choice but employers were not forced to recognize these unions.

'Funny law,' Karl said. 'Funny law.'

But if the union was not recognized by the management, what right has it to call a strike? What right had the workers to be disturbing the peace? They were breaking the law!

The police arrived at about eleven o'clock, sun beating down with such might, that the asphalt sank when their heavy boots landed on it. Four truck loads of them, siren still wailing and danger lights still flickering, baton in one hand, shotgun in the other, pistols on their hips. As they lined up across the road, their black boots, black pants with red stripes, checkered shirts, white helmets with glass shields over their faces, helped to draw the crowd. The army patrol cruised by regularly, machine gun mounted on a stand in each vehicle.

The inspector arrived in a brand new police car. His khaki uniform seemed a bit darker than the colour of his sweating face. The fat around his belly, made it difficult for his pants to stay firmly at his waist. He stopped the traffic from both sides, then walked across the road, like a cock chicken with a boil under each wing. Like a red tin god, who owned the street from Parade to Half-Way Tree, he stood before the pickets.

'Who is the leader of the strike?' he asked.

A deadly silence fell over the place. Deadly considering the noise from the traffic, from people going about their business, not too long ago. Now everyone stood and waited.

The leader of the union and Kwame moved towards the inspector.

'So you are the trouble-makers!' He pointed his staff at them. 'Ah, you are the black power man,' his red face getting redder, 'the communists! You are under arrest!' To the sergeant, big fat

107

with sweat dripping down his oily black face, barked: 'Take them raas away!'

But it was not so easy. The workers still holding their pickets, surrounded their leaders and Kwame. The squad started to move in. The tension, the hatred could be seen in their youthful faces, all sixty of them, their batons, their guns had been trained to maintain the law. The eighty workers, eight hundred, eight thousand, eight million if there were that many, could not be allowed to break the law. Maas Charlie, Mr Mayer, oh . . . Mrs Mayer lived by the law! Why should the 'Electric Service' workers want to break it?

'So after the . . . oh . . . ah . . . ' the pain could be seen in Kwame's face. 'After the clash . . . they carry me and some other brethren . . . to the station.'

The light in the ward was low, but his eyes could not stand the glare. He wanted to put his head further up on the pillow. His mother and Aunt Hilda helped him. Spots of blood could be seen through some parts of the bandage around his forehead.

He continued speaking slowly, 'The police carry me up here . . . in the same jeep . . . the same jeep . . . that they carry . . . two of them friends. Not the workers do it. The sufferer . . . sufferers who was standing by.'

'Then they arrest you?' Karl asked leaning over the bedside trying to hold back his tears.

'No,' Kwame replied in almost a whisper. He looked at Doreen holding Huey, the baby sitting on the bed, unconcerned about what was going on.

'Then what happen to the inspector, him get hurt too?' Karl asked again.

Kwame shook his head. He opened his eyes and looked towards the door, Mr Stone was coming in. He looked mad.

'This damn country, this damn country,' he said raising his voice. 'Workers, workers, farmers, poor people, them labour from slavery days, build this place. And yet . . . '

A nurse was coming across to them, 'Excuse me, sir,' she began.

Rachael put her hand over her husband's mouth. 'Shee . . eee, Vernal, not so loud,' she pleaded.

'But workers must get justice,' he continued in a lower voice. 'The poor man, the black man must get justice on this rock. Time now. Time!'

Mr Stone stood between Miss Rachael and Aunt Hilda. She had come so early to make sure that Kwame was well taken care of. Hilda was the 'maid' for that block.

'Then what going to happen now?' Karl asked.

The workers had decided to go back to work the next day. But until their union was recognised, their co-workers re-employed and their demands met, there would be power failures every day.

Power failures? And prevent the company from making a higher profit? The owners abroad would not have it! They would complain. Mayer was complaining about the same thing with his cement factory. The government would have to take action. What kind of action? Who controlled the police, the Electric Service, the government, the inspector?

Power failures? And make the company directors and the inspectors have to do without lights in their houses? They might suffer. Suffer? Delco plants give lights too!

Power faileres? And make the constables have to do without lights in their houses. Yet the constables and the workers were now feeling pain from the days strike. They had to be in bed with their women and children nursing their wounds in their houses. Their houses? What Houses? Rent houses!!!

Doreen finally met Aunt Hilda. As they left the hospital, some patients were just going home. Some had just got their medicines, others had waited in vain to see a doctor or a nurse. Some still had their grips. After waiting for one or two months with their illness, there was no space, no beds, not enough nurses to care for them if they had been admitted.

It was nearly eight o'clock. Karl began, as he passed through the hospital gate. 'How the poor man going afford that?'

Doreen, who was carrying Huey, stopped to fix the baby's shoes under one of the street lights. They had come on just over a hour before. It was a long day.

'So the poor man have to go to Public Hospital,' Karl added holding the baby, while his mother tied the lace. As they walked towards Papine, the conversation continued.

'Only about twenty public hospitals, forty, fifty miles apart, for nearly two million people. And every day—'

Doreen interrupted, 'But if they don't have enough trained nurses?'

'Train them,' Karl said. 'So many young girls, pass all kinds of exams, you pass Second Year Exam and did want to turn a nurse. Why not train people like you?'

'But, Karl, I didn't pass Third year.'

'Third year?' Karl stopped walking. 'Look how many girls I know who are nurses now. The only thing they pass was the Passport office and Palisadoes Airport.' He continued. 'We don't get

109

a chance here. People, human beings just put down to rest.'
They reached Papine.

'But who you going to blame?' Doreen asked, 'who but the black man. The black man too damn worthless.'

And that was where it started. Complete myths, myths with a grain of truth, half truths, near truths, complete truths but twisted and misinterpreted for centuries to suit the masters. The slaves and their children were made to swallow them—passed from head to sperm, then with sperm into womb, out of womb into head, out of head into sperm. The cycle continues for generations, though not really by this mechanism.

But what was more important than the mechanism, was the effect, the result, the way it had made the slaves and their children think. Doreen seemed to have been well molded by this process.

One by one, at Kwame's bedside, in the street, in the gardens, in bed, Karl had to fight the lies. At times, Doreen was not too difficult to teach, but at other times, it needed Kwame with his understanding, his deep knowledge, his patience, to help to keep the peace, but at the same time expose the myths.

'Most Africans, the men in particular, are worthless, have no ambition, and do not want to care for their children.' This seemed to have stuck deepest in Doreen's head, Huey's father and a few others are examples. If it was hard for a man to help the mother to care for his children, then the woman alone must have it double hard. True. But the men who did not know this, and did not care for their children were in the minority.

The majority of black people, like Kojo, Miss Birdie, Maas Joe, Miss Kate, Miss Rachael, had the greatest ambition and desire to better their lives. They were proud when they knew that they could take care of their families. Why else would they have worked so long and so hard although they remained poor? Why had they struggled so hard to care their children and send them to school? Yet the mass of Afrikans in this country are the poor workers and peasants.

As Karl explained, 'Sometimes we parents have to stay a whole day without food, but they still struggle to better them life and them children too. In the days when our fore-parents used to wear chains, a slave often saved enough money, if not to buy his own freedom, that of one or more of his children. Now many poor black people are buying the freedom of their children by going without food to send them to school. Which other race of people in this country have to do that?' Karl asked.

110

'Most Africans are lazy people.'

Karl showed Doreen that this one was folly, merely by asking her a number of questions. Who build the roads, the hospitals, the houses, the shops, the schools in this country? Who worked on the sugar estates, the farms, on the plains, on the hillside, in the valleys? Who drive the buses, the trucks, the taxis carrying people and goods from place to place? Who worked in the shops, the stores, the schools, the hospitals, the offices?

'Who plant the flowers at Hope Garden?' Karl asked.

Doreen smiled. 'True that is mostly black people or Afrikans or what you call we . . . is true because I never see a white man or a Chiney man with a hoe, not even as police.'

He asked her the last question, 'Then how you say that black man lazy? Eeen?'

'Most Afrikans are poor because they do not save enough money. They also waste too much money.'

'True, many black people use them money bad,' Karl began. 'But not more than the white man or any other man in this country. The amount of money Mr Mayer used to buy whisky or spend on race horse in one year, a poor black man would have to live a hundred years to waste this on rum or any other thing.'

The question was still deeper than that. Most Afrikans in this country are descendants from old time slaves. When the chains were removed from their foreparents' feet, they were driven into the hills. No house, no land, no money, only their bare hands. Since that time, the children of these slaves have been treated in much the same way. Unemployment, low wages, bad prices for their products. How then could they live and at the same time save something from nothing?'

Karl paused for a while and then continued,

'Doreen, I ever tell you how Mr Mayer get him money?'

'Yes,' she replied.

'Well, sister, I don't have to say anything more.'

But he continued, 'Yes, a few who were now rich, they had worked hard and saved. But this was only a few, very few. Besides, this only gave them a start. After that, because it took money to make money, they could now squeeze their way to riches. The more money one has the more he can get from a bank to make more money. To get richer and richer from the profits of other people's labour. But as for the majority, who were now rich? Legacy. Legacy from slavery days. Mayer's legacy is good land and riches and easy life. Kojo's legacy is rocky land, poverty and hard life.'

Karl turned to Doreen, 'You remember Mrs Mayer?' he asked.

'You remember who name so and her occupation? Yes, she work hard, but I won't tell how and where.' He paused, 'Then how you come to tell me that people like them rich because them work hard? Eh!'

Yes, many black people spent money badly. A poor girl paying fifty dollars for a wig, a man putting his money on race horse only to lose week after week. But he merely wanted to get quick money. After all, the law allowed this. But black people did not waste as much money as any other race, simply because in the first place, they do not hold much money.

From slavery the white man had the wealth. Many of them later gave their mulatto children education, good land, money and big positions. The same man gave black people the cutlass, the rock hillsides and the sledge hammer. Oh, they also gave some of them a little schooling and the whip. White on top, brown in the middle, black at the bottom, and black under the bottom. 'Out of many one people . . . that suffer,' the motto of this lovely land.

'Africans have no love for one another.'
There was more than a grain of truth in this. But it was far from the full truth. But this was not much more than how some white folks hated each other.

'Go to some countries where they are the majority,' Karl told Doreen, 'When my uncle come from England about three years ago, him say you should see how they treat one another over there.'

'But even then, they love each other more,' Doreen said.

'Never hear how we act loving to one another abroad?' Karl asked. 'Well, the reason why we so wicked to one another here is because for over four hundred years we all living like crab in a barrel. You expect them to be loving when they have to climb on one another back to get a little fresh air?'

Doreen then asked why the Afrikans in Africa hated us.

'We and them not in the same barrel?' she asked.

This was not true of all or even most Afrikans in Africa. The white slave master taught us that they eat people and that we are lazy and worthless. Then they tell us that we hate each other. They shouldn't want to mix with us, we shouldn't want to go to work with them, and help to build that continent. Divide and rule is the name of the game:

'First, them don't hate we like the white people in the country them that we always want to go to,' Karl told his woman. 'The

112

whole thing 'bout black people hate one another is pure shit . . .
white shit at that and many of we swallow it.'

Karl put his hand around Doreen's neck. 'Look how I love you
and you telling me 'bout black people hate one another . . . eeeen?'
He gave her a little kiss.

'The Afrikan race is the ugliest of all races of people.'

'Doreen, I have a question to ask you,' Karl began. 'Out of a
donkey, a mule and a horse, which one is best looking?'

The woman could not answer the question. But one can't if one
was sensible, because the donkey has its kind of beauty, the mule
its kind and the horse too. Compare a donkey with a donkey, a
white woman with a white woman, a mule with a mule, a yellow
woman with a yellow woman, a horse with a horse, a black woman
with a black woman. 'How the hell the donkey, probably the
smallest and the weakest, coming to tell the mule and the horse
that it is the best looking?' Karl stared at Doreen for a while. 'But
more than that, how come the mule and the horse in particular
believe the donkey. It mystic to me, mystic indeed.'

Karl, with the help of Kwame, explained to Doreen the real
meaning of 'Black is Beautiful'. They told her about not only the
beauty of Afrikan people, but its culture, its art, its music, its
traditional dress, the need for the black man to be proud of
himself, so that he can build himself and move forward as a
people.

Why should the educated, the best of the race, seek to marry
the worst of the other races? We must love and be proud of our
beauty, of ourselves as a people.

The words had not fallen on deaf ears. A few weeks later it
began to show. First the hot comb was on the oil stove less often.
Then, it was left in the kitchen. Then it disappeared. The bushy
afro, the fine cane-rows, the blooming head-ties came one after the
other, a woman proud of her natural self. Doreen was simply
beautiful!

But the mechanism had not only affected Doreen's ideas about
the African. The system also gave her ideas that were to be
the same for every country, no matter in which corner of the
world it was. The master, his school, radio, newspaper, and church
had done well.

Every country must have in it rich and poor people. The rich must be richer and the poor, poorer.'

'But, Karl, even the Bible say so,' Doreen explained. 'Is fly you want to fly in God face?'

Karl took a good look at her.

'Darling, I believe in God. From I born, Aunt Birdie teach me that there is a God. I don't even question that.' He paused. 'But I know that some one, I don't know if it is King James tamper with some parts of the Holy Book. What happen to the Maca Bee and the six and seven book of Moses?'

'Everybody cannot have education, food, clothes and good house to live in and no matter who ruled the country and how it was organized, things cannot be better.'

Kwame, Karl and Doreen were sitting around her table when she raised this point one night. Kwame spoke, 'But these things about every country having rich and poor, a country cannot do without rich people, and things cannot be better all come from the same source. How the hell poor people believe this is a mystery to me! True, sister Doreen, it is a mystery how poor people believe it. Them and them children will always be foot-stools working for rich man. I have to fight against this every day, even at my work place.'

He rested his glass on the table and reached for his bag near to the door. 'Let me show you something I cut out of a newspaper when I was in the hospital.'

Kwame was also working out some plans that he would like to write about. Some of the information, he had read from a university report, also when he was in hospital. But he would tell them more about that when it was finished.

Kwame handed the piece of newspaper to Doreen and sat down again at the table. He took a sip from the glass and then said, 'I don't write newspaper! And this is not American propaganda, is one of our own news reporter who go there this year.'

Doreen began to read the title, 'Cuba Appears Happy Under Castro.' She looked at Kwame and Karl around the table, then back at the newspaper.

'From all appearances, Cuba is happy and healthy and making progress under Fidel Castro. After fourteen years of the regime of the Revolutionary Government, the country shows signs of advancement especially in the areas of social and economic development.'

Doreen stopped reading. She shook her head. 'I don't believe that them happy.'

'Why you don't believe?' Kwame asked.

'How you believe when you read say them not happy?' Karl

got up from the table to sit beside Huey on the bed. 'Cho, read up the thing, man, and stop argue.'

'Education is freely available to all levels, in contrast to the pre-Castro days when the poor and the under-privileged could not go to school.'

Doreen stopped again. 'A lie this. Free education at primary, high school and University too?'

No one said anything for a while, till Karl snapped. 'Read up the thing man . . . Why is lie?'

'The literacy programme is succeeding. Medical and hospital care is free to all, the mortality rate has been reduced, and the population is increasing. Public transportation is adequate and well organised. A mighty effort is being made to overcome the housing problem. Fidel Castro inherited a legacy of bad housing in which the poorer members of society lived in levels known as "favelas", under the most primitive conditions.

Since 1960, a big drive has been make to remove these wretched conditions. A major housing programme is being carried out, which is providing modern living accommodation in multi-storey apartment buildings, mainly for members of the working class.'

'HIGH RISE. One such housing estate has already been established in the eastern section of Havana, the capital city. A complex of high-rise apartments in huge blocks of buildings, it is a virtual "city within a city", providing accommodation for 75,000 persons, mostly workers and their families.

'Former slum-dwellers live in these apartment blocks which contain two bedrooms, a living and dining area, kitchen bathroom and laundry. They are reasonably roomy and comfortable, and are rented at a basic rate of 10 per cent of the worker's wage or salary.'

Karl wondered if it was not true that such houses were merely a 'showcase' to the world. But even if that was true, why didn't Kingston and Washington clear its slums and put the slum dwellers to live in similar 'showcases' for ten per cent of their wages.

He exclaimed, 'Ten per cent! Who . . ooy! That mean a man working a hundred dollars, don't pay more than ten dollars. Ten dollars for two rooms, kitchen, bathroom!'

He was about to say something else, but Doreen did the hushing that time. She continued reading.

'A similar project is being put up in Santiago. These massive housing units are made of prefabricated cement components, which can be easily and rapidly assembled by workmen on the site. They appear to be the right answer to the problem of taking the people out of the "favelas" and putting them into decent living quarters.

FISHING. On the economic front, Cuba has developed a major fishing industry since 1960. As a result of this development, Cuba has increased its catch of fish to some 175 tons a year and aims to take it even higher. Many varieties of fish, as well as shrimp and lobster, are caught and there is a growing export trade to countries in Europe, including Britain, France, Italy, Germany and Spain.'

Doreen lowered the paper, 'Britain trade with them?' She looked across at Kwame. 'Then how Britain don't want we to trade with Cuba?'

Karl spoke, 'I use to hear Maas Joe have a saying, "what good for busha not good for him dog."'

Doreen raised the paper and continued reading.

'Cuba is one of the world's largest producers of nickel and production of this mineral is kept at a high level. Santiago possesses an oil refinery and a cement factory. There are other factories in the country producing a wide range of light-manufactured goods, including textiles and plastics.'

Kwame, who had been sitting at the table playing with his low cut hair, was about to say something. But before he could have his say, Doreen started to read again. Karl smiled, as he could see the woman was eager to read on.

'Agriculture is also being maintained and improved. The sugar industry has been retained as the mainstay of the economy, with an annual production of between six and eight million tons. Tobacco is another big agricultural product and there is a large export trade in Cuban cigars and cigarettes. Food-processing is being developed.

Unemployment which stood at an estimated figure of 600,000 before Castro, has been eliminated. There are jobs for everyone between the ages of 18 and 65, and every adult man and woman in Cuba is engaged in what is described in census-taking language as 'gainful occupation'.

Doreen looked up from the paper she was reading, 'Kwame, tell me something. When they say unemployment has been eliminated, they mean everybody who can work, have work?'

Kwame did not open his mouth. He just nodded his head over and over again as he played with some short strands at the side of his head.

Doreen looked surprised. Huey was turning as if he was about to wake up. Karl hushed him back to sleep.

Seeing the baby was sleeping again, Doreen took up the paper and continued reading.

'*MINIMUM WAGE*. There is a minimum wage of 95 pesos (about J$85) a month for the lowest class of worker. The figure rises proportionally according to the type and category of worker, and achieves an average of about 250 pesos a month.'

Karl quietly commented, 'So is not true that everybody get the same pay?'

Doreen read on, 'This is by no means luxurious when compared with what is obtained in some other countries, but is a reasonable wage within the Cuban economy, which is socialist and egalitarian.

'Food is not generally plentiful but is adequate. Some items such as meat, rice, sugar, milk and butter are rationed. But fish is in abundance, and there is a good supply of poultry. And of course there is plenty of rum and beer, cigars and cigarettes. Petrol is available on a controlled basis.'

Doreen paused, Karl spoke, 'Then how I hear that one somebody can't get more than three quarter pound meat each week?'

'But even if that was true, it wouldn't too bad,' Kwame replied. 'For instance, your family, Kojo, Miss Birdie and the five of you, would certain of 'bout four pounds meat every week.' He leaned back in the chair, 'How much family out here don't eat four pounds meat in a month?'

Doreen's voice could be heard again in the small room.

'Small cars of many makes, including Volkswagen, are imported and appear to be in fair quantity. The buses, some of them, are modern and comfortable.

'Life seems gay and cherful in—' she stopped in the middle of the sentence.

'How then life can cheerful when I hear that Castro pulling out them toe nail, and cutting out them tongue every day?'

Karl spoke, 'Maas Charlie say that one Peace Corps from America tell him that Castro cut out them balls too.'

Kwame shifted in his seat, 'I know why them tell people that,' he began. 'The white man in America used to do it to the black man if him look at one of them precious white woman.'

Karl's mind raced back to Beverley Hills, and the gracious Mrs Mayer.

'But not even them Watergate . . .' Kwame's tongue had slipped ' . . . not even them C.I.A. spy machine can prove that Commandante Fidel government do that'. Miss Rachael's slim son continued.

'Bet the Peace Corps would tell you, Karl, that General Idi

cut out the Indians and the white people balls, and eat one every day.'

Doreen continued to read. 'Life seems gay and cheerful in Havana and Santiago, the two principal cities. There are cinemas and night clubs, restaurants and cafeterias, all well patronised. The hotels are operating, catering to tourists and visitors from Europe, Canada and Latin America. As a people, the Cubans continue to be friendly and hospitable. Except for their undisguised lack of love for the United States, they welcome all visitors to their country. English is taught in schools and some Cubans go out of their way to practice it on English-speaking visitors.'

'People seem to have a special hate for Americans,' Doreen commented, 'Even more than for the British. Why?'

Maybe the Peace Corps worker who had told Karl about the wickedness of Castro could help, or maybe Maas Charlie could. No, no, he thought white Americans were God's chosen people.

'Like how that fucker so black, if him did live in them country, a mean the Red Indian country that them capture, him would know if . . . '

'How you love curse bad words so, buoy?' Doreen interrupted, turning to her boyfriend, still sprawled out on the bed beside her little son. The affairs of Cuba did not interest Huey, sleep was sweeter.

Cubans speak in words of friendship and fraternity of Jamaicans and Jamaica. There has been intermarriage between the two sets of peoples and many older Jamaicans live in retirement in Oriente.

So close is Cuba to Jamaica that it is only one hour flying time between Kingston and Santiago. So, if and when Cubana Airways starts flying here regularly, there should be an easy interchange of visits between the two countries. Many people in Cuba are looking forward to this happening.'

When Doreen was finished reading, she took a deep long look across the table at Kwame and then at her boyfriend lying beside her sleeping child. 'You know, Kwame, I did know all the time that you and Karl was black power man. But I never know that you was communist too.'

She was saying the same thing and almost in the same way as the manager in the Electric Service, the same thing and almost in the same way that Mrs Mayer had said it.

White people afraid of black power . . . yes, but black people afraid of black power!! Rich people afraid of communism . . . yes, but poor people afraid of communism!!

Karl broke the silence in the room. 'Ras Bongo tell me that is the same way the enemies of black people use to call Garvey, mad, a communist too.' He looked at Doreen. 'I don't even know what communism really 'bout.' He sat up on the edge of the bed.

It was after ten o'clock, soon he and his friend would have to leave for August Town. He got up.

'Cuba jus' ninety miles from here why we can't go and see how it stay? But we can go to America. Good or bad let me go and see for myself. Let me see.'

Kwame looked at his friend then at Doreen. 'Garvey say, Afrika for the Afrikans, Fidel say Cuba for the Cubans. What wrong with that, een?' He got up from around the table. 'The imperialis' don't want the oppress people to control them own destiny. Garvey and Fidel is enemy to them. But take this from me.' He pointed his thumb towards his chest. 'Whatever I believe is true, whatever I believe will help the sufferers in this country, I will die for it.' He emphasised every word as it left his lips one by one, thumb digging into his chest with every word. 'Call me black power man, call me communist man, call me shit-man if you want! But Kwame will die . . . die for what him believe will help to make the masses of this country better. Hear that? Well, believe it!' Then, his final words in the room, 'Good night, Sister Doreen. Sleep good.'

CHAPTER 10

'Everyday carry bucket to the well...'

Independence celebrations came and passed Karl, like the masses of the people in the same or worse position. For after a decade, the Festival was still the best thing that independence had brought to the majority of the people.

As usual the climax of the celebrations was the big show at the National Stadium. The stage was set with the white Queen and her troupe in the background. They played the music and directed the show, as the supporting actors led by a white-headed Chief and his Cousin ghost. But as the scene changed, the Queen and her troupe moved back-stage to play the music. The Chief and his Cousin ghost took their place in the background. The stage was now clear for their children and close friends to continue the act. And although the audience could no longer see, it was the same Queen and her troupe that played the music to which the golly-WOGS had danced.

But for the majority in the audience, the show brought no new life. For when the Queen and her set was on stage, they played not for the masses. Neither did they who always sat in the back, the bleachers, see much of the act, since the stage was so near to the grand-stand. And the script was written, the music and entire act far away from the roots of the masses in the bleachers. But the elite in the grand-stand enjoyed every minute of the show.

Yet it was those in the bleachers who had built the Stadium, the stage and all. When the Queen and her set went back-stage to play the music, many in the audience had thought that the golly-WOGS would bring more life for the masses in the audience. But no! How could these WOGS bring life with a dying script and the same dead music? For the majority and not the minority, in the audience to enjoy the Independence show, they would have to build the stage, write the script and play the music . . . and fuck off with the few in the Grandstand, the Queen, her troupe, the WOGS and the entire cast!

The Independence Celebrations was becoming more and more like Christmas. More and more money was being spent into the pockets of the big business people. Independence, like Christmas was a good thing for them. But for the masses of the people who were getting poorer, the true meaning of the Independence celebrations was becoming less and less . . . except as a big holiday and time for merriment. So that, it was no surprise that each day, the Festival became more and more important. There was the Festival Agency which operated for the entire year like all government agencies. As one Festival was off, it would begin to plan for the next one twelve months away. But strange as this may seem, the agency brought more happiness to the masses of the people than many other agencies with a similar budget. And all the plans and preparations of the three hundred and sixty four days was for that one day—the first Monday in August.

The centre of attraction in August Town on that day was the float. Aunt Hilda told Karl that for the last three years, it was Mr Wong who had sponsored the float. The same Wong who had the youths like serfs selling *Glee-News* for stale patties was spending money to pretty-up a tractor trailer with kite-paper? But there was a trick in it. Wong insisted that the tractor should be prepared on the barbecue at the side of the supermarket. During the week that the float was being decorated, many people would congregate to help and watch what was being done. Some would play dominoes, drink and eat a lot. That was good business. Besides, the sign 'SPONSORED BY WONG SUPERMARKET' was good publicity.

Karl was glad for the Festival holiday. He got the Monday off from slaving in the cement factory. He also got a chance to visit his parents in Guys Hill.

The next week, back at work his mind was very upset with many things. When he was working it was not too bad, but as he went for lunch, his mind would wander and he would think more and more about these things.

He had been working at the factory for over three months now. He had started the first week in May and it was now the middle of August. The pay at the factory was not bad compared to the eight dollars from Maas Charlie. His code of ethics, Charlie's famous words of wisdom, 'each man for himself', was true enough. Beggars standing at the doorway of banks would stretch out their hands for hours without getting a cent, remembering that each person passing had money either entering or leaving that place. Old women, old men, some sick with no one to care for them, their bundles tied to their backs, would either be looking for a comfortable bus stop or piazza to spend the night. The crowd coming from the cinema, party, or salons would pass them as if they didn't exist. But they had not failed to see the signs 'You can save for a home of your own'. By its sheer number, it managed to convince many.

The prostitutes, oh, yes, they got attention, but for a different reason. What will happen when they join the ranks of those who live on the streets? Would they join the homeless or the mad. But the mad were also homeless. Little boys, girls, though few in number, were as mad as the older folks roaming country and town, increasing in number each day, getting dirtier and looking more wretched each day. Some did not hesitate to expose their private parts to public view. People walked past them each day, they themselves bordering on madness, but not able to spare their probable fore-runners even a red cent. Others driving air-conditioned cars, were not even bothered by the antics of the mad folks. The rulers of the country passed them everyday—everyday except near to election time. Our humane rulers passed these human beings as if their votes did not count! But could they vote? And does it matter with many voters only a little better off?

They were deformed vegetables, human plants left to exist until they die, rot and become a part of the soil, the soil that will later produce more deformed heads. Was it the soil that really produced so many deformed heads? If not, what else? Oh, it's just another sickness. Send them back to Bellvue. Shock their bodies with a hundred volts this time. Put them back on the streets. Without a job, a place to live, a family and good God! one may as well use two hundred volts this time! That will send them to another world. In this would they are free, free to curse, to haunt a society that so hastily gave them that freedom. Their duppies wait, and wait patiently for the day when they will get a chance to drink blood—blood from the rich few who had sucked theirs like that of their fore-parents, and drove them on the streets to eat from garbage-cans and live as Scavengers. Their duppies wait for revenge. Ah, their children are but the remaining shadow of the dead parents.

'The roots, the roots,' Kwame said. 'We must get down to the roots!'

And in this country of 'each man for himself,' Karl was not really making it for himself. Over three months in the factory, and still no bank account. Not a red cent did he manage to save. No work for most of the time, low pay, and with the high cost of living! Yesterday the size went down, today the price goes up, tomorrow the size down and the price up. But the wages, that stays one place. Karl had no savings, nothing to help to make him into a man, a man who could care for a family.

'Then, young Kojo, you thinking 'bout children already?' Miss Freda had asked last September when he was coming to town.

'Freda, don't ask the young man any fool-fool question,' Miss

Merl her friend had said.

'How do you mean to ask him if him thinking 'bout children. You don't know that from a boy is sixteen him can plant him seed.'

It had taken Karl not sixteen but twenty-two years to plant his first seed. Only last week Doreen had missed her period the second time. The doctor had confirmed it, Kojo and Miss Birdie's first grandchild was well on the way.

'Somehow, I feel is that night,' Karl thought as he ate his lunch. 'Must be that night in May when the heavy rain was falling and I couldn't get to go home. I never plan to stay, so I never have anything on me. Not a socks, not a boots, nothing. He shook his head, 'Bwoy, life really funny. Funny bad.'

It was rough on Karl, because he had seen the rain, and was about to leave when . . . 'Come, come, pa . . . paaa,' Huey had called.

'Karl, you can't stay with the baby a little longer?' Doreen had pleaded, holding Karl as he got up to leave. Hugging him, kissing him lightly on his cheek. 'Cho, Karl man, is only seven o'clock now. If the rain even fall, it will stop by nine. Cho, Karl man.' She pulled him closer to her.

When he sat down again, Huey had all but jumped off the bed. 'Papa come, papa come . . . come pa . . paaa . . .'

The relationship had grown so much over the seven months. That day in January when they first met at Hope Gardens, it was Huey who had broken the ice between man and woman. And how Karl had been like a father to the child. Caring for him loving him as if the baby were his own. Doreen saw, understood and loved Karl for what he was. Poor, living in hard life, but still loving to her and her baby.

'Karl, I never believe I would love another man. But you . . . umm . . . ' She held on to his short beard and pulled him closer. A little kiss, short but spicy, flush on the lips. He deserved that and more.

'Karl,' she said, blushing. 'I would like to have a baby . . . a baby for you. But not now. I know we can't afford it.'

Yet that night the May rains had drowned their senses. The rain drops, beating down on the zinc roof had sent the baby to sleep by eight. Nine, ten, it didn't ease up.

'May as well we go to bed.' But once they were in bed and the lights were off, the feeling was on. Lips meeting playfully, breast against chest, genitals tormented by kinky hair, black as the bodies that pressed against each other. Soon someone or something had to give. Not animal. To hell no!

The man had great love for the beauty of the African woman, beauty much deeper than meets the eye. How she cared for him. His food, his clothes, his work, his everything. How could the woman treated like a mare by the master, like a beating stick by her slave husband, be so sweet? What he could not do to the man he did to her. Yet the African woman remained so strong. But her strength was now going. She and her man would have to fight or be swallowed up by that thing.

But how could they fight this feeling? Fight it when it was so strong. And inside so warm? As warm as it had been the first time. The strain had now gone. They had known each other so well, yet every other time, there was something new to learn. How long would it last. Till tomorrow? Oh, no! It was coming, he could feel it. Coming, coming, exciting every inch of his body. She, as if in another world, was pulling, pulling every strand of hair from his head. Coming, coming, come to an end.

Karl put the fork down on the edge of the plate. 'And from the time I hear Doreen say that she feel bad, from the morning we get up, I could tell.' He got up from the table. 'Could tell it. Tell any man that I breed her. Two months pregnant?' He started to leave the lunch room, 'Blood claute. Doreen pregnant! What I going do now?' he muttered. 'But no sense worry, it gone bad already.' He suddenly turned back and went to the juke box. Deposit five cents and made the selection. The machine started to hum, record spinning, a favourite old tune:

> See 'it dey now, everything crash,
> See 'it dey now, everything crash,
> Every day carry bucket to de well,
> One day de bucket bottom mus' drop out,
> Everything crash, Oh, oh, oh, oh.

When Karl went back to work that afternoon, a co-worker told him that his supervisor wanted to see him. The man was from Germany, and had come to the country to work in the factory as a machine specialist. Yet it was the foreman who had to show him how to start the compressor in the drying room. What an expert he was! None like him in the country, he had to be imported. Eight thousand plus car, house fully furnished with 'maid' and 'garden boy' was the price.

Karl went to see the supervisor. The man spoke the English language much better than he fixed machines.

124

'I zee zat you are heres at last,' then he paused and nodded his fat head. 'Kants understand you menz.' Leaning back in the high-backed chair in the air-conditioned office, he said, 'Ze managers personel ze'crtry . . . er . . . Mis'tress Mayer wantz you to do zome work at the ze house. You could takes ze eveningz off.'

But Karl told him he would prefer to go early the next morning. He had to attend union meeting that evening. Karl had become a member soon after he started working. Now the little union was gaining a few victories. Through the struggles, Karl got a raise of five dollars weekly. He had to go to the meeting.

He worked for the rest of the afternoon. Only now and again did Mrs. Mayer come across his mind. But after the union meeting and he was ready to go home, she was on his mind again.

'What that woman want see me for? And why now as her husband gone abroad on business?' Karl thought. 'I glad to do the little carpenter work. That is my trade. But is three time since I working down here that this woman send to call me. Every time is the same thing she always come to me with when I finish doing her work.' He walked towards the big iron gate of the factory. The sign 'No Vacancy' was always there. 'She pay me good . . . to do her work, her carpenter work. Nothing else. Not one damn thing else!'

As Karl passed through the gate, he thought. 'Well, tomorrow morning early, I going up to the Hills. And maybe, I just go home and rest for the balance of the day. But I going to see that woman first thing tomorrow morning.'

Karl went to Beverly Hills the next morning. Walking with Miss Rachael now, was just like the first morning. He still had to trail a little distance behind the slender woman.

Mrs Mayer wanted him to fit a wooden rail along the back step. That would keep him till ten or eleven o'clock. Then she wanted him to replace a broken mirror in her bedroom.

'Her bedroom?' Karl thought. 'While Mr Mayer is away! Umm . . mmm, ah, sah,' he commented as the Mayers' mansion came into view. 'What happen, Karl? . . . what happen?'

'Nothing, Miss Rachey, nothing,' he replied. 'Careful you know, careful, mind Bellvue catch you. It pack up already. Mind Bellvue,' she warned.

Karl was surprised when he reached the house to find that Mrs Mayer was up. Her white face looked rather pale in the early morning. Young Master Mayer was getting ready to leave for school. The boy now had a funny look, a kind of deep wicked look in his eyes as he looked at his mother. At nine years old, he walked rather girlish. They say that when parents, especially mothers, treat their children the way Master Mayer was treated, they might turn into real 'mama's boys'—boys who wanted and tried to be mamas. Faggots! And as soon as the boy had left, and Miss Rachael was back in the kitchen, Mrs Mayer wanted Karl to come and fix the mirror. Why? But it was she who had called him to do the work. And she wanted the mirror done first.

As Karl entered the woman's room and started to pull down the broken mirror, the woman's eyes was fixed on his every move.

'Karl, I want you to do something for me. Something special,' the Jamaican-American began. She lit a cigarette and sat down on the bed and took the house-dress off. See-through nightie as usual. Her pointed tits did not even strike Karl's eyes. He had his woman, the woman he loved, the woman bearing his child.

'Remember how I helped you to get the work at the factory,' Mrs Mayer said, handing him a cigarette.

He refused. True she helped him to get a job. But now he was working, working like hell for every cent, in fact for more than what he got on Friday evenings. If he and the other workers were paid fully for their work, how would the Mayers live?

The American accent continued to flow, 'Karl, honey, I want you to do something for me. I hear that you are a member of the union.'

'Yes, Mrs Mayer.'

'And you get along well with the leader, that black power communist fellow.'

Karl stood in the corner of the room, screwdriver in one hand and looking at the silky-haired woman.

'Why stand there, Karl? Something wrong? Come and sit down, or maybe you'd like a drink . . . you know, a little something to loosen you up.'

Karl shook his head. He was too tied down for a drink to loosen him up.

'Well, have it your way,' she leaned back on the bed-head, cigarette in hand, ash tray in the other. Long, thick drapes over the windows. The early morning sun could not come in. A bedside lamp was turned on in one corner of the big room. Smoke was slowly coming from her mouth as she spoke.

'Karl, you're a smart young man. You know that this country don't need no black power. The negroes here have power already. Your governor general is a full negro, your prime minister . . .

126

well, you could also call him a negro . . . ' she paused for a while to make another pull on the cigarette, 'like my husband, he is a negro . . . he doesn't like to know it, but I know.' She popped her eyes wide open, 'I know he is a negro.' She continued, 'Most of your government is made up of negroes . . . '

Karl was about to say something but changed his mind.

'Karl, did I say something wrong?' Mrs Mayer took another puff at her cigarette, then smiled. 'Hear some of these subversives calling themselves Afrikans, saying that they have claims to that dark continent. Yes, we got Europeans, Chinese, Indians, but no Afrikans in this country.' She took another draw and quickly let out the smoke.

'You are negroes, not a darn thing else. Why want to say you are Afrikans, when your foreparents came here four hundred years ago.' Mrs Mayer leaned back on the bed again. She put out the cigarette in the ash tray and looked at the thick coat of pink polish over her finger nails.

Karl thought it funny that the woman's fore-parents had come before his, nearly five hundred years ago, yet she was still a European by race, she was proud to say this. But black people should forget the home of their fore-parents, that 'dark continent'. Mrs Mayer and her kind, black and white feared that Afrikans all over the world might become aware of their roots and want to claim it. Then how would her relatives and friends in America, Britain, Canada, Rhodesia, South Africa, Angola, Mozambique, . . . Jamaica, get more wealth to plunder from the dark continent.

Afrika's wealth would not benefit Europeans, but Afrikans at home and abroad. They feared even the very fact of black people calling themselves Afrikans.

Mrs Mayer stopped looking at her nails and took up the cigarette again. 'Country independent, own governor, flag and all the works, you should feel proud of it.' Then looking straight in Karl's face, 'You don't need no black power, cause you have Black power!'

'Yes, Mrs Mayer,' Karl said. He was about to move from the corner of the bedroom, to start working on the broken window.

'Oh, Karl, come off that "Mrs Mayer" stuff. Don't you like to call me Edna, no more? Come off that.' The woman leaned up off the bed to put the ash tray back on the stand. Her breasts jumped a little. She put up one foot on the edge of bed. Where is the underwear? Oh . . . see-through too?

'Karl, you wouldn't like your poor father working all these years have ten goats . . . well, he might not have that much, but you wouldn't like someone to just come one day, come and take away one of your paw's goat. Sure you wouldn't!'

Mrs Mayer paused as if expecting Karl to say something. There was nothing. 'Me, my husband, our parents . . . yes, I know slavery was cruel . . . I feel ashamed of that too . . . but that's long gone . . . forget it. We now all have to work for what we got.'

'True, Mrs Mayer. True, mam.'

'Mr Mayer, although you may not know, as a boy used to walk bare-footed, his parents were not that well off. But they worked night and day, till now he is a 'big man' in this country.'

Karl wondered if the woman did not know that she had helped him to learn that from the first Mayer left Britain in the seventeenth century, the whole family had been living on legacy. But now Mrs Mayer was puzzled as Karl just stood in the corner of the spacious room, quietly listening but unwilling to talk.

'Karl, this is a free, free . . . free country,' she pleaded. 'Anyone, absolutely anyone with ambition can make it.'

The woman put out the cigarette butt in the ash tray. A cloud of smoke went up towards the roof of the fifteen by twelve room. 'Karl, do just this little thing for me,' she pleaded. 'Like talk to that fellow, find out what plans the union has . . . oh, that shouldn't be difficult. I could arrange a little more, a little extra pay, if you'd do just that for me.'

The woman got up off the bed. As she moved slowly towards Karl, he could remember Kwame in the hospital, blood seeping through the bandage around his forehead.

'No, Mrs Mayer. No. No, I can't do that, mam. 'No!'

'Oh, Karl darling.' She started to raise her left hand to put on his shoulder. 'Don't you love me any more, Karl?' she asked in a soft childish voice.

Karl moved away, 'Love? Love? Love who?' He was getting angry.

The woman's left hand fell off his shoulder. She took a hard stare at him, tightening her lips, her face changing from white to red to redder, Mrs Mayer raised her right hand to slap Karl. Left hand up to block the blow, Karl's right hand open and swinging with full force, sent the woman staggering back to the bed. She looked at Karl as if astonished. As if mad, she grabbed for the telephone on the bedside table.

'Use the screwdriver on her?' Karl thought. No. He quickly dropped it, held on to the phone and pulled the chord out of the wall. It dropped on the carpet.

'Raa . . . a . . . a,' she began the word but couldn't complete it.

The right fist landed flat on her face. A heavy blow from Miss Birdie's own Mohammed Ali and the woman's face became deep red, bordering on purple.

'You white f . . u . . cker you! Is prison you want to send me now? Rape, what?' Karl grunted in a low heavy voice. He felt like hitting her again. Mrs Mayer slightly stunned, Karl picked up his tool-box and moved towards the door. He locked it with the key from the outside.

'Time to leave this place. Time to dig up,' Karl thought as he shot out through the gate, down the hill, like a flash of lightning.

No one was at home, when Karl reached August Town. He locked himself inside the house for the rest of the day. The six hours before Kwame came from work seemed like six whole days. Every vehicle that passed sounded like a police jeep, and almost every one sounded as though it was reversing after it reached where July Road met May Road.

Miss Rachael had not told Mrs Mayer where he lived. But what if the police forced her to talk?

'Kwame, Kwame,' he called easing up one of the side windows as he saw his friend about to enter the house next door.

'Karl,' he crossed over the fence. 'What happen, man, you didn't go to work today? You didn't stop at Doreen this evening? How you down here so early?'

'Come in, man,' Karl said. 'Walk 'round the back.'

His friend came into the room.

'Kwame,' he paused, 'Man, I have to go back to country tonight. Tonight, tonight. This very night.'

'Why? Why?' Kwame asked looking frightened.

Although Karl had kept the story about Mrs Mayer and himself from Kwame so long, he felt glad to spill out the whole truth now— from top to bottom, the whole affair, the love-hate affair.

'Well, running to country is not how to deal with it, man,' Kwame began. 'I don't even think the woman going to the police. That would cause too much scandal. But what she might do, is try to get you out of the factory.'

'But, Kwame, I can't afford to lose the job now. Doreen pregnant,' the words flew out of his mouth. Kwame did not seem very surprised.

'Doreen really getting fat lately,' Kwame said rubbing his clean-shaven cheek and smiling.' He thought for a while as he looked at Karl sitting on the little bed.

'Kwame, I wish I could turn into a little ants.'

'Anyhow, know what, go to the brethren, go to the leader of you union. Tell him everything. That is the only thing that will help you now.' Kwame looked at Karl's sulky and fretting face. He slapped his friend on the shoulder then smiled.

Karl smiled too, the first one in hours.

'Do that, Karl. Do that . . . and jus' rest.'

The next day Karl waited at the factory gate to see his union leader. The man called a short meeting that very morning. Without calling any names he spelt out the message loud and clear.

'Any attempt to fire any worker from this factory, without the soundest of reasons, will cause an immediate strike.

The whole matter would then have to be investigated under the eyes of the public. The issue would be taken to the people.' The warning was clear.

A day, two days, a week, two weeks, all August and September passed and Karl neither heard of or saw Mrs Mayer—except when she visited as 'secretary to the general manager'. And although she saw him once, she said nothing to him. 'So you don't walk far from every policeman again,' Kwame asked his friend one evening over two bottles of beer.

'Cho, man, stop jive me, You know what, Kwame . . . ' he paused to take a sip. 'How 'bout going country this weekend.'

Kwame lowered his bottle. 'You carrying Sister Doreen and Huey too?' he asked raising his eyebrows.

Karl looked at his friend and smiled, 'But mus'.'

CHAPTER 11

'K . . . a . . arl, me son'

Karl, Kwame, Doreen and Huey took the Star bus at Parade nine o'clock the Saturday morning—Kingston to Spanish Town to Linstead to Guys Hill. Nothing unusual happened along the way, except for one little thing, When they reached near Spanish Town market they saw a large crowd. The story was that a man had been shot in the back. He had attacked a jeep load of policemen with a knife. That was the only unusual incident. But even then, it was not too unusual as similar happenings occurred almost every day.

The bus did not reach Guys Hill until around one o'clock that afternoon. Geney was in the yard when it stopped at the gate. The little four-roomed pink house, a few banana trees and the big ackee tree in the yard, looked much the same as when he had last been home in August. The two months seemed like only two weeks had passed since Karl's visit.

'Mamma, mamma, Miss Birdie,' the girl called running into the house.

Miss Birdie got up from the sewing machine in her bedroom. 'What happen, Geney? Is what?'

'Is Brother Karl! Him and some more people,' Geney started pulling her mother out on the verandah. They came face to face first with Karl.

'Ka . . a . . arl, me son,' Miss Birdie said hugging and squeezing her first child. 'Karl, how you do?'

'Well, Aunt Birdie,' Karl replied putting down the little travelling bag and hugging Geney with the other hand.

Miss Birdie loosened her squeeze. 'Laud, you don't shave off the little beard yet?' she asked.

Karl did not answer.

'And this is the young lady? You is Miss Doreen?', Miss Birdie asked taking a good look at the young woman while stretching out her hand. Her eyes moved from Doreen's face to her bulging stomach, to Huey, and back to Doreen's face. She stretched out her hand and held Miss Birdie's. 'Yes, Miss Birdie, pleased to meet you mam.'

'And this is Maas Huey,' she said and bent to take up the little

131

boy. He just stared at Miss Birdie as if he was seeing the first ghost.

'Huey, Huey baby,' Geney toyed with the child, holding on to one of his hands.

The child looked at her and smiled.

'Then who is this young man?' Miss Birdie asked.

Kwame who had stood to one side watching the family reunion stepped forward. 'Kwame is the name, mam.'

'Oh, Kwam . . . Kwamin,' she stuttered. 'You is Rachey big son.'

'Yes, Miss Birdie,' Kwame replied, his hand still in her grasp.

'The last time I come to August Town and see you, you was jus' a boy. You didn't even start grow, much less shave beard yet. Karl always tell me how you nice and help him out over town.'

Karl went into the house, Doreen and Huey followed.

'Come, come in, Kwamin . . . '

'Mama, is not Kwamin, is Kwame,' Geney corrected her mother.

But Miss Birdie would not learn that easy.

'I get so used to hear 'bout Amin, Amin . . . So forgive me if I call you Kwamin.'

His friend had to smile. The name caused his mother and Miss Hilda much more trouble.

Now, in the house, Doreen sat on a chair with Huey in her lap. Kwame sat at the other side of the room. A framed picture of Miss Birdie and Kojo was hanging above Doreen's head. Karl went somewhere through a door leading to the back of the house.

'Then Miss Doreen and Maas Kwamin,' Miss Birdie began.

But Geney interrupted again, 'Mamma, is Kwame, like Kwame Nkrumah, the first President of Ghana.'

'Geney,' Miss Birdie gave the girl a stern look.

'Alright, me little brainy daughter,' she was holding back a smile. 'Anyhow go and finish wash up the plates till I come.'

Karl stepped back into the room.

'Aunt Birdie, what happen to Papa, Pat and the others?'

Kojo had gone down to Maas Joe's farm to help him plant some banana suckers. They wouldn't usually work whole day Saturday, but the farmers wanted to set the young suckers before the heavy rains started. The year before when Karl was leaving for Kingston, the two farmers were just selecting suckers for planting out another field. Pat and Junior were gone to Maas James's shop to take up the week's groceries. They would soon be back.

Well, as for Tom, Miss Birdie was not certain, but she believed that he was playing cricket down the community centre.

'Remember the young teacher up the school?' Miss Birdie asked.

'Yes, Mr Annan,' Karl replied.

'Well, him form a youth club and get many of the young boys to join it.' The woman continued, 'But it helpful, you see. Them play all sort of games and learn 'bout history and all kinds of things.'

'Mama, mama,' Geney called from outside, 'the pot boiling over.'

'Geney a coming,' Miss Birdie said looking towards the kitchen. 'Yes, the club really helpful, because now even Tom don't spend so much time round Maas James' shop with all them man drinking and betting race horse.'

'That good,' Kwame said, 'Karl tell me about him all the time.'

Miss Birdie got up, 'Yes, man. Mr Annan really helpful to the young people. Him even trying to get the government to set up a trade centre for boys and girls. That was the last thing we hear him say at community meeting.'

Karl spoke, 'Him have to write to the Ministry of Youth.'

'Yes, but him say him write for over six months now, and them say them will send someone to see him. Nothing else.

Kwame said, 'Since the people up here vote and pay taxes, it is up to them to see that whoever them vote for, do things to improve the people and the community.'

'Mamma, mamma!' Geney again yelled from the kitchen.

Miss Birdie turned towards the door. 'Young people, excuse me a minute.'

Karl spent the rest of the day showing Doreen, Kwame, and Huey around the district. Maas Joe and Miss Kate were first. They were so glad to see Karl. Huey took a liking to Miss Kate instantly. The woman almost wanted to take away the child. She smiled when she saw Doreen's pregnant stomach. It was there that Doreen and Kwame first met Karl's father. Like Miss Birdie he would have preferred if Karl had taken a woman who did not have a child before. But now that they had seen Doreen and Huey, they looked forward to the day when Doreen would bare them their first grandchild. Kojo wanted a boy. Miss Birdie wanted a girl as the boys were too bad. Karl would take anyone.

Karl also showed them Maas Charlie's house. He had robbed Karl, took his labour in return for a miserable eight dollars a week. Now the man was not getting Karl's labour but he still had men working for almost the same pay. They either work for that, steal or starve. They preferred the first as they did not want to be hung by the forces of law and order. The same forces overlooked the crimes that Charlie and Mr Mayer or Mr Wong committed daily. As Karl passed Maas Charlie's gate, he remembered the favourite words 'each man for himself'. He looked at Doreen in her roomy dress.

'I would hate if my youth have to grow up in a country where him at the mercy of people like Charlie.' He shook his head, 'I would really hate that.'

Levi Annan was not at the school's cottage when they stopped there. Karl left a message that he would come to see him the next day. Being Sunday he should be home and Karl was hoping that the teacher would be able to spend the day with them.

It was now getting dark. The crickets started to tune up for the night's singing. The pene-wallies flew around in the trees by the roadside. The green lights that shone from the insect's head had Huey's head moving from side to side as they walked up the road. Doreen was afraid of the frogs on the road. Soon they came to the little shoemaker shop. The red, green and black painted on the door could be seen from the light of the gas lamp hanging from a beam in the roof.

A man was standing near the doorway. The Ras was behind the counter.

'Ras Bongo,' Karl called as he approached the door.

'Love, Brother Karl,' Bongo replied in his same cool manner. The Ras bowed his head as he looked from Karl to Doreen to Huey and then to Kwame. 'Love, love . . . ' Smiling through his thick beard and moustache he asked, 'How life treating the brethren?'

'Well, you know, Ras,' Karl continued, 'it dread out there. Truly dread. But man have to live.'

The other man who was in the shop before they came said good-bye and left. Kwame had been standing near the door and taking a good look at the man he had heard so much about. He now moved nearer to the counter where he could see some shoes and sandals that the Rastaman had made. They looked strong and were very neat, although most of the work was done by hand. Why was this man, like many others with all kinds of skills, being wasted? he thought.

Bongo had given Kwame and Doreen two stools to sit on. He had often heard the names before. Karl had written to him a few times and the two or three times he had been back to Guys Hill since he met Doreen, Karl told the Ras quite a lot about the woman. Bongo, although quite a few years older than he was that Karl could trust almost completely. But it was the man's own eyes that had to tell him about the seed in the womb.

'Yes, I, bring them forward,' Bongo said looking at Doreen and pulling his locks as he spoke. 'Whether in the motherland, that is Afrika, or in the outside states where Afrikan dwell, then Jah children need the youth. Forward with them on the father-land.' Then raising up off his stool behind the counter, his eyes wide open. 'I and I woman should no longer be graveyards. No more dumping ground for the unborn.'

Karl looked at the Ras. 'True, brethren, it dread, but I not killing it. It mus' come and live too.'

Kwame and Doreen just sat watching and listening. Ras Bongo took a pack of cigarettes from under the counter. He gave one to Karl, one to Kwame and lit one for himself. He gave Doreen and Huey some sweets. That was their cigarettes. Everyone in the little shop was now smoking.

The Rastaman again sat on his stool. He puffed his cigarette. 'True if the white man desire to make his woman into a grave yard,' he paused to exhale the smoke, 'although I Bongo don't agree, I cannot stop him. But the Afrikan woman? No, Jah!'

Always the same thing. Once Bongo started to talk his forcefulness, his conviction seemed to grow more and more. And as it grew, so he spoke more and more.

'I man, never going forgive the slave master or him children or them negro puppies who practise genocide, be it the master cutlass, the police bullet, or the doctor knife on black people.'

Doreen was slightly mystified. The doctors knife was clear. Yes, he must be talking about abortion. The police bullet, the blind could see that.

'But what you mean by the master's cutlass, brother man?' Doreen asked, still holding Huey in her lap.

The Ras came from behind the counter. 'You see you, sister Doreen,' he began, 'a woman like you in the old slavery days, could be carrying a child for either you master or for a fellow slave . . . Seen?'

Doreen shook her head as to say that this could not happen.

'Yes, sister. If you don't forward it with you own free will, then it will be by force. Him may even have to tie you up, plant half you body in a hole, cut out piece of you flesh and put lime and salt in it; or, if you lucky him might just throw boiling sugar over you body and leave you for flies and maggot.'

'Then I wouldn't have no use to him then?' Doreen replied.

'True, true,' the Ras replied, 'so him may do that to one of you

135

friends or you sister . . . get the message?'

Then opening his eyes wide Bongo said, 'Them was the first rapist. Not only Afrika them rape.'

The words struck a bell in Karl's head. Oh, yes, Kwame changed his name from John because John Hawkins was a rapist. ' . . . but them rape the daughters of Afrika. And if the woman pregnant, and the master want to win some quick money, he could bet one of him friend if the child is boy or girl and . . . '

Some one passed on the road and hailed the Rastaman. He stopped and looked out to see who it was.

Kwame completed what Bongo was saying. 'And right there him would order some of him good slaves to hold the woman and them would cut her belly wide open with a cutlass.'

Doreen opened her mouth as if shocked.

Kwame continued the argument. 'Now them say, kill it in the womb. Tomorrow will be kill as long as it not three months. But the basic thing, the roots, them don't get down to it.'

Ras Bongo took over from Kwame, 'Why should life be so hard that young women have to make butcher push all kinds of things inside them and cut up, cut up them structure? Why should life be so hard, so hard on the sons and daughters of the black continent? Why this barbarism? Overpopulation? No, I man don't think two hundred people live between Linstead and Guys Hill. Overpopulation? No, I.'

Doreen spoke, 'But still the brethren must understand that whether it illegal or not, some suffering woman have to do it. Better they do it than the youth come and suffer. More suffering on both the poor parents and them coming in to the world.'

Ras Bongo pulled at his locks, Karl and Kwame looked at Doreen without saying a word. Huey sat and leaned back on his mother's breast. There was a lot of truth in what she said.

The Ras did not drink any form of alcohol, but he always had a bottle of 'ital juice' made from chainey root and strong-back and a little herbs mixed with milk, in his shop. He always had a mug and a 'veedal can' under the counter. Kwame got the veedal can, while Doreen got the mug. Karl would have to share the bottle with the Ras. What about Huey? Doreen did not want him to get any. 'It might make him mad. He was not even fully three years. The ganga in it might make him mad like shad.'

'You don't want the youth to become a strong warrior?' Ras Bongo asked. 'You don't want him to become a strong Afrikan like I man?'

Doreen looked at the Rastaman. She asked, 'Ras Bongo, why

you saying that you is Afrikan?
'Because I and I fore-parents is from Afrika.'
'But you don't come from Afrika—you is Jamaican!'
Karl looked at Doreen and was about to say something to her.
So many times he had tried to explain the relation between race
and nationality to her. The sister was coming, but still slowly and
sometimes he was to blame. Too impatient and sometimes not too
clear. But Ras Bongo was the right person for her to have asked.
The Ras pulled his beard and his lips parted.
'Sister Dee, know anybody name Wong?'
'Yes,' she replied. 'Him is a Chiney man.'
'Where him born?'
'Jamaica.'
Kwame smiled and Doreen glanced at him, then back at the
Ras.
'Sister Dee, know anybody name Maragh?'
'Yes,' she replied. 'Know a Indian girl.'
'Where she born?'
'Jamaica.'
Kwame did not smile, but only cleared his throat. Karl kept
quiet, he too wanted to clear up the matter in his mind.
'Sister Dee, know anybody name Cargill?'
She thought for a while, 'Yes, I know two black man and a white
man name Cargill.'
Bongo smiled and shook his head from side to side. 'What you
know about the whiteman Cargill.'
'Him is a land-baron, a backra man who is a good friend of the
man who own the drug store where I work.' She turned to her
man, 'That same one telling my boss to fire me because I pregnant
and not married.'
Karl lowered the bottle from his head, 'That sucker.'
'Then, sister Dee, what race the white man Cargill claim him
is?' Bongo asked.
'A funny name cau . . . , something or the other,' she answered.
'Caucausian or European,' Kwame added.
'Where him born, you know that, Sister Dee?' the Ras asked.
'Yes, right up Highgate way . . . somewhere up in St Mary,' she
replied and then took a sip from her mug of 'ital' drink.
Bongo's mood suddenly changed. He looked very serious, staring
at Doreen as he spoke, 'So you have Chiney, Indian, European
born in Jamaica . . . but no Afrikan . . . e . . eh!'
She did not answer, neither did anyone else. There was silence
in the little shoemaker shop for a while. Against the background

137

of people passing, Bongo continued, 'Wong is Chinese by race and Jamaican by nationality. Maragh is Indian by race and Jamaican by nationality. Cargill is European by race and Jamaican by nationality.' Bongo pointed to himself, 'I and I is Afrikan by race and a captive of Babylon.'

'But, Ras,' she said. 'Why not only say that we is of Afrikan ancestry?'

He replied, 'The people of European ancestry is European; the people of Chinese ancestry is Chinese; the people of Jewish ancestry is Jews. Then how come the people of Afrikan ancestry is not Afrikans?'

The Ras went on to explain that the mulattos, most of whom are confused about their race, were the main ones who should talk about ancestry. They are a cross between Europe and Afrika and as such are the ones to say that they are of Afrikan ancestry. They were neither Afrikans or Europeans—but mulattoes.

'As for me,' he continued, 'I and I am Afrikan . . .'

'But, Ras,' she interrupted. 'Why you don't say then that you is a negro?'

For a moment Bongo looked up at the lamp hanging from the roof. His locks rested on his shoulder as if it kept his head and body in touch with Rastafari in Zion.

'Sister Dee,' he began, 'you ever hear about the negro and the negress?'

'Yes, one is male and the other is female.'

'Ever hear about the lion and the lioness?'

'Yes, one is male and the other is female.'

'Ever hear about the Chinese and the Chineseess, or the Indian and the Indianess, or the European and the Europeaness?'

'No, Ras.'

'So the negro and the negress, and the lion and the lioness are one. The negro and the negress are names the white slave-master give us to show us that we is black animals with no origin. Him don't want us to identify with one another our roots, so him don't call us after the land of our fore-parents, although all other races of mankind name after the land of their fore-parents.' He paused and then asked, 'Where the negro originate?'

Kwame who was finished drinking, put the 'veedal' can on the counter and replied, 'In Negrola . . . that on the dark side of the moon.'

It must have been sometime after eight or nine. No one had the exact time. There was silence in the shop for a little while. It was broken only by the cries of the crickets and the croaks of

138

the frogs coming from outside. Karl was ready to leave.

'Ras Bongo,' he said, 'we want to spend the day at the river tomorrow and cook some food. So you know, we would like the brethren to forward.'

Bongo stroked his beard for a minute, then half smiling his lips began to move. Two words were enough, 'True, true.'

CHAPTER 12

'So we mus' rub off the polish . . . Seen nyah?'

The Sunday morning was a bright one. There was no fog in Guys Hill that morning. By about ten o'clock, Karl, Kwame, Doreen, Huey, Ras Bongo and Junior were on their way to Guys River. Junior had escaped from Miss Birdie, who wanted him to go to Sunday School. Huey was enjoying the ride on the boy's back. When they reached the school gate, Levi Annan might join the party.

Although a teacher, he was just a little older than Karl, about Kwame's age, and in the two years he taught in the community, he had become totally involved. He was now almost accepted, as if he had grown up in Guys Hill. But when they reached the school, they found out that Annan had not yet returned.

Because of Doreen's six month's pregnancy, they had to move slowly down the track from the road to the river.

Karl remembered the last time he had been to Guys River, about a year ago, just a few days before he left Guys Hill to go to Kingston. Then he was filled with disgust, bordering on almost deep hatred for Maas Charlie. He had been to the river all by himself. He had left Guys Hill, had also suffered in town and seen much more of the country. Yes, he was now going to the river with friends. Yes, he had Doreen, he had the seed that he hoped would be mature in another three months. That made him feel good. But where was the better, or a chance for the better life?

Ras Bongo led the way from the road, down the shaded track. He had a paper bag with some ackee in his hand. Kwame next, carried a paint pan, then Junior with Huey on his shoulder. Doreen with a big tie-head she had borrowed from Miss Birdie looked a much older woman than she really was. She and Karl were some distance behind the rest.

Karl looked at Doreen walking in front of him. Her bottom, like that of most black women, was round and attractively so, but the baby in her stomach seemed to push it further back.

As they walked Karl wondered how he was going to manage when the baby was born. If life was already so hard, what would it be like then? 'And Doreen will have to stop work too'; he thought. 'How I going manage?' The sight of the river broke his thoughts.

Guy River had changed little over the year. A few places were a little wider, and one or two pools nearby looked deeper. The last October rains had removed much material from the river banks to deposit further down stream.

The bank, where they stood was not so high. A part of the bank and some of the trees growing on it, had been washed away by the river in spate, but not the big guango tree, not that tree where Ras Bongo frightened Karl with the frog that morning. And now as the six people shared the experience as Karl and the Ras told the story, it seemed such a short while back. They sat on some big stones in the shade of the big guango tree. The place was so peaceful as the river flowed silently below.

They decided to cook. Junior, with Huey on the bank, was catching shrimps in the shallow pool a few yards up stream. He wanted them so that Huey and Doreen could taste them, not dried and pickled as they were used to getting it in town. They were to taste fresh shrimps.

Ras Bongo started to make up the fire. He wanted as much practice as possible. 'A time will come when I man shall have to make up the eternal fire. Then all the people, fathers, mothers, children, who downpress the children of Afrika . . . the people who hold back the forward motion of humanity . . . I Bongo, son of Rasta shall cast them in everlasting fire . . . Let them burn in the fire for their wrongs . . . Oh Jah . . . Rastafari.'

But now it was not the eternal fire, just a few bits of dried wood and a flame enough to cook a pot. A pot of what? Flour or rice was the choice. Flour was chosen to go with the national dish, ackee and salt-fish, part national, part imported, but still national.

'See what we eating,' Kwame began. 'Flour or rice, to go with ackee and salt fish . . . where the flour, the rice, the salt-fish come from?'

And so it started. Nearly a whole day of chatting about almost every problem the district, the parish, the country faced. Kwame held the floor, or better yet the bank, for most of the day. His three weeks in hospital was not spent only in nursing wounds from the struggle at the Electric Service. He read and thought over many things, adding one moment, subtracting the next. Kwame's friends, and enemies too, born, unborn and Guys River could bear witness that he had been thinking seriously. He knew what he was saying could work. It was based on some of the information from a university report and was the plan he had

141

been telling Karl about, the night when they read the newspaper clipping on Cuba. Now Miss Rachey's big son was ready to rap.

'Only when a country own and control it resources . . . land, mineral, everything in it, only that time it can feed all the people. And feed them well,' Kwame stressed. 'I know people going to say is communism, but . . . '

Ras Bongo cut in, 'If Jezus Christ was on this earth today, the enemy of greater humanity, the people who uphold slavery today— as I and I live under a new form, a twentieth-century slavery . . . for in 1838, slavery was not abolished it was only polished—the downpressor and him follower would say Jezus was a communist.'

Ras Bongo was still sitting near to the fire. The wood was cold and smoking too much. But the Ras was doing his best.

Between Kwame with his plan to better the country, and the Rastaman with his '20th Century slavery' the day at the river was a full one. What was Kwame's plan?

'To get our country right,' he said taking a seat on the stone, 'we must get down to the roots of our woes. The roots of our woes is the riches of a handful and the poverty of the mass of the people. Control of most of the wealth of the country, in the hand of foreigner, capitals' or imperialis', and a couple local capitalis' and them puppets.'

'It mus' end,' Ras Bongo stopped blowing the fire. 'The riches . . . ' He caught his breath, 'The riches of the few slave master on the agricultural estates and the industrial estates, then the poverty of I and I, the Afrikan slave. I man overstand fully . . . and it dread Jahman. Dread a tell you.'

Doreen sat near the root of the tree leaning her back against it. As she listened to the Ras and Kwame, she kept watching her man. He was busy kneeding the flour in the big paint pan. When he was finished, he would rest the flour on a stone and put the pan with water on the fire. Some friends fishing nearby hailed them.

Kwame was speaking. 'But to get the mass out of poverty, first, must get agriculture right.' He emphasised, 'The land mus' be in the hands of the people, not a few, but the majority of this country. First we mus', we mus', so we can feed ourself. This is one of the main task of the working class and the peasants to build socialism to free and feed the masses.'

Ras Bongo wanted to go back up on the stone. What a hell of a day it would be at Guys River that day! Kwame was a great talker, but the Ras was a greater talker. Both were learned men.

'This land mus' no longer be in the hand of the absentee owner, or him children. No, no, I,' the Rastaman said. 'Nor can I and I continue to live on barrels of pickle fish and flour from the master stock and trading company. Live on what we get from the imperialis' country. No, I!'

He pulled off his black, green and gold tam and dropped it on the big flat stone. The locks were now resting on his shoulders. 'The imperialis' feed him slaves, them work for him . . . so in the beginning, so it is now.'

The sun was now shining more brightly and its light was now penetrating through the leaves of some parts of the big guango tree. As the two men talked, Doreen, who sat down so comfortably, now started to get up. Junior, with Huey watching from the bank, was turning stone after stone, catching one shrimp after another. But now the baby was walking towards the water.

'Karl! Karl!'

'What happen, Doreen?'

She pointed towards the baby. 'Huey, Huey come back,' she shouted.

Junior looked up, jumped out of the water and put the baby farther up on the bank.

Ras Bongo smiled, 'Then, Sister Doreen, is so the daughter easy to frighten?'

Karl who now got up, went back to making the dumplings. 'Spee . . . ew;' he hissed his teeth, 'I don't know how woman easy to frighten so.'

Kwame continued to unravel his plans. First, the land of all foreigners must become the possession of the people of the country.

'Death to imperialism,' Bongo shouted. 'Our fore-parents was captured from Afrika, bound in chain, like beast of burden, pull the ploughs . . . yes, pull plough like cow and mule to work this land. What did them get apart from whip 'cross them backs'? Them blood, them sweat, them tears more than pay for the land. Yet, the best lands in the country, who own it?' Bongo asked.

As usual he gave his own answer, 'Sugar estates, owned by children of the master from the fifteenth or sixteenth century. Some never see sugar cane from the day them was born.'

Kwame butted in, 'Rasman, Daddy Stone tell me that a estate owner come out here once, and when him look on the sugar cane, guess what him say . . . 'Oh, what giant grass!''

Then who did the sugar estates help? Sugar from this country sold cheaper in Britain than here, also they have sugar there when we have none here. Yet they grow none. Spanish Town in the

143

middle of three such estates was only better than Lionel Town and Little London, these two also well placed in the heart of large sugar bowls. The lives of their people, though producing sugar, miserably bitter. The land of the country should be owned by the people and used to benefit all of the people of that country.

Bongo asked, 'How much people from Jam-down, own a square of land in America or Britain or Canada?'

Yet Kwame said that the imperialists owned nearly half of the country's best land.

'Then how much small farmers like Kojo and Maas Joe have?' asked Karl.

'They have about a quarter of the land. And the worst land too,' Kwame emphasised.

'But mus'. Them is the children of the run away slave, those that fled to the hillside, some before, some after 1838,' Bongo said. 'Them did not want to see much less to work for the white man no more. So is the hillside them capture till now. I man don't blame them for fleeing from the master.'

But in Kwame's plan, they could work for themselves, mainly on co-operative farms. They would do the production while the government could handle distribution and sales. And as more and more was produced, less and less food should be imported from abroad. In that way, there must be market, the farmer would get a better price and the people would get food cheaper. Most important, the agricultural, industrial, all workers and the small peasants like Kojo and Maas Joe, would now be free from the oppression of the landed 'backra' class.

Doreen kept quiet for most of the time, listening to the men and gazing at the river with its lush vegetation on both banks, or at the activities of the few people in sight. She said,

'Because a tin of condense milk cost so much, sometimes I can hardly buy any for Huey. Then is pure milk water and sugar in the tin,' she paused. 'Then with this one coming soon,' she rested her hand on her stomach 'laud have mercy on them.'

It was now about twelve o'clock. The sun was directly overhead. The food did not take long to be cooked. Karl who was in charge of the cooking started to share it in the two plates that were there, and, for some he shared the food on banana leaf. He used a long piece of stick as there was no long spoon.

'Then, Kwame,' he began. 'What you think should grow on the co-op farms you talk 'bout?'

'Cho, Karl,' Doreen said jokingly. 'Hush up you mouth over the pot. Mind you spit fly in the food.'

144

Kwame did not answer Karl's question immediately. 'First, land taken from the imperialists, land that was level or sloping slightly, but too stony for farming, should be shared up among the people who did not have land for themselves.'

Ras Bongo remarked, 'Yes, a square for each single working man or woman and a little more for a family without land, should provide space to put up a little shelter over the head of the uprooted children of Afrika.'

'Not only them, but all poor people,' Kwame added. 'The poor Indian people work hard too. All poor people mus' get land. Them can't buy it. Time to stop make people squatters, . . . squatters in them own country!'

'Then the country has sand, board and cement to house us'?

'Yes! Every day Mayer say him love this country,' Karl said getting up from around the pot. 'Him should be willing to prove him love. Sell the cement to the people cheaper.'

Each person got his share of food. They started to eat and even then Kwame continued to talk. According to him, houses could be built along the roadway or on the borders of these co-operative farms. After the people got the land, then by organising themselves under community basis, they could build their houses.

The young carpenter in the group said, 'I personally, if I get a square of land in a community, I would prefer to work there, teach people the carpenter trade and help to build the house them.' Karl took another bite of the stubborn dumpling, 'I prefer . . . to do . . . that . . . ' The food was still in his mouth, 'than . . . work . . . for nothing from either Maas Charlie or Mayer.' His mouth was now empty, 'cut down the rent house business. Too much landlords live like ticks on people backs.'

Kwame ate very slowly. Most of the time he was not even eating. He was chatting. 'Hillside land could be used for forestry. This would provide lumber for buildings. But not only that, it could provide pulp, that could be used to supply our own paper factory. House, paper and employment for our people.'

Huey got up from beside Junior, passed Doreen and was coming to Karl, 'Umm . . umm . . pa . . pa.' He put a shrimp in Karl's mouth. 'Umm, eat, eat this, papa.' Karl munched the little red piece of food. But then Huey started pointing up the stream. Everyone looked. Three little boys, about the size of Junior, less than a chain off, were stoning a brown donkey.

'But them little boy not suppose to be in Sunday school?' Karl asked.

'Aay, Jah, I man can't tell why the youths this day so vile.

145

Won't do the Father commandment . . . look what them doing.'
The Rastaman got up, 'But is no Brother Joe donkey them
fooling 'round?'

Yes, it was Maas Joe's donkey, the same one Karl had seen
that evening nearly a year ago, and had thought it was a naked
woman bathing in the river.

The boys, now about half-chain away, saw the Rastaman and the
rest of them, they ran back up-stream and disappeared behind a
clump of bushes.

Everyone went back to their eating. Karl told them about that
evening with the donkey and then the chatting about Kwame's
plans continued.

'But you still don't tell we what you think could grow on the
level lands,' Karl reminded his friend.

Kwame told them that one or two of the sugar factories, could
provide enough sugar. The rest of the level land could be used for
crops and livestock. Vegetables of all kinds. Grow the ones that
people eat most and is rich and good for the body. Some could
also be grown for export to other countries, he had said.

'I read a book, a professor from the Netherlands write. Him
say that things like cotton, hibiscus, mango leaf, cashew leaf,
banana leaf, cock-comb, poinciana and plenty more things . . . '
Kwame paused and looked at Ras Bongo. 'Even the top and flowers
of herbs is good food.' There was silence for a while.

'You mean that ganga can eat?' Doreen asked.

The Rastaman replied, 'Yes, Sis. true, true.'

'Research could be done on these plants to see how it could
help to feed our people. This would help to get rid of 'bang-belly',
malnutrition and starvation in the country. Nearly half the
children suffer from malnutrition! Disgrace! It must stop!'

Doreen agreed with him. 'Yes, I know that many people in
Papine don't eat a leaf of lettuce and two slices of tomato in a
week,' Doreen said. 'All them eat is pure rice and flour, and that
is when them can get it. Them mus' suffer from malnutrition.'

'And where the rice come from?' Kwame asked. It came from
abroad. Then why should the country import rice when it could
be grown on the plains. Import rice when there is a rice factory in
Spanish Town, which for most of the year was not even used? With
Co-operative rice farmers on some of the land there would no
longer be the need to import so much rice. Co-operative farms
owned by the farmers and state farms owned by all the people
should supply enough rice to help feed the people.

Karl asked, 'But since when we start eat rice for breakfast, lunch and dinner?'

Bongo answered, 'The slave master create the taste for what him want I and I to eat.' Co-operative growing of yam, banana, cassava and other food crops . . . on a large scale on the level or gentle slopes . . . not only on the rock-sides of the country.

Kwame who had been chatting so much and the only one still eating, took up one of his dumplings on the piece of stick he was using as a fork. Even a couple of friends passing, ate and left.

'You see this,' he said pointing to the dumpling on the stick, 'you see this wheat flour, it can't sweet like cassava flour. You know that?'

Junior still trying to get Huey to eat the shrimps, had his say, 'Miss Birdie make bammy give us all the time, it nice you see.'

'That is true, youth,' Kwame said still holding the dumpling on the stick. A wasp landed on his leg. He tried to brush it off quickly to avoid being stung. In the haste, his left hand accidently hit his right, and the dumpling fell to the ground. It rolled gently like a loose cartwheel and into the water it fell. The dumpling floated in the shallow pool at the root of the guango tree.

'See that,' Kwame pointed to the white object. 'Bet if it was a cassava or banana or breadfruit flour make it, it would be heavier than that. It couldn't float like that. It couldn't.'

No one, not even Ras Bongo made any comment. Strange how he sat down on the stone, quietly listening for so long. The Ras was now taking something wrapped in brown paper from his pocket. 'Sister Dee, you not afraid of herbs?'

Doreen did not reply.

'Oo . . oh,' Bongo said nodding his head. 'So afraid that you mouth can't open.'

Corn for man, sorghum for animals, both were rich in protein. Whether people ate the corn, or fed it and the sorghum to live-stock, they would benefit. And so on, and so on Kwame named them . . . cocoa, coffee, tobacco with factories to process them, not owned by foreigners, but by the people to whom the country belonged—fruits: sweetsop, soursop, citrus, mango, pear, nase-berry, pineapple, ackee . . . yes ackee on large farms to supply plenty, and prevent it from selling for thirty and forty cents a dozen.

But that was not all. What about cotton? People in other Caribbean lands can grow it. Why can't we?

Ras Bongo made the 'spliff' and was smoking. He lowered

147

the herb from his lips. Smoke gushed out of his mouth and nose at the same time.

'Yes, I man know too say, that Arawak Indians use to grow cotton right here. Them use to grow it before the Spaniards wipe them out to get them to work as slaves. Then the syphylis . . .' The Rastaman took a draw on his herb. He seemed at peace with the world. 'Yes I know that cotton can grow here,' he puffed out the smoke. 'Hear that rubber trees grow in some of the hills in Jamdown. You know if anybody ever check it out? 'Cause like most of Afrika . . . ' He took another draw. . . . 'this land in the tropics and many things that Jah put on this earth, can grow here.' He leaned his head against the root of the guango tree, picked up a pebble and threw it in the water. Ripples moved away in circles from where the stone landed.

'Cotton industry to make garments for I and I, rubber industry to make wheel for the charriots.' Bongo paused. 'Not bad. Still not what we have when Afrika liberate, and we drive the white devils out of the motherland. But still, not bad at all Jah son.' The Ras raised the spliff to his lips, 'Some say socialism, but is sosoism'.

The others smiled, the Ras was dead serious.

'Many things we import can grow here,' Kwame emphasized. 'But the capitalis' who live by import and export would get hurt. But neither Sir Chief nor Mister Manlie government don't want to hurt the big capitalis' them.'

Kwame then went on to say that crops were only one side of the story. Livestock was the other half. Small livestock . . . sheep to supply meat and wool, with the cotton no one need to walk naked any more. Goats, poultry . . . pigs . . .

The Rastaman pushed up his nose after hearing the last word. 'Swine!' he exclaimed. 'Anyhow most of you is unclean people, so you eat the viper.'

'But it not nastier than fowl, Brother Bongo?' Doreen asked.

'You hear I,' Bongo said. 'It not going to touch I man mouth. Seen?'

Cattle, beef and dairy would also play its part. According to him cattle would not only provide beef and milk.

Kwame continued, 'We could make some leather and some shoe factory, so that poor people can get good cheap shoes to wear.' That was where the skills of people like Ras Bongo could be useful, to train unskilled youths, to be good shoemakers. Some of the vegetables and fruits could be processed and canned for export, when there was a surplus.

'In the same way, we could have factories to process the meat and milk. A butter and cheese factory could be built where we could use up our milk.'

Doreen butted in, 'And the tin meat from abroad so trashy. I always wonder why we have to get butter and cheese all the way from New Zealand.'

Stop importing saltfish. Develop our fishing industry. The island was completely surrounded by the sea. Small boats, large ones co-operatively owned, bought by loans from the people's bank would provide cheap fish. Kwame said, 'We can press fish, and dry and salt in our own factory. The oil good, especially for old people and children. We might not have the big long saltfish but we would still have saltfish.'

'But the most serious question I have to ask,' Doreen paused and looked around for her son. Junior had taken off the little boy's clothes and was bathing him in the river. 'If the government know them things, why them don't do it to help the country, een?'

Before Doreen was finished the Ras started to chant. 'Death to imperialism! Death to colonialism! Death to neo-colonialism!'

Ras Bongo must be going mad. What song did that line come from? Doreen was confused. And the Rastaman just sat there without saying another word. Four boys catching shrimps passed.

Kwame put his plate aside. Oil was still running down the side of his mouth. He continued with his plan.

The people of the country, not a handful, but the mass of the people as owners of co-operatives, and state enterprises would now for the first time be the owner of the land that had been stolen from the Arawak Indians and developed mainly by the labour of Afrikans past and present. A 'familyram' and two sisters stopped.

What would happen to the wealth, the produce got from the land? In wages, in clothes, in food, in education, in everything each person according to his skill and how much work he did, would share the fruits of work. One getting a peg of the fruit, another two, another three, but never one getting four, five, or six with another getting one or none. Seen! The 'cocksman' and company left.

Karl turned to Kwame, 'Then what 'bout bauxite and things like that?' he asked getting up as if he were now tired of sitting on the flat stone. The river in spate, carrying its bolders, bits of stone, gravel, coarse to fine grains of sand, had done a good job on that one. The mighty sandpapers of different grades had worked the stone down to almost a perfect finish.

'You mean the industries,' Kwame asked, looking at Karl then to Ras Bongo who was now leaning against the root of the guango tree. The green giant had been so kind to them. It had tamed the

149

midday sun, and now somewhere near three o'clock, it was even cool.

'Who work in the factories them in this part of the west?' Bongo asked.

'No one but I and I,' he answered himself. He threw the butt of his spliff in the river. Slowly it floated away. Guys River flowed lazily by, undisturbed by either the hours of talk on its bank, or the voices that came from the church up the road. Karl was almost certain he could hear Mis Birdie's voice as the people sang:

'My home is in Heaven,
Jus' waiting for me.
And when I reach there,
How happy I'll be.
My home is in heaven,
No rent to pay.
My Jesus paid it,
Paid it all for me.'

Doreen asked if all country people kept church that long.

Karl asked why is it that mostly the poor and few, very few rich people went to church regularly. The Mayers went to the race track every Saturday, but went to church only every first Sunday in the month. Didn't the rich have more to praise the Almighty for? Then why was it the poor, and not them, that was always praising the Lord?

Ras Bongo knew the answer, 'Lay not your treasures on earth where moth or rust doth corrupt, or thieves break through and steal, but lay your treasures in heaven. The poor did not have treasures on earth, not even food, so how could they work to give the earthly treasures to other people.'

Karl said, 'The black man from we great great grandparents laying treasures in heaven, we must be the richest people up there.'

Kwame added, 'And we must get the most milk and honey to drink too!'

Doreen was not religious, but she had a deep fear for the Almighty, so she kept quiet. She looked at Kwame who was about to talk again.

'How I see it you know,' Kwame began, 'is that we must drink even a little sugar and water so we can live. When we go to heaven, the milk and honey can flow while we play with the lion, the leopards and the archangels.'

Ras Bongo who had been keeping quiet for sometime now spoke,

150

'The brethren talking 'bout white angels that the slave master, the imperialis keep showing Jah-jah children.'

True, at Sunday School, through to sixth class in school, Karl had said he had not seen a drawing with a black or even a brown angel. Certainly, the Almighty did not have all white angels around his throne. But Jesus and all the angels had to be white! If they were not, their pictures would have to be placed in the back, but more certainly outside the church where white people worship. In short if the white man did not have a white God, white Jesus surrounded by white angels, he would not worship him. White Jesus! Do the people of the Middle East have pale faces and blue eyes?

Bongo who had been leaning against the tree said, 'Then if Jesus was on earth today, if him was not a white man, him would have to use the worst shit-house in America or in England or South Afrika. And if that man, son of the most high, was in Jam-down, and him not white, him might have to rest down Trench Town. True I.' The Rastaman continued, 'One thing I man Bongo say, as the Prophet Marcus Garvey say, the Afrikan must create him own, worship images in him own likeness . . . Seen?'

The Rastaman then suddenly started talking as if he were vexed. 'The blood claute slave master been fucking—excuse me Sister Doreen—fucking with the teachings of the most high, Jah Rasta, the most High who dwell on Mount Zion!' The Nyabinge paused, 'When the slave come off the boat from Afrika, them brand him with hot iron on him chest and back, and what next?'

He paused as if waiting for an answer. 'The accomplice of the master hiding under flowing black gown and broad felt hat, Bible in one hand and cross in the other, would start teach. 'Servants obey your masters . . . the will of the Lord'.

As the Ras spoke, Karl could tell that the bearded man would soon come to the phrase he often used to describe people like Maas Charlie, who claimed that they are Christians, but were really just church-goers.

Bongo spoke, 'As in the past, so today . . . Death to the Churchians.'

Kwame was longing to get back to his plan. Three weeks in hospital with a bandage around his head, had prevented his body from working well, but not his mind. The cool breeze, the river flowing by, and a full belly made him feel fit. Foreign-owned industries and services like the bus company and the electric service should also fall into the hands of the people. The co-operative farms would be owned collectively by groups of farmers, young and old. But the industries and the services should be owned by the people through its government. Pay the imperialist for them? That would depend on how long they were in the country. The ones that were operating for a short time, yes. But the ones that had been underpaying, overcharging our people and sending back millions to their countries abroad and sucking the country? Pay them? The 'cocksman' was having fun in a pool down stream.

Kwame asked, 'How can we make a few people own we bauxite, the city bus, factories, electricity, telephone, the oil refinery? Then on top of that, is a few people who don't belong to this country.'

Karl asked, 'Why them should own so much in this country and we can't own much in them homeland. Why?'

Kwame took up from what Karl asked. 'When we own we can charge reasonable, give reasonable pay,' he said. 'Need no profit to send abroad. Can stay here to make life better for the people here. Then them won't have to line up to flee to the white man country. Then nobody will need to insult or kick we in we ass, neither on Duke Street, Fifth Street, or Downing Street.'

'End of dictatorship of the capitalis' class, time for national liberation. I an I die for salvation.' Ras Bongo added.

Junior was at the edge of the river. He was washing the plates with some 'quaka' bush. It gave a fair amount of suds, Huey stood beside him. There was going to be hell when that little boy was to leave Junior to go back to town!

Karl had just got up off the stone and turned up the track that led back up the road. He would soon be back. The dumplings, ackee and saltfish were bubbling in his belly. Karl had to leave to lose some weight.

It was only Kwame, Doreen and Bongo left under the tree. The Rastaman took off his shirt, and after the spliff, was still resting his head against the big guango tree. Soon Ras Bongo started to doze off, his mouth began to open. Kwame got up, took a short slender piece of stick from the fire. He put the unlighted end in Ras Bongo's mouth. It stayed in place for a few seconds, then slowly it started to drop out of his mouth. Doreen got up, but too late.

'Lightning and fire!' Bongo shouted as the fire stick touched his belly. In one action he sprang to his feet, nearly bouncing down the pregnant woman and almost falling into the river.

'Satan! Satan!' Bongo said looking half-grieved with Doreen.

'But . . . but, Ras is not . . . ' Doreen tried to explain but she was only wasting her breath.

'Sister Dee, is only Rasta-fari could come down from Zion to tell

I that is not you.' Bongo said. Then he smiled, 'But I man forgive you. Seen?'

But no powers would make her forgive Kwame.

After a while, Miss Rachey's slim, clean-faced, self-educated electrician son, continued to reveal his plans. The country was not on some world maps. So small, yet one of the world's largest suppliers of bauxite—not coal, but bauxite, such an important mineral in the world today. But what do we have to show from it? Deep holes and the red mud river near to some plants. What do they have to show? Millions of dollars taken out each year. Skyscrapers, blast furnaces in aluminium smelters, employment for ten times as many people in their countries.

Do they invest money here because they love us, or because they want us to get rid of poverty and make our lives better? Then why didn't they do the same to wipe out the ghettos and stop people from digging up garbage in their own countries?

'But them may not want to buy the bauxite from us.' Doreen said.

'We wouldn't want to sell them bauxite, or even aluminia,' Kwame replied. 'The real thing aluminium, they need that. Yes them have to buy that. What they going use to make them cars and chimmy? Them can make plastic chimmy, but the plastic car only at Christmas.'

Kwame moved towards where Karl had left his shirt. As he searched for a cigarette, he continued.

'Besides if them don't want to buy the aluminium, let them go to hell! Them is the ones who teach we to think that the whole world make up of four countries in the west.

Ras Bongo was now fully awake.

'But how the brethren sight up making the metal on this rock?' he questioned Kwame. 'The man overstand that it need plenty power.'

Kwame had found the cigarette in Karl's pocket. As he bent over the dying fire to pick up a fire-stick to light the cigarette he remembered the incident with the Ras a short while before. He could not help smiling.

The problem of power to smelt aluminium could be solved by working with other countries in the Caribbean. Any country that was willing and able. Cuba the biggest one, is just ninety miles away.

'We cannot tell America how to run them business. So how them want to tell we who we should deal with?' Guyana, has many great rivers that can supply enough power to make aluminium.

153

They make our aluminium, we make something else for them, not only bauxite but almost everything . . . every raas thing', were Kwame's exact words . . . We should co-operate with other countries in the Caribbean, especially those fighting against imperialism.'

The Ras quickly added. 'And Afrika, the homeland of our foreparents, the cradle of science and the new civilization.'

Kwame agreed with the man and said that while the countries in the Caribbean and the Black Continent were our first allies, we should trade and get help from any progressive country that is willing to help us to break the hold of the slave master on our country.

Kwame soon finished smoking the cigarette. He threw the butt in the river. It had not reached far, being tossed about by little waves blown up by the cool evening breeze. The lengthening shadows could tell that it must have been well after three o'clock.

Karl came back from the bush toilet. He felt much better and wanted to go for a swim. It had been such a long time since his last one in that same river. The Ras wanted to have his regular bath in the river. It was his bath tub and swimming pool all in one. Kwame was not too keen, but he would go with them to the deeper hole, a little further down. Doreen could not go. For one, she was too fat, then, the Ras was not a man to bathe in any form of clothing. Junior would stay with her and Huey.

The split did not prevent Kwame from revealing his plan.

'We can make our own aluminium right here,' Kwame continued. 'All we need is a nuclear reactor.'

According to the University report, a nuclear reactor could provide power to run, not one but two aluminium plants. Kwame had studied the figures carefully. The annual export value of this aluminium would be about one hundred and thirty million dollars! This would be more than what the reactor would cost. And it would supply a hell of a lot of power, for other uses too. Power enough to change sea water to fresh water. With this water, wells, dams, to catch the waste October rains, the country could not be short of water either to use on farms, houses or for industrial purposes. Enough water for Miss Rachey's bath pan and the Mayer's swimming pool . . . that is if they were still around to watch school youth learn to swim in it. The reactor could also supply power for fertilizer factories. We have some, if not all the raw materials we would need. But that was not all the blessings of the nuclear reactor. Power convert the 'red mud' from bauxite into steel. Not to fatten any one man, white, mulatto or black, but all the people . . . all the people of the nation. Power to help to make more of the things we import, especially equipment like tractors and so on for our co-operative and state farms.

'With aluminium and steel,' Kwame said, 'why couldn't we do it? Why?'

Then there was the problem of transport. First, more railway lines, especially to serve the farms and industries were needed. Use up the rail fully. Use it up. It will take much of the people and vehicles carrying loads, off the road. City transport? Karl said a little about the conditions and the amount of time wasted on the buses. For him, about two and working days to get to work each week. That was about twenty-five working weeks in every working year. Some friends further upstream were getting ready to leave.

Ras Bongo also said something about what he had seen when he went to town to buy leather. 'And the condition, how I and I ride on the white man chariots, for it is black people—worker, driver, police, conductor and all, drive on the bus. It not much different from the way we fore-parents drive in the slave, waggons to the plantations three hundred years ago.' The Rastaman continued, 'True the condition on the bus not as dread as the wagons. But equally true, the big chariots that carry the master today, not the same as the buggy that use to carry them three hundred years ago.'

According to Kwame, the city transport should belong to the people. 'Express buses, reorganise the routes. Conductresses and drivers getting reasonable pay, low cost of living, their children well cared for. Then they could be working to build their country instead of Britain and South Afrika, and so would run the buses well. Those who did not, would run the tractors on the farms better. The friends who were upstream, said 'bye' to Doreen.

There should also be transport to carry children to and from school. Few people wanted to carry them now as children paid only half fares, took up almost the same space as adults and gave more trouble. 'But the youths must reach school, fairly comfortable and on time,' Kwame said. 'Country transport? Between the buses, mini-buses and the trains, that would be well taken care of.'

The young electrician, trade unionist, poet and Miss Rachael's first son, spoke from the remains of a log on the bank of Guy's River. Ras Bongo and Karl in the pool below listened like candidates for a baptism, listening to their parson before the ceremony.

And Kwame's low trim and clean face made him look so much like one that just left the seminary, looking so different from the Ras with locks and beard hanging down, or Karl who sometimes

155

didn't comb his hair for a few days, and had a stubble. One would expect that Kwame would be busy preparing sermons, instead of thinking of such earthly matters as crime, unemployment and poverty. But looks can be deceiving, and one should not judge others by their looks. As Kojo told Miss Birdie many times something that nearly everyone in Guys Hill knew, 'the parson that stole the church money last year, looked like a saint.'

And yet there were many people fighting for change, who would want to fight against Kwame, because of what he looked like. He had this trouble when he first started working in the union at the Electricity Company. Some workers said that he looked like a 'society boy' that would sell them out. But the works of a man are more important than his looks. True the Afrikans must cast off the image, the standards of what look good or bad as set by the the white slave master. But could we afford to go to the other extreme to judge people by how much unlike the 'good' white image they looked? Could one say that Kwame was a parson because of his clean face and low trim?

It was now approaching five o'clock. It was almost time to leave. Doreen and Huey and Junior were waiting. Bongo took up his tam.

'In 1838, the form of slavery change.' The man shook his head. His locks swirled from left to right issuing a light sprinkle of water over his shoulders. 'True dread. The form change from old slavery to the new one, neo-slavery. Same way, the Osageyfo Kwame Nkrumah, show us how many of the countries that now say them independent, only change one form of colonialism to a dreader form, neo-colonialism!'

As the Rastaman started to fix the black, green and red tam over his locks, he began to recite. 'The essence of neo-colonialism is that the state which is subject to its . . . is, in theory, independent and has all the outward trappings of international sovereignty. In reality, its economic system and thus its political policy is directed from outside.' Bongo paused. 'Yes, the words of Nkrumah great fighter for Afrikan unity following in the footsteps of the prophet Marcus Mosiah Garvey.'

Karl was now coming out of the water, he had been taking his last dip. He was finally coming out towards the bank where Kwame and Bongo stood.

'So, Jah,' Bongo continued, 'I man know that we could have ten governor to open a thousand buildings, and a dozen flags, until the people here—and the Afrikans being eighty per cent of the population control eighty per cent of the country's wealth . . . then all talk 'bout freedom and independence is folly!' Ras Bongo sat down on the fine sand, to put on his sandals. He put one foot on then the other.

'Slavery not a law, or a set of laws. It not a chain or a set of chains. It cannot be abolished by a new set of laws or pulling off chains. Slavery was and is a situation . . . where the slaves worked and lived in poverty, hunger and baracoons, for the master in his riches, luxury and mansions.'

Bongo stared at Kwame, 'Seen I.' He sat down to buckle the sandals. 'When the down-pressor can control school, church, police, army, court house and all him weapons of destruction of Jah children . . . why keep we in chain?'

As the Ras spoke Karl remembered a few lines from his favourite record:

'I am used like a tool day by day,
Cause I'm black and still in chains.'

And as the Ras spoke, Kwame realized that the man was not talking merely about wage slavery. It was not just economic and political, but also cultural enslavement. What Bongo spoke of was nearly a change in form and substance of what the black-man had experienced from the time they set foot on the slave-ship in Afrika.

Ras Bongo got up, 'Until agricultural or industrial estate no longer belong to absentee proprietor, until what the master have become the property of the slave, so that them can eat the fruits of them labour, is still slavery'. The Rastaman got up and stared across Guy river.

'I Ras Bongo, son of most high Jah, Rastafari, know that in 1838, slavery was not abolished, it was polished.'

Karl quickly cut in, 'So we mus' rub off the polish . . . and abolish it NOW.' He turned to Ras Bongo. 'Seen nyah.'

The man fixed his black green and red tam, 'True, true.'

Kwame exposed most of his remaining ideas during the walk back up to where Doreen, Huey and Junior were. The river just flowed on, not in the least disturbed by the hours of groundings.

There were some more vital questions that Kwame had to answer.

'Can we get enough money to carry through such a plan?' Karl asked.

'Definately . . . def . . . in . . . ately,' Kwame replied. 'Firstly, such a plan would benefit the people—I mean the masses—in such a way that no one would have to tell them to work. We people not willing to work on things that people have to tell them 'bout the benefits'.

'Why?', Karl asked.

Bongo answered for Kwame. 'Because I and I can see no fruits from it.'

'Yes, we would have to depend on our people.' Kwame continued. 'Don't mean that one set would work and the other get the benefits. 'Don't mean that again . . . again the Afrikan and the Indian bear the burden and the white man, the Chiney man, the Jew man get the sugar.'

Bongo spoke, 'I dread, sight up the 'operation' this and the 'operation' that, and the voluntary works, and all I man see man flying the 'lass is only Jah children I and I see using the lass you know.' The Ras stopped in his track. 'And how them love to tell I and I bout 'out of many one' and when you check it out is' true . . one man use the lass, chop the coal, sledge the stone, dig the yam hill, drive the dray, drive the bus, live in the slum, and full up the prison . . . you sight that?'

Karl broke in, 'And is the same people love talk how black man lazy, and don't want to touch ground.'

'When is only I and I hand touch the soil,' Bongo said. 'Chiney man, Jew man, malatto and white man scorn the ground, but come to tell me that I man lazy and don't want to touch ground . . . folly!'

But in Kwame's plan, all hands would have to touch either the ground or some machine in a factory.

'At least one month work from every fucking person in this country. Every Jackman . . . same pay as if in him normal job. But we all, all who belong to the nation must work.'

Karl smiled. 'Mean like Mrs Mayer, too?'

The three men walked slowly along the river bank as they spoke. Doreen, Huey and Junior had moved a little distance away from where the men had left them. Very few people were now at the river.

In reply to Karl's question, Kwame said that with the people of the nation working together, much less money would be needed. Many of our people who had valuable skills and who were living like chinks in imperial capitals, would be glad to come home to build their nation.

'But we are still going to need money,' Karl stressed.

'Yes, more money would be needed, and none would come from the people who had controlled our land, industries and labour. A

158

'People's Bank' with small compulsory savings from all who worked, would be a good start. It should almost be like a 'partner', a kind of co-op bank for the entire country. The People's Bank would replace the 'Imperialist Banks'. Loans from a Caribbean Bank would also help. And if more money was still needed, loans from countries that would lend but not tell us how to spend it, would help. The socialist countries of the world could be counted on, and others fighting imperialism too?

Kwame continued, 'But no more loan, or aid from them who used to oppress and rob us. The aid is just that.' He shook his head. 'Not aid from them to us, but aid from we to them.'

'I man did know long time that the imperialis' vampires . . .' The Ras squeezed the last word. 'Imperialis' give with one hand and take back with two. I man did know lo . . ong time.'

Doreen, Huey and Junior were only a few feet away. They stood and waited patiently. The Ras knelt down to play with Huey at his mother's side.

'Jaa . . a . . come, man, come,' the baby said. He was now able to call many more words than many months ago, when he had somehow brought Karl and Doreen together.

She turned to Karl. 'How you stay so long.' She tried to look serious, but was half smiling. 'You know five o'clock must gone long time.' Their shadows on the river bank were so long, that for some, it stretched off the bank and unto the lush vegetation' nearby.

'Must be that damn one,' she looked at Kwame, "bout him have plan.'

And while collecting the things to leave, Kwame went back in motion.

'Reorganize our schools. Scrap the masters education system. Educate our people to help themselves in nation building. Give technical education to all. Teach history, literature of all people, but mostly that of the Afrikan people. Education for all, free up to university level, when the country can afford it. Not for a few, but for all as long as they have ability. And not to further divide . . . 'oh, I went to a higher school than you, so you are not as good as me'.

From the child can learn, till death, education in the school buildings, the churches, the fields, the community centres, education for young and old. 'We have enough people to teach our children,' Kwame emphasized. How can we be taking in people from imperialist countries, countries that hold us back for centuries, and are still holding down the progress of our people. How can

159

we expect them to educate our children to move forward? Why don't they stay and educate their own people? Why do we allow these tourists calling themselves 'Peace Corps to come here saying that they are teaching us, but really spying on us?

In Vietnam they found that the people believed in astrology. They used this to tell the people all kinds of lies, stories of doom in the stars, if they drove out their good French, British, and American war-lords.

In Jamaica they will tell us that rolling-calf will eat us, if we drive the master off the land, the burial place of our fore-fathers.

'We mus', we mus' teach our own people,' Kwame continued. 'Primary school students help basic schools, fifth class help first class, sixth class help second, high school help primary and so on.' Crash programme work, Christmas and election work, what do they produce? A burden on the taxpayer's pocket. Same cutlass, pick-axe and mattock used. Why not on land to produce some food? Give our people a chance to improve their skills and feed themselves. Big people, youths on the streets everyday with cutlass and rake.

Fuck off with that! Uplift the people!

Money from exporting certain products from our co-operative farms, our industries, our aluminium would be used to build, not only more recreation centres, more schools, but more hospitals and health centres to keep our people strong and well. Young women who pass through primary schools can be trained to become nursing assistants. Then a system that allows progress to highest ranks. Anyone who could work well, could even become a doctor.

Doreen asked, 'You mean a girl who pass through primary school even from a poor family?'

'Girl or boy,' Kwame replied.

'But that wouldn't make the doctor them vex?' she asked again.

'Sometimes a doctor get about forty patients one day. Them charge say five dollars for every patient, they wouldn't get so much money again!'

They were getting too much, they, although providing a good service for the country, were sucking the masses dry. It must stop!

'Beside what they get from the drug store,' Doreen added, 'in the one I work, the doctor get twenty per cent of everything we sell one of him patient.'

Karl spoke, 'So that is why nowadays them don't want to give you medicine? Man, them think really wicked. When will it stop? No wonder the poor mus' poorer.'

Kwame added, 'And incomes must share out different, one set, one thousand dollars, another two, another three. But, my God, why some twenty thousand, and some none? The masses of the people must get freedom from the capitalis' and other blood suckers.'

They were now almost ready to leave the river. Only Junior was still in the water. Karl called to him, 'Hurry up, man. It getting late.'

'Five more minutes, Brother Karl, man,' the boy replied, lifting another stone.

Kwame still on the floor, rather on the bank, continued, 'Reduce the police force and the army too.

The government of the working people will stop training the young black men and women to kill their own people.'

And while they were doing this, they, their children, their parents, were still living in poverty. When they die from a bullet, from another suffering and rebellious youth, the medals and the praise cannot feed their children.

'Send them to the School of Agriculture.'

'The school near Spanish Town?' Doreen asked. 'I know a man who used to go there. When him was first year, them used to call him grub. Him say one night, him drunk and drink off a bottle of pepper sauce. Him vommit till him nearly dead. The next day him wake up and find himself in a toilet bowl. Him flush him head.'

'The daughter not serious?' Ras Bongo asked.

'Yes. And is not only that him tell me. Him say a second year send him to milk a bull. Him say him was coward, so him get a pail and start to pull the bull balls. One kick. One rib broke. One month in hospital.'

But no ex-police or soldier who went to school would have time to milk bull. One year training in crop and livestock would make them well suited to work on the farms and help to run them. Other policemen and soldiers should also get some training in either agriculture, industry or some other skill apart from beating and shooting their own people. Sell back the new police cars and long guns to the country that we bought them from. Each car could be exchanged for a tractor. The armoured cars for railway cars, the machine guns for sewing machines.

Junior was coming out of the water.

'Then what happen to the criminals?' Doreen asked.

'No man is born a criminal, society makes him so, and the only way to change things, is to change the social conditions.' Words of Kwame Nkrumah, coming from Ras Bongo's mouth as he sat patiently on the river bank.

Kwame spoke again, 'Take away all the guns, him use the cutlass, take away the cutlass, the knife, the glass bottle, then he will use the rock. We will soon have to give a man life sentence to have a rock stone in him house. Ever stop to think why after Mr Joshua come in power for about a month any man could walk through even Trench Town in peace?'

He paused as if waiting for an answer. 'Everybody, criminal and all hand in their guns, waiting for real change, a better life. Jobs with good pay so that them can buy food and clothes. A man don't have a job, high cost of living, how must him live but by stealing? How else? And nobody don't tell me shit 'bout they don't want to work.'

As Junior came out of the river, Karl got up, he reminded them, 'I who is a skilled man did have to walk for months to get a job. Even your old man too, Kwame.'

Kwame got up off the river bank too. He said that everyone must oppose all forms of crimes, whether of the factory owner who underpays, the supermarket owner who overcharges or the man who comes through the roof at nights. But how to solve such crimes? Increase the police force and army? 'It is the sufferers who join them, not the rich man's children. And is the sufferers come through the roofs at nights. With uniform and gun at his side, who need a roof?'

'Get down to the roots, the roots!' Miss Birdie's clean-faced son said. 'Houses for the people, clear the slums, the breeding ground for rape, robbery and all kind of evil . . . we need to get rid of capitalis' oppression and all the bad things that it breed.'

Kwame looked towards the river for a while, then back to his friends. 'And more than that, train all juveniles, all prisoners and let them out gradually. Them is our own people, our own brothers.' True they had done dread things to their own people. But beating, castration, hanging, chop off head, that was being done since the fifteenth century. It is now the twentieth century!

Kwame pleaded once again. 'The mad man out of the prisons, off the streets to where they belong. Train them too to fit into our country. We must get . . . to the roots. The roots!'

There was silence for a while, broken only now and then by a cricket or bird, delivering its Sunday sermon. The sun was casting its dying rays, it was now well past five, if not yet six o'clock.

Ras Bongo got up, 'And how I don't hear the brethren say anything 'bout them white people who come in Jamdown, camera round them necks and racism in them hearts.'

162

Kwame looked at the Rastaman, 'Who own the ships and planes that carry them here? Who owns the hotels that them stay? Who run the whore houses? Who it benefits?'

Karl spoke, 'As for me, people could always hold them down, ease them body in them face, cork up them nose and feed them with castor oil.'

Doreen's parents were from MoBay, the chief tourist area. She knew that what both Kwame and Karl had said was true. Her father had been prosecuted for going on a private beach owned by a Canadian. She like most black people had never set foot on Doctor Bird Beach.

The Rastaman took a good look at Karl and then Kwame. 'So the brethren agree that we should end whorism? Mash it up, since it is not I and I business. Well is love.'

The party started to leave Guys River. Karl led the way, Doreen next, then Junior with Huey on his back, Kwame and the Ras bringing up the rear. Only the 'cocksman' and the girls were left.

'I have one last question to ask,' Doreen, said holding on to her man's hand as he helped her over a stone in the track.

'Kwame, you don't believe that the government must know some of these things. Then how them don't do it?'

Ras Bongo did not give Kwame a chance to answer. 'Them playing the master tune to get the fish-head. 'Divide and rule' is the name of the tune. Encourage I and I to fight politricks and tribal war. When Jah children going wake up and cease them folly? Stop killing our own brethren for politricks. Who benefit? Who end up in jail? Who end up in Prison?'

Then the Rastaman continued, 'I and I will have to fight down family politricks . . . fish-head politricks. Up with people politics!'

Karl was taking care to move slowly with his baby mother. He commented, 'In power them don't do it, but out of power them willing to do it. Promises, promises, is all them make. But that can't full hungry belly.'

Then Ras Bongo made a funny statement. 'Criminals versed in the art of criminology. Politricksters versed in the art of trickinology.'

He continued, 'Them use the people money to carpet the floor of public buildings, yet the people have no floor. Them use the people money to travel around the world, yet the people have no world of their own. Them talk 'bout liberation abroad, yet the people in their own country suffer under the yolk of down-pression!'

'Not all of them, Ras man.'

163

'True, Sister Dee, but most of them stay so!'

Then the Rastaman continued with his strange talking. 'In school, I and I learn that one and one make two. But here, one and one make one.' He looked up at those before him, 'umph . . . umm. Think that corruption only in sore foot?'

Kwame said that the people should choose only those willing to serve the majority, and not just a handful. Let them prove themselves. End political tribalism—One people united behind a socialist party to serve one nation and better the life of the masses, to free the poor people from oppression of the rich and their obedient servants.

Kwame looked back, 'Seen Nyah?' he asked.

The Ras answered, 'Yes I.'

'Is one last question I would like to ask,' Karl said still leading his woman up the track. It was getting dark.

'Remember we would take over many companies that use to oppress we. You don't think them going to send soldiers from abroad to do some other thing to stop we?' Bongo jumped on it. This was a question that he had heard so many times when someone spoke about plucking the country from the hold of imperialism. The Rastaman said that, it was true that the absentee proprietor would not want the slaves to take over the industrial or the agricultural estates. The downpressor had tried to crush the Mau Mau in Kenya, bombed the babies in Vietnam, invade Cuba at the Bay of Pigs, supporting not in words but in deeds the massacre of the people in South Africa, Rhodesia, Angola, Mozambique and Guinea.

Yes, the same absentee owner had used his muskets on the Maroons, on Tacky, on Sam Sharpe, on Paul Bogle . . . 'and more than that,' Bongo allowed two or three seconds to pass, 'every year him send soldier here to train to fight guerilla warfare. Training to fight in them country? Them have jungles? . . . except concrete jungle. Why train them in the Cockpit Country to fight in Ottowa or in New York or London? Tell I dread. Why?' The locksman continued to express himself.

'Them training to fight slave rebellion here, in Afrika or anywhere I and I and all sufferers try to cast off the yolk of downpression. So I sight what young Kojo dealing with.'

Because of Doreen carrying the 'pumpkin', they had to walk slowly up the track. Many times they had to stop. Karl was pushing now, pulling the next moment. Kwame pointed out that there were people, many people were getting benefits from the imperialists. They were paid to hold down the masses. They would be willing to sell their souls to the imperialists.

'Yes, yes,' Ras Bongo began. 'The red and black puppies of imperialism are deadly! But one thing I and I mus' learn. Nothing can beat the united will of the people. More than that, the vampires have to fight I and I in the Carib sea and in Afrika, then him have to deal with Latin America, Asia and anywhere him suck blood! But even more, the youth, the people who have heart, the people who suffer in him own country especially the black people, will support a just cause. Then with the powers of the east ready to launch them rocket . . . and a thousand Vietnam on him hand . . . the red, white and black Philistines must fall. Babylon must fall!'

Then as if everything had suddenly changed and he was going home to free Afrika, 'I Bongo man, son of the conquering lion, feel high when I sight up victory against the forces of downpression and freedom for their children of Afrika, wherever I and I lie, and the forward movement of all peoples . . . '

Another line from a strange song, began to pour out of the Ras' jaw. He began to shout, 'Down with slavery, down with colonialism, death . . . death, death, de . . a . . th to imperialism!'

And even as the Rastaman chanted, Karl, Doreen, Junior, Huey, marched up the track, the river behind, the road ahead and the night coming down, the poem written on his sick bed came to Kwame's mind:

OUR ROOTS

I sit, I gaze and behold I see,
The sight that stabs my heart,
A lonely tree that's near to me,
By violent winds is torn apart.

And with no protection from the
hills around,
Its chance to stand, do I mourn,
For though, to many, it is an ugly tree,
In it a deep beauty I do see.

But can this lonely tree withstand the wind?
I do not know, I cannot tell,
For now I look, and what strikes me,
Is twisted leaves scattered far and wide,
The shoot's left but scant,
By the violent winds that threaten the plant.

165

I rise to my feet and walk to the tree,
I turn my eyes and stare to the ground,
My lips have parted, I can't help but shout,
'Good God! Where are its roots?'

A tree with weak roots cannot stand,
Is tossed and torn by the slightest wind,
To the east in the morn, to the west in the eve,
It commeth and goeth, but never of its will.

A people like a tree must have strong roots,
Without the land, they cannot stand,
To face the rage of the mighty brutes,
With greedy hands and evil plans,
They try to blow and tear apart
The lonely people that's close to my heart.

GLOSSARY

Since this novel contains certain terms familiar only to Jamaicans, a few words about them might be an aid to communication for non-Jamaican readers.

Pages

1	Wash-belly	last, youngest child
2	Ward-maid	female orderly in hospital
3	Load	ground provisions
3	Cling cling bird	a Jamaican bird that makes a beautiful musical sound
3	dig up	leave; go away
4	Whites	very potent local rum
4	trust	get goods on credit
5	ganja	marijuana
5	devil soup	white rum
6	Corn	hardened blisters
7	Ras	title of address for male members of the Rastafarian sect.
8	Nyah	another name for the rastaman
8	ital	ganja
9	dunny	money
14	side-men	men who load/unload baggage on trucks, buses, etc.
19	J.S.C.	Local examination—Jamaica School Certificate taken at grade 9 level
19	Partner	a kind of small cooperative bank practised by most Jamaicans
36	bowson	hernia (swelling) of the male sexual organ
41	short day	day during the spring season
47	de-gey	only one
56	draws	female undergarment
47	dawg	dog
60	leggo beast	person who roams
63	buddy	penis
65	backra	person in authority
68	cocky	penis

75	black-eye peas soup	A situation where the great majority of people/children are white with just a few token blacks
87	bone-ache	erection
88	Grandmarket day	Day before Christmas
89	Three-card men	Card tricksters
96	Second year exams	An examination which used to be taken at Primary school level before G.C.E. was introduced
101	Reggae	rhythmic music indigenous to Jamaica
137	Pene-wallies	fire flies
149	bang-belly	a disease caused by protein deficiency in which the stomach protrudes
150	spliff	marijuana cigarette
150	familyram	A man known to have sexual relations with women in the same family
150	cocksman	Man known to have great sexual prowess
167	pumkin	feotus

Other titles from Bogle-L'Ouverture Publications

Poetry
Dread Beat and Blood by Linton Kwesi Johnson
Ammunition! by Sam Greenlee
At School Today by Accabre Huntley

Children's Books
Rain Falling, Sun Shining by Odette Thomas
Getting to Know Ourselves by Phillis and Bernard Coard
Joey Tyson by Andrew Salkey
Danny Jones by Andrew Salkey
The River That Disappeared by Andrew Salkey

Economics
Minerals in African Underdevelopment by Samuel Ochola

Anthologies
One Love by Audvil King (ed)
Writing in Cuba Since the Revolution by Andrew Salkey (ed)
Caribbean Folk Tales and Legends by Andrew Salkey (ed)

Short Stories
Anancy's Score by Andrew Salkey

History
The Groundings with my Brothers by Walter Rodney
How Europe Underdeveloped Africa by Walter Rodney

Forthcoming Titles
Novel
Sign Post of the Jumbie by Faustin Charles

Religion
The Complete Rastafari Bible by Robert A. Hill

Karl Black leaves Guys Hill and goes to Kingston—'the city of Killsome' as Ras Bongo calls it—seeking a 'better life'. But where is that better life? After two months in town, with no job, Karl wonders if he has done the right thing. He asks, 'Why life so hard for most of the people in this country?' Amid the squalor and hunger faced by the mass of people Karl sees another Jamaica, Beverley Hills—the heaven of the rich few, with swimming pools in nearly every yard when the masses below cannot even get water for ordinary use.

Through his friend, Kwame, Karl gets a better understanding for the reason for the plight of the poor people. Labelled a black power man and a communist for standing up for the workers' rights, Kwame is beaten up by the police for being one of the leaders of the strike at the Electric Service. To make things worse, Mrs. Mayer, the wife of the owner of the factory where Karl eventually gets a job, attempts to bribe Karl into selling out his friend. It is through Doreen, his girl friend, that Karl comes to the realisation of how brainwashed and misinformed the people are about their own situation.

Countryman Karl Black vividly portrays life in Jamaica for the poor working people—the anger and frustration of waiting for buses that never seem to come; the hostility and callousness of the bus conductress, and the people beating the youth nearly to death for stealing a woman's purse; the deprivation of the tattered youth selling *Glee-News*. Neville Farki clearly brings out the contradictions in the society as he constantly points to the bloodsuckers—the Wongs, the Mayers, the Goyles—who benefit from the destitution and deprivation of the poor.

Neville Farki, a graduate of the Jamaica School of Agriculture, also obtained a B.Sc. Econ. at the University of the West Indies, Jamaica in 1974.

Neville has written several books for the National Literacy programme of Jamaica as well as "A Week in Blue Hole". He is presently at the University of the West Indies, St. Augustine, doing graduate studies.

Cover Design by Errol Lloyd

A Bogle-L'Ouverture Publication
141 Coldershaw Road, Ealing W13 9DU